THE INADVISABLE MARRIAGES

THE INADVISABLE MARRIAGES

Pamela Hill

I need a Man for my Health.
Hester Thrale Piozzi

O, ... live single forever!
Fanny Burney

Chivers Press • G.K. Hall & Co.
Bath, Avon, England • Thorndike, Maine USA

For Terry here and Jacqueline there

This Large Print edition is published by Chivers Press, England, and by G.K. Hall & Co., USA.

Published in 1997 in the U.K. by arrangement with Robert Hale Limited.

Published in 1996 in the U.S. by arrangement with Robert Hale Limited.

U.K. Hardcover ISBN 0–7451–4834–4 (Chivers Large Print)
U.K. Softcover ISBN 0–7451–4845–X (Camden Large Print)
U.S. Softcover ISBN 0–7838–1732–0 (Nightingale Collection Edition)

The text of this Large Print edition is unabridged.
Other aspects of the book may vary from the original edition.

Set in 16 pt. New Times Roman.

Printed in Great Britain on acid-free paper.

British Library Cataloguing in Publication Data available

Library of Congress Cataloging-in-Publication Data

Hill, Pamela.
   The inadvisable marriages / Pamela Hill.
      p   cm.
   ISBN 0–7838–1732–0 (lg. print : sc)
   1. Large type books. I. Title.
[PR6058.I446I63   1996]
823′.914—dc20
                                                                 96–10460

CHAPTER ONE

On a darkening late evening of August, 1811, a woman aged forty-six lay dead in one of the upper rooms of a great bleak sparsely furnished house in Nottinghamshire, which in former times had been an abbey. Beyond, acres of blazing gorse retained the last of the day's sun. From among them a disturbed pheasant suddenly rose whirring, then vanished in the dusk.

The room itself smelt faintly of whisky and already, somewhat, of corruption, the corpse having by now lain two days. A cupboard door, partly off its hinge, showed however that the few necessary furnishings, which were all that the bailiffs had left, were not quite all that remained of forgotten grandeur, however brief. In her youth Catherine Gordon Byron had loved fine clothes.

O, whaur are ye going, bonnie Miss Gordon,
Whaur are ye going, sae bonnie and braw?

That was as she had once been; and now, hanging inside the lopsided door, could be glimpsed, once again, a satin gown. It was dark in colour, as became her age and widowhood, with short sleeves and a low neck trimmed with what, two years ago in order to have her

1

portrait taken, had been finely laundered lace with a pointed edging; there had been, unaccountably, some money at that time. By now, the lace had grown grubby and limp. The gown was of immense size because, in life, its wearer had grown excessively stout, though never tall. Her hair, which had turned grey but which she resolutely dyed black, needed curling and straggled now beneath her nightcap, which they had not yet removed. The sheet with which the servants had covered her face upon death had since been turned down to reveal the features, which gave nothing away. She had died quietly, and alone.

The young man who had turned down the sheet waited now by his mother's body. He had resolved to sit with her all night. It was the custom in Scotland, where she had been born, to hold a wake, and there was nobody left to hold it except himself. In any case he had neglected her in life and had not, despite making all speed, even arrived in time to see her die. This was perhaps a way of atonement she would understand, if her spirit lingered in whatever manner; of that prospect he was uncertain.

His own head and profile were of singular beauty, although he was still haggard from the journey made in all possible haste from London when he heard on arrival from abroad that his mother was dangerously ill; but to come at all he had had to borrow forty pounds, which necessarily delayed matters, and so halfway they had come to tell him Mrs Byron was already dead. The news had shocked him: he had not seen her since returning from his travels, but had written to her often from Greece and Albania and the other places he had visited, telling her some of his adventures but not all. The former thought salved his conscience, remembering as he did how it had always embarrassed him less to write to his mother than to be in her company. It occurred to him now that he had, nevertheless and despite everything, loved her after his fashion: but it was better to be elsewhere.

He sniffed at the pervading smell of whisky. He had brought a libel action lately, then abandoned it, against some mention in the newspapers about her drinking. It was true enough that she drank. No doubt she had been driven to it by solitude. Few could endure her outbursts of temper; the neighbours had long ceased to call, here or, earlier, at Southwell. When he was there, while the Abbey was let, he had spent such time as he might with the Pigots across the way, seldom with his mother.

Yet she had not always been so. He tried to think of her as she must have been as a girl, before the vast increase in flesh had made her unwieldy. She had first met with his father, he knew, going down the dance in Bath Assembly Rooms; a healthy and bouncing creature then, who had loved dancing always. There had even been a dancing-master later on, when he himself was old enough to take note; he recalled the man; it had been about the same time his mother had come clamouring and making a fool of him while he was briefly at school in Dulwich; the other boys had laughed at her. Well, all of that was best forgotten now.

He thought again of her impulsive marriage with his father Mad Jack Byron. Bath society had held aloof, it being nobody's concern to warn the uncouth Scots heiress that she was encouraging the advances of a fortune-hunter with one marital scandal in high life already to his discredit: the Carmarthen affair of a few years back, leading to divorce, remarriage and the birth of Augusta. Catherine Gordon would have heard, could not have failed to hear it, but from Mad Jack himself and no other; and the fascinating wooer who had reft away an earl's daughter, a marchioness who would in time have become a duchess, from her husband and young children was the same man who, by then, had scattered Kitty's accustomed shrewd Scots wits as though they had been straws on the wind.

It was probable, Byron now thought, that her father, after whom he had been named, the late George Gordon, twelfth of Gight, had he not recently committed suicide by drowning himself in Bath canal, would have tried to prevent his sole remaining child and heiress from falling prey to a debt-ridden and

4

improvident, though certainly most charming, widower whose own family had understandably cast him off. Nothing of the kind would, however, by then have altered Kitty Gordon's mind. She had instantly and wildly loved Mad Jack; had handed him all her worldly goods without even waiting to secure a settlement; and, after he had squandered her fortune, sold her inheritance, and abandoned her, grieved sincerely when she heard at last of his death in France. This had almost certainly been by his own hand.

That made three suicides, leaving aside the violent history of the ancient line of Gight. A great-grandfather had likewise drowned, in the Ythan when it was swollen high with snow. They tried to give out that he had been bathing, but who bathed out of doors in a Scottish winter? No, it had been the black depression that often settled on oneself; and that had maybe overtaken Mad Jack also, alone and in debt and despair at Valenciennes, with no more fortunes to spend, no more heiresses to cozen.

'He looked after me for an evening once, in Aberdeen,' the young man thought. He recalled the slight, negligent figure of his father, powdered hair disarranged as was the fashion then, cocked hat laid aside on the table, a French novel in his hand. Kitty, for once, had been out visiting; her husband had come north again to try to extract the last of her money from her. He himself, demanding the usual attention, had proved too much for Mad Jack; it had never happened again that they were left alone together. Byron however remembered now a thing his father had been heard to say: that not the twelve apostles themselves could live with his wife Kitty two months, for she had a temper like the devil.

Well, it was stilled now. There had maybe been reason for it then, and after; Gight had been sold, Gight of her ancestors, and before that the fisheries and the forests, with the herons long flown from their tree-nests. Thomas of Ercildoune, Thomas the Rhymer, had written centuries ago:

When the heron leaves the tree,
The laird of Gight will landless be.

This was the thirteenth laird of Gight; his mother, lately dead. Thirteen was an unlucky number. The first laird had fallen at Flodden, grandson of a king.

Gight had been a place of high degree once, a place for nobles and royal company. *There was a day when they were young and proud.* Those were his own lines, written in praise of the lost tower high on its rock above the flowing Ythan; Gight, with its carved panel of the sufferings of Christ which had survived the hackings of the Covenanters, last century but one, and which was still to be seen above the

6

stone arch beyond the ruined entry. His mother and Mad Jack had somehow contrived to live there for a while, and his father set up stag-hunting and stood for the borough, but the creditors came clamouring about the doors instead. They had fled then, his parents, to England, then to France, then London where he himself had at last been born. His mother had been alone by that time: and all of his childhood he been left alone likewise, with her, save for that one remembered evening with Mad Jack.

Gight had been sold by then, like everything else. He himself should have been reared there; among strange ancient stories like the one about the servant who had been sent, a second time in fear and trembling, to dive for the treasure known to lie at the bottom of deep Hagberry Pot; and his fleshly fragments were found afterwards floating on the water's surface, torn asunder in the depths by guardian demons. There was a tale of a ghostly piper as well, whose pipes could be heard playing. Byron's mother had told him all of them, the stories, when her temper was good enough, in the cheap lodgings where she had been left alone to rear him in near-poverty in Aberdeen. Alone together, for cuffs or kisses as the mood took Kitty; alone with her as now, when she would never move or speak again.

It was fitting, no doubt, that she should have died here, at Newstead. They had come down when he himself inherited the title as a boy of nine. The nurse, May Gray, of whose familiarities with him he had never dared speak to his mother, had been with them. He, George Gordon Byron, was become sixth Baron Byron of Rochdale, having got the title once his kinsman the Wicked Lord was dead. An army of tame crickets, evidently the only creatures to feel affection for the Wicked Lord, had marched in a body out of the house as soon as this happened.

Death. It was incomprehensible: there was no avoiding it. At some point, from some cause, in some place or another, he himself would die. He hoped it would be at Newstead; he loved it; it was his own, the place of his ancestors, as no other place now could ever be. It must never be sold; he himself, now his mother was no longer there to garner his money when she could contrive it, must of necessity marry money.

Marriage. He was considering the thought of it with Admiral Lord Keith's daughter, Mercer Elphinstone. He had already sent her a gift, an Albanian costume of bright colours collected on his travels. Mercer would manage him, no doubt; no question of being left without a settlement there; but the thought of so much money in fact deterred Byron. He knew he would squander it, like Mad Jack, as far as he might, unable to help himself, if it was available. His mother had scrimped and saved to get his finances in order all his boyhood, then he had got into debt at once again at Cambridge, buying a carriage and taking to wild ways and keeping a tame bear, as they would not allow a dog there.

'You deserved a better fate than the pair of us,' he said aloud to the corpse. It was strange—the light was growing now a little—to see his mother's face without its remembered high colour. She had known, after all, how to love: in France, before he was conceived, she had looked after Mad Jack's daughter by the first marriage, little Augusta, who had a fever such as had killed her mother, the erstwhile eloping marchioness. After the child was better her grand relations had taken her away to England, to be brought up.

Augusta. Her mother had died of following Mad Jack out to the hunt too quickly after the birth. There was no doubt that both his father's wives had been devoted to him.

Augusta. They said Mad Jack's only real love had been his sister Frances. There was no doubt a pattern in such inheritance.

Footsteps sounded outside, in the dark of the passage; it was a servant, oddly enough named Mrs By. She stared in, aware that Lord Byron had sat in the room alone all night. He turned to her, despair in his voice.

'Oh, Mrs By, I have lost my only friend!'

After she had gone he knew it was not strictly true; there were others; Murray,

9

Hobhouse, the rest: but would anyone do as much for him, with so little in return? He rose, and looked down a last time on his mother's face.

'I wrote to you, did I not?' he asked, as if she could answer. The light was growing now beyond the windows. His voice, whose deep vibrant quality had been much remarked in London drawing-rooms, echoed now in this room that was almost bare of furniture, wholly so of comforts. The room's walls had been built out of the stones from monks' destroyed cells. The monks had cursed the Byrons who came to take possession of their abbey at the Dissolution, and had said that no son of the direct line would ever inherit. Mercer also had a family curse, ruling out sons for two centuries. Well, it remained to be seen. He had in any case not made up his mind. There was no doubt she would accept him were he to ask; but he might not, after all, do so.

The dawn had come, with veils of mist rising from among the roots of the gorse-bushes, disappearing slowly with the growing warmth of the sun. 'Fare ye well,' he said to his mother; and some unforeseen echo in his mind predicted eerily *Then for ever, fare thee well!* He had found himself addressing her, at the last, in the Scots vernacular they had used together when he was a child, when she had at times loved and laughed with him and at others hit out at him, calling him a lame brat. 'I was born

10

so, mother,' he had replied then.

He glanced down now at his club-foot, concealed in its false outer shoe made to match the other; but it was impossible not to limp. That was a thing he had blamed her for; pulling at the foot during his birth, thinking she knew better than the midwife. Mrs Byron's crookit de'il. So they had called him in Aberdeen, the neighbours who crowded to stare at the fallen heiress of Gight, reduced to common lodgings in the town after having foolishly married a man who had spent all her money and then abandoned her.

'I will have it put on your coffin-plate that ye are of the stock of kings,' he told her, still aloud. He stretched out a hand halfway, the hand that held his pen and made him famous; but found he could not bring himself to touch her cold body. He turned and went out, limping downstairs, and presently gave orders for the funeral. Then he went into the lower room where he often sat alone, drinking claret out of a skull he had unearthed in the Abbey chapel and had caused to be rimmed with silver to fashion a wine-cup. He thought of past and future, and of the corpse upstairs; they were moving it by now. Poor woman! They said she had had The Sight, and could foretell the future; could she not have saved herself and him?

If only Augusta were here, he would not be

11

as lonely. He had always known that he himself was damned.

* * *

He could not, despite having ordered mourning-clothes, bear to attend the funeral. He stood at the door to watch the weighty coffin borne out, then stripped off his black coat, donned boxing-gloves, and fell to sparring with a young page named Rushton, becoming violent in the process. Later still, exhausted, he stared at the portrait of his mother painted by Stewardson only two years back. It hung on the wall, the painted lace delicate and crisp, the dyed hair carefully curled against the plump red cheeks. Her dark eyes regarded him with shrewd understanding. She had never, when one thought of it, seemed surprised at anything he might do.

* * *

Byron caused the wrong Stuart princess to be inscribed on the coffin-plate, obeying his mother's confused recollections. It was her last misfortune, and a minor one, before she was lowered into the Hucknall vault above a coffin placed there much earlier. Over the years her weight would crush it. So ended Catherine Gordon Byron, last of Gight. Her son found her jewels to be of some value; they had been kept by her carefully elsewhere, out of reach of the bailiffs.

CHAPTER TWO

Lady Keith had made her way downstairs to the Piccadilly drawing-room early, as she liked to do each weekday to ensure that everything was in order before callers began to arrive at three. Having inspected the great prosperously furnished room with its naval souvenirs, she ensconced herself in the chair in which, almost half a century later, at ninety, she would be found dead: and placidly looked about her at what was by now, after four years of late, well-considered and most successful marriage—the Admiral's disposition and her own continued to agree perfectly—a familiar and edifying scene. The draped curtains had, of course, been chosen by herself and hung at the time of the wedding, as during Lord Keith's long widowerhood he had paid little heed to such things, being seldom at home, and Mercer, his daughter by his first marriage, had not been old enough then (and was not now) to consider other matters than herself. She had however executed, competently enough, certain paintings on china plates and bowls of her father's battles, with everyone in ancient Greek costume; and these were proudly displayed. Other objects in the room had been

13

brought by Lady Keith herself from the houses at Bath or Brighton, some of them personal mementoes from dear Streatham itself. The rest belonged to Lord Keith, and were variously from Naples, America, Cape Town and Aboukir, also a few from his boyhood in Scotland at Elphinstone Tower. These had of course come by way of his old mother's suddenly acquired house in the Marylebone Road, given up at the time of that extremely independent lady's death some years ago now.

One's own portrait by Saunders was however perhaps the most notable object in the room, and commanded instant attention. He was in demand at present: the Princess had had herself painted.

Queeney Keith—her real name was Hester Maria, but the other had been given her in childhood by the great Dr Johnson, who had taught her Latin and other things, and she preferred to use it if only to distinguish herself from Mama—surveyed the recent fashionable rendering of herself in oils. She saw a majestic woman who looked less than her forty-seven years, with a swan's neck in good repair, and magnificent white exposed shoulders. Her face had its habitual faintly haughty expression, as though the somewhat prominent pale-blue eyes stared down unacceptable persons, which was in fact the case. The low-cut maroon gown, and the white turban set off by small bright feathers, Lady Keith wore again today, the

14

toilette not yet being ready to discard. She was fond of it; the colour set off, she knew well, the notable beauty of her white hands. They were smaller than Mama's, and Mama had always been audibly proud of her own, nevertheless calling them, in her unpredictable way, her huge Salusbury fists. It was no doubt an excuse to mention her maiden name of Salusbury, which she believed, almost certainly in error, to have come down from a mediaeval personage named Adam of Salzburg. In any case the exploits of grandfather Salusbury were best forgotten.

Mama. One did one's best to forget her also. It had been bad enough for her to have been, all one's own youth, embarrassingly affectionate and repressive by turns, demanding all the attention for herself as the respected hostess of the literary and philosophical group gathered regularly at Streatham; but at least she had had fair fame in those days as the wife of Henry Thrale (it must be tacitly forgotten that Papa was a brewer) and the constant, beloved and revered hostess of the great Samuel Johnson himself. Then, just before Johnson's death and promptly following Papa's, that unforgotten escapade despite all advice to the contrary, the appalling second marriage to an Italian music-master! Society had turned its back. She, Queeney, had departed at once with the younger sisters and, except for Cecilia, had brought them up herself. She had been nineteen.

By now, the Admiral was a great comfort to her in that matter: had been so from the beginning of their acquaintance. He had stated in his down-to-earth way that Mrs Thrale Piozzi's conduct had been most improper and that now she was widowed a second time, she would have leisure to regret the position she had lost in the eyes of everyone of standing. However Mama, it must be admitted, showed no signs of open penitence.

Queeney tried to reassemble her thoughts suitably, using the method recommended long ago by Dr Johnson himself. *Encourage in yourself an implacable impatience of doing nothing.* He had then recommended, if necessary, snatching the broom from the maid. Well, one could not very well follow such advice while waiting for exalted company to arrive. Everyone seemed to be late. It was a fine day, which was no doubt the reason; most people would be driving or walking.

The filtered sunlight from the Park, where at this season the leaves were thick and green, reflected itself not only on Lady Keith's portrait but on the magnificent full-length of her stepdaughter, painted by the German, Hoppner, when Mercer Elphinstone was thirteen. It showed a handsome child of promise, one shapely arm flung pointing out to sea. Mercer was portrayed as Miranda, in compliment to her father the Admiral's

16

preoccupations at that time. Her white gown, which in Queeney's opinion was by far too closely cut and transparent, was relieved by a drifting scarf of rose-colour across its folds. Mercer's mature young breasts had obviously given pleasure to the painter. He had done his best not only to emphasise so desirable a feature, but also to underplay, by causing her to look downward a little, his subject's determined nose and jaw. Nevertheless it remained a face which already showed character and a decided will of its own; unsurprising when one thought of the circumstances of Mercer's birth and upbringing. By now, she had refused various suitors including the Duke of Clarence, but that was of course to be expected. It had angered her father less—Tarry Breeks would have been an expensive, if royal, son-in-law, and much of Mercer's vast fortune would have gone in paying off his debts—than Mercer's own persistent refusal of the Admiral's own preferred choice for her, Lord Cochrane, tipped early for promotion by the Admiralty. It was true that Cochrane had shown signs of eccentricity lately, so perhaps Mercer was right to decline; but it showed an undue desire to have her own way, as usual.

Queeney moved her arms a little on the chair. Mercer's latest fancy might not be altogether pleasing to her father; one awaited the outcome. A poet, even a titled one, was an

17

uncertain speculation, despite Lord Byron's recent creditable speeches in the Lords. His heredity on both sides was disastrous; his parents' incautious and hasty union was still food for gossip in Bath after more than twenty years. Catherine Gordon of Gight had as it happened been exactly the same age as oneself, and there at the same time; and Mad Jack Byron's mother Sophia, Admiral Foulweather's wife, had been a close friend of Mama's. Queeney banished the recollection of the bouncing young Scots heiress going down the dance with their son Mad Jack, light of foot, to her doom. Had her father not drowned himself in the Bath canal some time previously, there might have been someone to warn the stout little person, but as things stood it had been nobody's concern after such a scandal earlier. In any case Miss Gordon's manner was unpleasing, being a Scot. Queeney smiled to herself, having since married one; there was no doubt that they were an independent race, frequently unpopular in England still, owing to the memory of Lord Bute and his incomparable leg, not to mention the Jacobites. Years later, as far as all of that went, long after Mad Jack was dishonourably dead like his Gordon father-in-law, one had encountered Kitty, sadly run to seed, with her son, by then a young man, at a Bath masquerade. That had been in 1809, when she herself and the Admiral were not long married and Georgy on the way. Young Byron had been dressed as a Turk, which helped to disguise his lame foot.

Queeney herself had thereafter welcomed the interesting son of so ill-fated a marriage—it was known that Mad Jack had squandered almost every penny, Kitty having been too greatly lacking in prudence to wait for a settlement to be drawn up beforehand—to her drawing-room as early as that same year, after Georgy's birth. That of course was before Lord Byron became famous on return from his travels in the East. He had meantime written an epic poem which everyone read. Lady Keith herself preferred Dr Johnson's more solid writings, and permitted her mind to wander back from contemplation of *Childe Harold* to recall that Byron had inherited the title as a boy by way of a great-uncle, the regrettable brother of Sophia Byron's reclusive husband Foulweather Jack, who had never sailed a ship but it fell into a storm; he had been shipwrecked for five years in Patagonia and since his return, had evinced a distaste for human company, no doubt having ceased to be accustomed to it in those strange parts. In any case there was a curse on the Byrons; it was said a son would never inherit from a father. 'Mercer's family also has such a curse,' reflected Mercer's stepmother placidly.

At any rate, young Lord Byron's epic poem had made him the lion of London society; as he himself put it, he had wakened up one morning to find himself famous. He had also improved remarkably in looks while abroad. Earlier, he had been almost as *farouche* as his mother, and she, Queeney, had had to request him, when he first called, to wear a stock or cravat. His appearance had otherwise been most singular in that open collar, with nankeen breeches and the clumsy boots that hid his crippled foot; that of course was a misfortune. Byron bit his nails, moreover; but there was something that appealed to one in him, and evidently appealed even more to Mercer.

Mercer. She had naturally been given her head for far too long, spoilt by aunts and her eccentric grandmother while the Admiral was away at sea. By the time his protracted courtship of oneself—it had lasted six years— had been concluded to the satisfaction of both parties, Mercer was twenty, a difficult age to start reforming any young woman. It was certainly not desirable for the girl to have control of her own money, and so much money! That of course had come from her mother, the Admiral's long-dead first Scots wife Jean Mercer. *Her* family, one understood, had been a very old one. She had died of a fever caught while returning to London from Scotland when the only child of the marriage was no more than seventeen months old. Her widower had thereafter resisted offers of remarriage from almost everyone of note, especially after he acquired titles in Ireland in gratitude for his victories in the service: the Scots one was of course his by right. She herself had always said she would like to marry a lord.

It was in fact an ideal marriage, the only cloud being the existence of Margaret Mercer Elphinstone herself; and if only Georgina, conceived as it were miraculously at once and born when one was forty-four, had been a boy, the Keith title would have gone to him. It could not be helped, however; there would certainly be no more children now; and one must be thankful that Georgy continued strong and healthy in the nursery upstairs. Mama, when permitted to see the child, had said that she resembled her, Queeney, at her age exactly; but a great many children had died at Streatham, though she, the eldest, had lived. Harry, her brother, should have lived also. Queeney closed her eyes, remembering.

A distasteful thought occurred after that. Mama had had a miscarriage to the unspeakable Piozzi at forty-seven, one's own present age. It did not bear thinking of; she had also had one latterly to Papa, and twelve of a family before that, not only at Streatham Park but in the unfashionable town house they kept at Southwark, near the brewery. How different life was now! The Admiral, who respected the learning instilled into his wife by Dr Johnson and others, said repeatedly that until he had made her, Hester's, acquaintance he had not

21

encountered a mind suitable to be a companion to his own, especially in retirement. It was true that he had the unrewarding post about Clarence's household, with its straggle of bastard children: but otherwise, his time now was his own.

That her own mind had been carefully fostered there was no doubt. Queeney dwelt once more on childhood at Streatham, when all was at least outwardly smooth, and there was the constant presence of the enormous lumbering body, scorched wig, and incomparable sayings of the great man her mother had deserted at last when he was old, ill and dying. One could not forgive that; or the fact that the reason was Piozzi. That Italian! One always came back to that, and remained coldly angry, even though, on his death, the erstwhile music-master had left her, Queeney, his harpsichord as though in atonement. Even prim Miss Burney, who had almost been swallowed up by Mama at Streatham, had deserted her on news of the marriage. 'Poor self-deluded Mrs Thrale! Dear, lost, infatuated soul!' Fanny Burney had always gushed; it was one sign of her lack of early education.

Why had nobody arrived yet, and where was Mercer? One could never be certain, and it was improper in a young unmarried woman not to state her whereabouts beforehand. She might be with the young Princess at Warwick House, or else—Queeney frowned a little—with the

Greys at Portman Square. One hoped Lady Grey was in residence; Mercer was beginning to be known as the Grey Mare, presumably because of her vehement Whig politics, but one had to remember also that Charles Grey, since his marriage the most respectable of men and a devoted husband, had in his day been the lover, like a great many others, of Georgiana, Duchess of Devonshire.

In any case it was time Mercer settled down. Perhaps Lord Byron would call today. One could not however predict it; since *Childe Harold* he had after all become society's lion. If he and Mercer did marry, one however assumed that she would manage him; she had managing ways.

How finely the sun shone! It was tiresome not to be out in it, but one would give the expected company a little longer. Soon, and it was pleasant to think of it, she and the Admiral and little Georgy would be down again together at Purbrook, where the Princess had visited them last year from Bognor and Mercer had ridden with her to visit the Forest of Bere fortune-tellers, to Princess Charlotte's great diversion. Such entertainment did not often come her way. This year, though, Mercer had said she herself would not be coming to Purbrook, or not at once. She had evidently made other arrangements; well, there it was.

Queeney stared again at her portrait. There had been a copy taken to send to Tulliallan,

Admiral Lord Keith's beloved house built by himself on the Fife coast; she however found it cold. Saunders was, on the whole, better at painting miniatures; it was for that that he had become so well known in Bath, where she had encountered him. He was a Scot by birth—how many of them seemed to come down here!—and had begun his three-quarter length portraits after making the one of Princess Charlotte, who had afterwards impulsively sent him a present of a chair. 'Why?' Mercer, who of course saw the young Princess daily, had asked her. The Princess had replied that she knew Saunders liked chairs. 'It is the kind of thing she does and can't afford,' Mercer had remarked herself in one of her few exchanges with her stepmother. Queeney had looked disapproving. She was aware, having a finger on the town's pulse, that there had been gossip about the young Princess's visits to the studio in Vigo Street, though she had of course not ventured there unchaperoned; but there was gossip about most of the things Princess Charlotte did. She had no doubt inherited, from her mother, a certain lack of propriety. Queeney, herself a past mistress in the art—she had reared her younger sisters strictly, taking them away at the time of the Piozzi marriage, though Cecilia, being under age, had unfortunately by law had to be returned to Mama, who later most disgracefully let her elope to Gretna Green—Queeney knew this quality was bound to be lacking at Warwick House, the Princess's residence, despite the habitual seclusion of the Regent's only child by order of her father. However the Princess herself was engaging enough: she had only been allowed to visit them all for the day at Purbrook that time from Bognor—'and I always go down to the baker's and eat his fresh buns while they're hot'—and her pretty hands had been red with constant riding and she, Queeney, had suggested that the child use white butter on them. Mercer also was shrewd enough to take trouble with the Princess in such ways, ingratiating herself with a view to pending importance: though no doubt the presents she had made of a hat and gown had seemed a trifle patronising to a probable future Queen.

There was the sound of a carriage arriving below. Presently Mercer came in, still in her bonnet. It was trimmed in what her stepmother considered too much profusion for an unmarried young woman, with artificial flowers of all colours. Seeing nobody in the room the young woman's face hardened. 'Nobody has come,' she said, in a slight Scots accent.

'It is the good weather, no doubt,' replied Queeney equably. 'It is in any case still early. You had best go upstairs and remove that bonnet; it gives away the fact that you have arrived in haste.'

Mercer Elphinstone's blue eyes, of a deeper shade than her stepmother's, sparkled beneath their somewhat heavy brows at receiving orders, as she had not been used to have to do before Papa brought this formidable new wife home. However it was still possible that Lord Byron would come, and Mercer accordingly wanted to look her best, with her dark hair, which she wore long now and profusely curled, seen to freshly by her maid; so she went. She already determined to marry Byron and to use her money to promote him in politics; she herself was a convinced Whig, and so was he.

Arrivals began at last to be announced in the drawing-room, among them the old Admiral himself, home from his unrewarding assignment in Clarence's household, firmly still in pigtail and powder, which few wore these days. His men had been near mutiny at being compelled to stick to the old fashion long after other crews had been instructed to cut and wash their hair as others did on land. Lord Keith stood erect beside his wife, and welcomed the company in his laconic Scots fashion. He had joined the Navy as a boy of fifteen, and by now had had the honour of being named Admiral of the White, then the Blue; Commander-in-Chief of the Mediterranean Fleet—he'd fallen out there that time with that damned irregular feller Nelson, who had however justified himself at Trafalgar seven years ago—then the Irish barony had come as well as the Scots title, and the building, at last, of his beloved Tulliallan where the winds blew straight off the Forth. That was his only difference with Hester, a mild one; she had confessed that she disliked the snell winds and preferred the warmer south parts, so the south it was. George Keith had a respect for his wife's good sense and her learning; by God, besides the Latin of a scholar she knew fortifications, perspective and Hebrew! He had been fortunate in finding such a woman, after long search, to content his old age. During her unexpected pregnancy he had walked about in a dream, picturing perhaps a son at last to fill his cup to the brim, and deciding already that the boy would of course go into the Navy. Alas—well, it was not such a tragedy—there had been born another girl, one hoped less trouble than the first was turning out; but the main point was that Hester—the Admiral eschewed the name Queeney as fanciful, it having been bestowed on Hester herself long ago by the Grand Cham after some children's play—had survived the birth at her age, none the worse in health. The Admiral looked down at the white turban now, not displaying his affection openly for that was never his way, but proud of his wife; her white hands dispensed tea to the company, with grace and competence, from a heavy silver pot which had been his mother Clementina's. He spared a thought for her, a Fleming of the old

27

Wigtown family of Galloway as she had been, a childhood friend of wild Duchess Jane, later on mother of twelve including himself. Hester had no wildness; she was predictable, dependable, placid, different from her own mother; thank God for that.

*   *   *

The Honourable Miss Mercer Elphinstone meantime, upstairs having her long thick dark hair combed out and curled with hot tongs, had dismissed her mild irritation with her stepmother from her mind, this being, as usual nowadays, full of Byron. Mercer knew herself not the only young woman to be in this state, and it was to be hoped he would call today: since he had become society's lion he was also becoming unpredictable. Mercer, accustomed to have all eligible men, old and young, at her feet, was intrigued by this very quality in Byron. How fascinating, as well as mysteriously handsome, he had become since returning from his travels, having lost the boyhood fat he had had when they first met; he told her he contrived it with charcoal biscuits and soda-water! He had been fierce with shyness when they first became acquainted, but now it was turning to arrogance: shortly she must give him a set-down, to which he was no doubt not used. The secret of everything was to make him laugh. He hadn't had enough

28

laughter; his childhood must have been very sad. Queeney had known his mother, who sounded extremely difficult, in Bath, which was why he himself had been invited early to Piccadilly, before all London knew him. One forgot by now the clumsy boy with straight hair pulled over his eyes who had first come here; by this, his curls ravished all credulous women. He must, like herself—Mercer smiled—torture it with curling-rags by night and tongs by day. Such knowledge did not hinder love, and she knew she loved Byron and intended that he should become her husband. She was ambitious for him as well as for herself, with the Princess's friendship firmly established now. Byron would become a great political leader, as great as Fox. His maiden speech in the Lords about the Luddite frame-breakers had impressed everyone who heard it, including Charles Grey. With her money—till now this had been somewhat of a weight about Mercer's neck, with everyone fawning, and Papa's selected applicants safe and dull, as the rest were bound to be fortune-hunters—with that, Byron and she, as his wife, could go far indeed; further even than Charles James Fox and the Duchess of Devonshire, who had given a kiss to each of his voters and had carried a fox muff for all to see. Beautiful Duchess Georgiana was dead long since. Her son, lately succeeding as Duke but still called Dearest Hart by his sisters as formerly, was in love with

29

Princess Charlotte and that young lady kept his portrait balanced on a chair.

The Princess liked Byron—'Do not burn my neck,' said Mercer to the maid—and had been permitted to see him fairly often, after her father the Regent had met him and amicably discussed the novels of Walter Scott. Almost two years ago now, in the Forest of Bere, the gipsies had foretold two dark men in both their lives, hers and the Princess's; the one in her own must certainly be Byron.

Well, she must go down to tea. Would he yet be among the company? By now one had heard several carriages arrive, but Byron of course would walk; it was after all only a short distance from his new lodging in the Albany.

Mercer descended the stairs at last, skirts hushing prosperously; and entered the drawing-room with her usual confident step. Byron was however not there, though others were. Mercer, too adept to let her disappointment show, accepted a cup of tea from her stepmother, having kissed Papa. Then she went to the window to talk to Mrs George Lamb. She already had a plan involving Byron, perhaps even a way of causing him to declare himself formally. She was convinced that he was not indifferent to her, though as yet he had never made her the subject of one of his short poems; that mattered relatively little.

The murmur of polite talk continued as it

30

will at tea-drinking; many persons were already out of town, but Lady Keith's drawing-rooms would never be entirely deserted. She was a valued link with the past, having taken the place of her eccentric mother, who, as was still remembered, had been hostess to Dr Johnson and had since published a series of slightly suspect memoirs and collections of letters of his, probably added to by herself. Her daughter was less of a chatterbox, and more trustworthy; Lady Keith would never, after all, betray her class. The old Admiral was a figure to be sought also, with his long history of service at Toulon and other places and—this was never of course mentioned—his connection with the old Jacobite families in Scotland, though one understood that had been mainly through his first wife, if not perhaps altogether.

However—and this particularly concerned the gentlemen present, correct in uncomfortably starched stocks and tight-fitting coats, their hair, unlike the Admiral's fashionably *en brosse*—as a more tangible result of that almost forgotten first marriage, here was Miss Mercer herself to be encountered, though her flirtatious ways made it difficult to know whether she was seriously interested in one or not. The thought of the fortune tempted the gentlemen, most of whom were in debt; but Mercer herself would make a handsome, if somewhat less than biddable, wife. She was spending an unconscionable time by the window today, talking to nobody except mousy little Caro George Lamb; to what end? George Lamb himself, despite the handsome dowry old Devonshire had provided with his plain little bastard daughter, spent no time at all with his wife.

* * *

Queeney also was wondering the same thing. Mercer's manners were becoming a little *outrée*; it was impolite not to divide one's attention among callers. To spend a full quarter-hour with the duller of Lady Melbourne's two daughters-in-law— thankfully, William Lamb's half-crazy little wife, the other Caro, had not come today— was, to say the least, extraordinary. George Lamb's disdain for his illegitimate bride was somewhat comical when one reflected that George himself was known to be the son of Prinny. Betsy Melbourne had had too many fathers for her children ever to attain the peak of respectability, no matter how valiantly she endeavoured, now her youth had passed her by, to do so.

Well, there it was, and time to refill the tea-cups. Behind her, Queeney could hear her husband's voice referring to Bonaparte, in the way he always did, as Bonny. It was one of the set habits that increased her affection for him;

32

such a comfort to know that what was expected to happen would continue to! It suited her own taste perfectly.

*   *   *

The company having dispersed to its various evening preoccupations, Lady Keith made her way upstairs at last to change her dress for dinner: and on the way paused once again in the nursery to visit Georgy. Thank God the child was well and a good colour; there had been so many illnesses and deaths among one's brothers and sisters in childhood at Streatham that it seemed almost incredible that her own, born so late, should survive, besides resembling her so closely. It was, one recalled again, Mama who had noted that, having earlier been refused entry to attend the birth itself as she desired. The Admiral had distinctly forbidden it, and Queeney herself had not wanted the presence of a personage who always expected to be at the centre of everyone's thoughts, even at such a time. Hester Lynch Salusbury Thrale, now Piozzi, had been a bad mother despite her frequent, and embarrassing, emotional outbursts; her habit of dosing all of her children with tin pills was certainly harmful. Harry and Ralph, the only two boys out of the twelve, not counting the miscarriage, had died; with Ralph it was just as well, as something had been the matter

33

inside his head; but Harry should have grown to manhood. He had died of some internal complaint at nine years old; and when he was writhing in pain the tutor had threatened to whip him for disconcerting Mama. Well, Harry had proved clearly enough that he was not pretending. She, Queeney, had mourned him greatly; they had been close companions, and after his death there were only the remaining sisters, many of the rest having died earlier. Mama had seemed to care rather less than a cat which has mislaid some of its litter of kittens, except perhaps for losing Lucy. She had had favourites among them and those less favoured. Hester Maria had often been told that she, being the eldest, was also the dearest; but Mama was in fact jealous of her, especially as regarded the admiration of Dr Johnson. In fact, Mama had never cared in truth for anybody except herself.

Lady Keith's pale-blue gaze came to rest on the late Gabriel Piozzi's harpsichord. Its lid was closed, as nobody played it; she herself had naturally been given music lessons along with everything else, but after marriage one lost interest in such things. Why had Piozzi left the instrument to her, of all people, in his will? Granted Mama would have no use for it either, nor would that regrettable adopted nephew: but she, Queeney, had made it clear from the beginning what she thought of the marriage, even before it took place; initially she had persuaded Mama to send the Italian abroad, but Mama had manifested such tantrums in his absence that it had become necessary to call Piozzi back again. The instant the banns were announced she, Queeney, had, she again reminded herself, removed all the young girls to Brighton, to be reared correctly under her own care; she knew more of propriety at nineteen than her mother at any age. Piozzi and Mama, once married, had taken to travelling about with this same harpsichord, which folded up, in the carriage during their journeys on the Continent, necessary until the scandal should have died down. By then, Dr Johnson himself was of course dead.

Queeney stared balefully at the instrument. After their return Mama and Piozzi had settled mostly in Wales, as was prudent. The damp weather had affected Piozzi adversely and he had died there six years ago now, evidently of gout. The years did not, with one's own courtship and marriage occupying one's mind to the exclusion of almost all else, seem as long.

Lady Keith ran her white finger across the polished surface of the closed instrument. It was as well to ensure that the maids carried out their daily dusting. The extraordinary nature of the late Piozzi's bequest remained in her awareness as she had herself unlaced from the maroon gown. Mama, of course, subscribe to concerts as she might, had never been in the least musical; her voice was extremely harsh.

Mercer meantime was dressing for dinner also. As it would be *en famille* this evening, there was no need to decide on anything elaborate to wear. She gave more thought to her recent conversation with Caro George Lamb, who as expected had proved entirely amenable to her wishes. Poor Caro, brought across from France and only upon marriage informed who her real father was, led a sad life between her contemptuous husband and her demanding mother-in-law. Old Betsy Melbourne's past was so far from puritanical that by now, nobody could be more outwardly particular about the conventions than she. Only the dead heir, Peniston, had in fact been the son of Lord Melbourne, who condoned his wife's affairs thereafter, no doubt not expecting Peniston to die while still a young unmarried man. Emily's father—Em had had her marriage to Lord Cowper arranged early by her mother, and was one's own great friend—beautiful dark-haired Emily had some father or other, but nobody by now was certain who; William Lamb's father was decidedly Lord Egremont; who Fred's had been no longer mattered: and everybody knew, from George Lamb's sideways appearance in a buttoned-up frock coat, who *his* father was. Prinny's affairs did not as a rule produce such solid evidence as George: it was astonishing, given all the circumstances, that the young

Princess herself had been conceived by him so promptly by way of his loathed German marriage. However, the Regent never denied that Charlotte was his daughter.

At any rate, Caro George Lamb would make an excellent chaperone for oneself at Tunbridge Wells while Papa and Queeney betook themselves down to Purbrook, or wherever they chose. It had all been arranged, without trouble, this afternoon, under the eye of everyone. It had of course been disappointing that Byron himself had not been present at tea, but one could console oneself with the reflection that had he so been, the arrangements could not have been made. Mercer Elphinstone prided herself on her efficiency and her clear knowledge of the eventual goal.

Looking in the glass after she was dressed, she decided, not for the first time, that she was not unhandsome either. No doubt Byron was still a little shy because she was taller than he, but he was after all a small man. He was becoming more elusive, as already noted, for other hostesses desired his presence; but Tunbridge would provide the answer. Mercer smiled, and thought again of her lesser preoccupation meantime, the young Princess; the latter, in one of her frequent impulsive letters, had written 'I have seen a *great deal* of Lord Byron lately!' It was all to the good that Byron should ingratiate himself with royalty to ensure a sound political future. Princess Charlotte, after the Regent and the old mad King were dead, would be Queen of England. She was already a firm Whig by upbringing, and naturally one fostered that inclination, despite the Regent's recent political *volte-face*; that had of course been because of Wellington's victories against the French in the Peninsula; Prinny had told her so himself, during a long scolding at Carlton House after Princess Charlotte had burst into tears and left the dining-table on hearing that the Government had fallen, and the Regent had blamed Mercer for the whole exhibition, saying she had too much influence over his daughter. It was the first occasion on which he scolded her, indeed for a full half-hour: there was to be a second.

Mercer's mouth firmed a little beneath her strong nose. There had been considerable gossip about the Princess, even last year at fifteen; her visits to the grumpy middle-aged painter Saunders, whom Charlotte said she found most agreeable, showed the unnatural restraint under which she was kept; that was however understandable, knowing how her slovenly and mischievous mother Caroline, Princess of Wales, deliberately spread rumours and also tried to compromise her daughter with scoundrels like Captain Hesse, said to be the Duke of York's bastard son and Caroline's own lover. He was more of a danger to the young Princess's reputation even than Augustus Fitzclarence had earlier been, Tarry Breeks' bastard as he was, and thereafter it had been necessary for Princess Charlotte to be seen driving daily in the Park with a lady-in-waiting to prove that she was not, as had been whispered by way of Kensington Palace, in a certain condition. Hesse unfortunately had received letters later on from young Charlotte, who at the time fancied herself in love with him, and Mercer had already tried in vain to get these back; it might be necessary after all to ask Papa to do so.

Certainly Charlotte must be married suitably, though not quite yet. The Regent's estrangement from his deplorable wife meant that he might seize any excuse to divorce Caroline of Brunswick and remarry, whereupon the Princess might be superseded by a resulting son. Meantime the Regent kept his daughter out of sight when he could, 'but she is by far more popular with the common people than he,' Mercer reminded herself. It was something the same, after all, in its way, as her own situation; it had somewhat shaken her confidence when Papa not only married again after so many years when she herself was twenty, but fathered a child who might, after all, have taken away the anticipated Keith title. Little Georgy however brought no such danger: Mercer had grown fond of her half-sister.

Byron. Where had he been this afternoon, as he had not come here? It was possible that he had called on his own half-sister Augusta Leigh, who held a position about the old Queen and had apartments in St James's Palace accordingly. However Mrs Leigh was usually down at Newmarket with her unsuitable husband and their various children. One would therefore never know where Byron had been this afternoon; perhaps it was as well. Certainly the lines *'Weep, daughter of a royal line! A Sire's disgrace, a realm's decay!'* could fortunately not be blamed on him at the time of the Whig débâcle last year: he would have signed his name to them. In any case the whole matter, as Lord Grey had murmured today over luncheon, would never have arisen had Charles James Fox, lately his leader and the Prince's own close friend before the latter became Regent, not died in the same year as Papa had married Queeney. Concerning either happening it was quite useless to repine.

CHAPTER THREE

Mrs Piozzi settled her customary large white hat upon the flaxen wig she as usual wore despite the heat, took her stick and set out with determination to walk to the Pump Room, Bath. There would be some acquaintance
40

there, to be sure. Her black clothes trailing—
Hester Lynch Salusbury Thrale Piozzi had
worn no colours since the death of her second
husband—the tiny body with its large gloved
hands moved with confidence along the street
as though it was making an entrance on stage.
As she progressed, Hester Lynch Salusbury
Thrale Piozzi reflected on love.

It seemed only yesterday that the adored
Gabriel had died, and yet the three years were
like an eternity. His death had been a mercy,
however, after the screaming years of agony in
Wales with terrible and pervasive gout.
Nobody would have wished him to live as he
had become, yet Hester herself still felt the
emptiness. Her passion for Piozzi had survived
the necessary loss of all physical love between
them: cruelly, the gossip everywhere had said
that that was why she had fallen madly in love
and married the Italian in her mid-forties when
she should have settled down to respectable
widowhood like others. Did they suppose that
at that age, at any age, one was no longer
capable of feelings? Her own sensibilities had
always been excessive; yet Dr Johnson, who
had so long professed admiration for her, even
love, had written most cruelly when she
informed him that, for the second time, she was
made a wife. *Madam, if I interpret your letter
aright, you are ignominiously married.* As for
that little serpent Fanny Burney, she had
pretended to be all sympathy while, at the same

time, deploring the marriage with Queeney behind one's back and setting daughter against mother.

Queeney. It had never been possible to obtain any sign of affection from her, the eldest and favourite child of all. Why? She herself had lavished caresses on the girl, had even sent Gabriel Piozzi away once at Queeney's request, then found she could not live without him after all and that he must return from Italy, and he had come, and they had been married and she, Hester, for the first time since the arranged and passionless union with Henry Thrale when she was fifteen, had known bliss. It hadn't even mattered that Queeney had departed promptly with the girls. Later, she herself had got little Cecilia back again. Her recollection of all that was still clear; painfully clear, to the last detail. She had always had an eye for that, as well as sharp wit. Fanny Burney should have appreciated her more and stayed on with her at Streatham; why had the young woman—not so young by then, after all—been so determined to return to her family? Her father had denied her an education; *Evelina* had been a miracle, coming from the pen of a young person so greatly and constantly suppressed at home. Fanny had hardly had the confidence to utter a word when she first came to Streatham. Perhaps it was Dr Johnson's fault that her prose had grown too heavy later on; the last novel of all had been unreadable:

42

one could not even remember its name.

A passer-by raised his hat and Mrs Piozzi bowed amiably. It was not expected that she should ordinarily be met with in Bath in summer. Generally, she spent the warm weather at dear Brynbella, enjoying the green slopes of the Flintshire hills, the clear Welsh air, the house she and Piozzi had built together and had named half for her native tongue of Wales, half for his Italian. How happy they had been there together till the cruel gout prevailed! Piozzi had meantime turned himself into a country gentleman, taking great care of the tenants. She, Hester, had had no money worries at all while *he* was in charge, dear prudent soul. There had been a larger attendance at his funeral by far there than would have been the case in London, where those who know no better looked down on Gabriel Piozzi and on herself for having married him.

The bright lively gaze hardened for moments, thinking of the ostracism he and she had endured for some time following their marriage. Queeney had been particularly unkind. Queeney, naturally, resented what looked like one's own betrayal of Dr Johnson, but how could she, Hester, have continued the relationship they had so long enjoyed in Thrale's lifetime without marriage, and how in any case could she have married a sick old man of seventy-three who was in addition growing

43

extremely demanding? Johnson had come to regard Streatham Park as his home for so long that he had no doubt begun to think he could order matters there. Long before, she herself had told Queeney, a child then, not to trouble him with letters. 'He won't want to be bothered with your stuff.' Was that why she had never been loved enough by her daughter? It had hurt greatly that Dr Johnson's answers—oh, they had begun in such ways, to a child, as *My Dearest Love, Dear Miss, Dear Sweeting*—had been withheld by Queeney and refused for inclusion with one's own in a volume which was otherwise a little too short. One had had to pad it out. Then, on the marriage to Piozzi Queeney had of course gone away to live her own life; there had been a gap of six years when they did not even write to one another. Thank God, that at least was mended now.

Mrs Piozzi's full underlip, made fuller by an accidental scar at one side, drooped a little. Having Cecilia returned in the end had not been all joy; she had been troublesome over the years, and in the end had fallen in love with young Mostyn and eloped with him. He had treated her badly afterwards; there had been lawsuits and money difficulties. It was one thing to say the path of true love never did run smooth, but her own and Piozzi's had been smooth as a lake after returning from Italy, where the priests had however not approved of his choice of a Protestant wife. Well, she had

44

persuaded him to join the Church of England in the end, and he had died in it. She herself continued to attend the Laura Chapel.

One should not perhaps have condoned that elopement of Cecilia's to Gretna Green. Had she secretly been glad to be rid of her daughter? She would never have admitted it to herself at the time, but now, looking back, a great many things could be seen more clearly. At least the child was widowed now, at Segroid, and seemed contented enough with her three strapping boys; one had visited there not long ago and it was pleasanter by far without Mostyn. *Plus ça change, plus c'est la même chose.* She herself had had her first marriage to a rich brewer arranged by Mama, to whom Henry Thrale had paid far more attention at the beginning than he had to herself, apart from getting her with child from the wedding night and yearly without fail thereafter. She, Hester, had taken to wearing rouge constantly to hide the paleness of inevitable pregnancy, and still wore it by habit although there was now no need; in the glass, she looked, she thought, as usual, and certainly felt as usual; one remained, after all, forever oneself.

Twelve children in fourteen years, and a miscarriage; that had come after her struggles on behalf of Henry Thrale, her husband, at the by-election, when Henry was no longer in a fit state to appear in person to stand. Dr Johnson had certainly aided her then, with his ready speech, but the electors were not deceived; Thrale that time had been placed at the bottom of the poll. The miscarriage had been most painful, worse than the births. Later, there had been a further one to Piozzi, and that had been a great grief; of all things, she, Hester, would have liked to bear a child to the man she loved.

How she had indeed loved Gabriel Piozzi! 'I suppose you know,' Sophia Byron had said years ago, 'that that man is in love with you?' There had never in fact been such love. Piozzi's gentleness, his slight bewilderment over the English language (but both she and Queeney of course spoke Italian), his preoccupation at all times with his violin and harpsichord, and his carefulness with money, had totally enchanted Hester. It was all of it so different from Henry Thrale, losing large sums as he had on rash enterprises; one year he had brewed bad beer on the wrong advice, leaving out the hops, and the entire result had been unsaleable. She had given Thrale her own advice, naturally, earlier on, but he never listened to much she said. Also, he kept women in London and—this had hurt—one, Polly somebody, was a magnificent rider, which she, Hester, had in her youth been also, but Thrale had forbidden her to ride, saying it was unfeminine. Piozzi had been different. There was no unkindness, no coldness, no such forbidding quality, in him. No doubt Queeney took her formal nature from her father.

Queeney. Queeney had the harpsichord by Piozzi's will. Well, oneself would never have played it. Queeney, naturally, numbered music among her accomplishments: oneself had seen to that. No expense had been lacking for the girl's education, no matter how hard times might have been as money went up or down. There had been the Latin lessons for Queeney with Dr Johnson, his scorched smelly wig—he would burn it forever reading by candlelight—bending over the child, his great face with its shrewd oblique eyes peering down intently. Queeney had been a pretty child; both Reynolds and, earlier, Zoffany, who had also painted Mama in widowhood, had taken her likeness, once with a bowl of cherries. For Zoffany she had been posed embracing Mama's dog Belle, the same which had wolfed Dr Johnson's buttered toast on one notable occasion at Streatham. No doubt that was what had given Queeney persistent worms all through her childhood. One dared not ask if now, as Lady Keith, she had got rid of them; such intimacies were not encouraged. Why, she herself had not even been permitted to be present at the lying-in which had safely produced little Georgy, and Queeney had also prevented her, Cecilia's own mother, from going to Cecilia at such a time. Truly Queeney seemed somewhat cold and unresponsive: there had been the six years' silence between them, now healed, but even so one's loving and

47

frequent letters brought only formal replies.

Love. Dr Johnson had written to Queeney that he 'had loved her mother as long as he could'. In the days when she had had fresh linen laid out for him constantly at Streatham, and a new wig for the footman to put on the great bearish head as Sam Johnson came into dinner, he had no doubt loved her well enough. He said he had loved Henry Thrale also. Well, she herself had done her duty by Thrale; nobody could say otherwise.

The old lady she admitted she was now—she was however not quite the age Johnson had been when he died—came at last to the Pump Room, where the statue of Beau Nash, who had held her, Hester, in his arms when she was a baby, looked down from its alcove, keeping an eye as always. In his day everything had been very strict. He would no doubt have forbidden her entry here as Mrs Piozzi, saying she had unclassed herself.

Dr Johnson had written to Queeney at the time that she, Hester, was the most abandoned woman in the world. That was harsh as well as sudden. Also, she had been widowed again by now three years, and never thought of taking a third husband; the correspondence with dear Sir James Fellowes was merely flirtation of a harmless kind; he was many years younger than she. Perhaps he would be here today. Others had gone. Sophia Byron, Foulweather Jack the Admiral's Cornish wife, would not be elegantly present as formerly: she had died long ago. What a singular family that was! Sophia had once sent one an obscene poem about a geranium. They said her husband in his youth had been shipwrecked for five years in Patagonia, or was it seven? At any rate, Mad Jack had been born to them, with the rest. Sophia had been a good friend, and might even have welcomed one now. She had after all had to weather the Carmarthen scandal, when her son ran off with the wife of the future Duke of Leeds. Sophia had not lived, fortunately, to hear of Jack's death in debt and disgrace in France, after squandering the poor young second wife's fortune. They said the son of that marriage was becoming very famous, but she herself had no time for these so-called romantics; another was the Shelleys' son, reared no doubt on dumplings in Sussex, and getting himself ejected from Oxford for distributing some pamphlet or other saying there was no God. Well, she must be getting old after all: such notions wearied her, and were neither interesting nor probable.

She moved about the company, chatting and being listened to amid the sound of the splashing water. She felt however like a visitant ghost; and other ghosts were Sarah Siddons, who had so often come here; and the little serpent Burney, who despite her advice to Queeney to stay forever single had ended, *après tout*, by marrying a French royalist

49

officer, an *émigré*.

Hester Piozzi turned away early at last: it was not the same here, or anywhere, as it had been in the days when she, Thrale the brewer's wife, had been accepted by everyone as the great Dr Johnson's hostess and inspiration. Yet she still had her wit, her constantly published writings; they respected her, surely for those? She must begin writing yet again, but what? Perhaps a symposium of where words came from, with little anecdotes regarding each, only she was too greatly inclined, they said, to run on and on. Well, it remained to be seen.

She left the rooms, and went slowly back down the street. There was the doorway in which she had first seen Piozzi himself standing, all those many years ago. He had bowed coldly when she had asked him to come and instruct her children, saying he was here for his health. If either of them could have foreseen what would blossom from that first meeting! He had come to Streatham later, of course; later.

The black mourning garments trailed in the summer dust. Bath seemed empty; her tongue had wagged today to little purpose, and to nobody much of note. She would return to Wales, and Johnny. Ah, John, Piozzi's nephew, arriving to them years ago as a little dark boy with a shaven head, off the ship from Milan! How she loved him! The very best must be perhaps a scholar. She had that comfort, that prospect, now Gabriel was dead.

She reached her lodging at last, and went in. Presently—the day yawned before her, Sir James was away, no one would call—she began to ferret among certain papers she always carried with her. It was in her mind that she would begin to make notes about the notion she had just had concerning the origins of words. It was the kind of thing she could have discussed in the old days with Dr Johnson, and on perceiving his handwriting among the bundle she smoothed the paper out. It proved to be the letter he had written to her after taking his first stroke, hoping she would come to him; but her mind had been full of Piozzi's absence, for they had made her send him away about then, hoping she would recover from what they all considered a madness. Madness! Her own dear love!

She re-read the note. It touched her now, as from a dead man; Samuel Johnson had died not long after.

I have loved you with virtuous affection. I have honoured you with sincere esteem. Let not all our endearments be forgotten, but let me have in this great distress your pity and your prayers. You see I yet turn to you with my complaints as a settled and unalienable friend; do not, do not drive me from you, for I have not deserved either neglect or hatred.

There it was; but the note about her

ignominious marriage had followed on the news of it. Earlier, the *Morning Post* had had the effrontery to say that Mrs Piozzi and Dr Johnson were about to be pressed between the same sheets. It had not been at all, not at any time, that kind of attachment.

Well, he and Piozzi were both of them dead. She herself must go on living.

CHAPTER FOUR

Mercer Elphinstone and the sixth Baron Byron of Rochdale were riding on donkey-back among the conveniently enveloping trees of the Kentish Weald. They talked and laughed immoderately with a shared and sparkling excitement, jogging along in their Swiss saddles in almost Dionysian fashion. The rabble of small boys who had followed them on first departure, hoping as usual for pennies, had long been left behind. Society was about its own business in Tunbridge Wells. The daring nature of the adventure became more evident as Mercer and Byron plunged even further into the wooded depths of summer shadows beneath the thick green leaves.

Caro George Lamb, chaperone, recruited by Mercer on purpose that time in the Piccadilly drawing-room, followed in silence on her own donkey, keeping a little behind as was expected of her, now as throughout her married life.

Before the marriage to Lady Melbourne's son by Prinny (but of course *that* was never mentioned) she had been Caroline Rosalie St Jules, a happy enough young girl brought up elsewhere. Now, she was wretched. She had always understood that her real father lived in France, but not, or not till her wedding, that he was in fact the old Duke of Devonshire himself and her mother the famous Bess, now second Duchess, but not quite in time. George despised Caro for her bastardy, and it would of course never do to retort about his; he was in any case presently away on circuit. Caro was a trifle disturbed at the present situation in which she had unwittingly become involved; was it entirely correct? Mercer was so persuasive. Caro's own position in society depended almost entirely on correctness; lacking either beauty or wit despite the old Duke's handsome *douceur* of a dowry, she found herself just suffered by reason of being Lady Melbourne's daughter-in-law and was accordingly much in thrall to that efficient lady. The mildest deviation from propriety was unsafe, and had she, Caro, realised what all of this would entail, she would never have left London to accompany Mercer to what was, when all was said, a relatively secluded lodging by no means near the centre of the town. Then, that improper business of the frank! It hardly bore thinking of; she herself had fretted several nights concerning, it, but there was nothing to be done.

53

Caro surveyed Mercer's jogging back view with increasing disapproval. It seemed a trifle too flamboyant, almost—the despised young wife allowed herself an unwonted flight of imagination—like some gorgeous parrot in company with a slightly smaller, if extremely handsome, eagle, or perhaps a Greek god. Polite society, having been shunned by the pair, would certainly draw its conclusion; if only she herself were not held to blame! As it was, she had lent her name, or rather George's, to the whole mildly dubious business. For Mercer to have written, almost immediately upon their arrival, to Lord Byron in London to ask for a frank was singular enough; but on receiving it, with a letter, to write again a second time inviting him down to Tunbridge 'as he says he is dull in London' had been *fast*; there was no other word for it, and Caro's timid conscience trembled accordingly. Anyone of substance hereabouts would have provided a frank, as Mercer must know quite well; there had been no need to send all the way back to the Albany. It had been, one feared, a deliberate and fully intended *snare*. Caro herself had been ensnared also, as a means of lending respectability. It made one uncomfortable in one's conscience, and the flies were troublesome.

Ah, Byron! For the present hour, he even made poor Caro George forget the customary object of her lonely adoration, the up-and-coming lawyer Henry Brougham. Byron

54

hadn't noticed *her*, of course; few did. He rode ahead beside Mercer, his lame foot concealing itself for the time, his poise in the saddle easy like other men's, different from the limping walk one noticed as a rule, unable to help it. Lameness mattered to Byron greatly, no doubt, in the same way as illegitimacy mattered to herself: scars one could not be rid of.

Mrs George Lamb heard the couple's shared laughter as they rode on, with the green leaves making dappled shadows where the sun pierced through. It brought more flies, which troubled the donkeys; and these flicked their long ears restlessly. Donkeys were patient creatures, beaten and despised. She, Caro, though fortunately, so far, not beaten, resembled them, no doubt; certainly George himself took no notice of her. He was, as one again remembered, away at present; it was uncertain what he would have said had he known of all this. They seldom saw one another or spoke. How it had mortified him to marry her, even with the handsome sum the late Duke had disbursed! It mattered nothing that her mother Bess Foster was the second Duchess of Devonshire, now Dowager: she, Caro, had evidently been born with the rest in the lifetime of the first, the glorious Duchess Georgiana: and *she* had had a lover, Charles Grey; some said Dearest Hart was Grey's son, and there had certainly been a daughter, Eliza. At any rate the Duke had not loved Georgiana as he had, then and later, loved and married plain Bess. One had, at any rate, a large and affectionate family of sisters and half-sisters and brothers and a half-brother; if not Lord Grey's perhaps Dearest Hart was Bess's, smuggled into Duchess Georgiana's bed in Paris by a man-midwife named Richard Crofts. It would never be certain; but they all of them loved Dearest Hart, with his gentle responsive nature and his interest in fine and beautiful things. Then there was little Harriet, married in the north: and called Hary-O by the family, and *she* had married Granville Leveson Gower who already had two illegitimate children by Duchess Georgiana's sister Lady Bessborough, who was Caro William's mother by her lawful husband. It made everything extremely complicated. Princess Charlotte, who of course would never be permitted to marry Dearest Hart although they danced very well together, had, they said, balanced his portrait quite openly on a chair at Warwick House, and old Cornelia Knight, the companion, had prudently told an enquirer it was a likeness of the Pretender when young.

Caro's thoughts scattered as Mercer, who had a kind enough heart, reined in her mount for moments to have a word with the drab little creature: a model of propriety was useful in the circumstances, if necessarily somewhat dull. Caro was aware of Byron's intense and considering dark-blue gaze summing her up;

the sensation was disturbing.

'I wrote to tell Lord Byron that you would be angry if he did not come, and he says that he was so much afraid that here he is,' remarked Mercer, laughing. Byron raised his shapely brows and added that Miss Mercer had also written, most untruly, that Mrs George Lamb was grown quite fat, and he had come down to see that phenomenon, but it was clearly not the case. The famous moonlight pallor, its owner having addressed itself politely, turned then again to the flirtatious Scots heiress, who despite Byron's misgivings attracted him: she made him laugh, like Augusta. He had been amused by Mercer's lack of pretence in writing to him with the transparent excuse of the frank. It was probable that if he proposed, she would not refuse him; but did he want to be tied to so immense a fortune owned by a lady slightly larger than himself? He would not end like his father, having squandered a wife's money without let: but did he want to be controlled and ordered? In a way; but at the beginning of their ride today Miss Mercer had been the one to hand silver to the donkey-keeper, saying that the party was at her invitation and not permitting him, Byron, to put a hand in his pocket. It made him feel like a sponger; and how would he feel if this happened all the time? Mercer talked politics incessantly, even while they laughed together: marriage with her would be like, as it were, a daily, a nightly seat

57

in the Lords. No, he would not propose after all: an old Scots proverb said that when in doubt, it was best to do nothing. They rode on, still laughing uncontrollably: and presently rode back to Tunbridge.

*   *   *

Some time thereafter, Elizabeth, Lady Melbourne was engaged in putting the final touches to the great room of her new house in Whitehall, ready for an evening party on behalf of the wilder of her two daughters-in-law, Caro William Lamb. Lady Caro, despite her tantrums which made her disliked by all of the family except William, who continued to adore her, had been a Ponsonby, and so despite everything could be expected to shore up, a little, Betsy Melbourne's own not entirely unassailable social position. Betsy had bolstered it herself to a certain degree by letting the Duke of York exchange her Piccadilly house for this because he fancied the former; this one was a little less convenient, but on the whole quieter, without the constant press of carriages in the street outside, though it lacked any view at all of the Park except from the rear.

Lady Melbourne caught sight, as she passed, of her own fading beauty in a wall-glass; her mouth had grown loose with the loss of teeth, and it had become necessary to dye her hair. Nevertheless she still made up in spirit and

58

efficiency what she lacked by now in youth, and for William's sake, rather than that of his flighty and high-born wife, would dare anything. Moreover, Lady Caro's spirits needed lifting at present; it was understandable at her age of twenty-seven, for the sole surviving child of the marriage, poor little Augustus, would never be like other children. That weakness must be from the Bessborough side; Betsy's own healthy Yorkshire Milbanke strain was certainly not responsible. Dear William was always patient with Lady Caro, but George could be discourteous; lately when Caro William had asked him in her fantastical way what was the eleventh commandment, he had replied brusquely 'Thou shalt not bother.' Well, Lady Caro was not George's responsibility; as it was, adoring dear William as she, his mother, did, it was needful to keep an eye. He might be Lord Egremont's son, but since Peniston had died there was no other heir.

Betsy permitted herself to sigh a little then among the shining glasses and silver and jellies and elaborate creams. There would be elevated company here tonight, but persons of wit seemed to have departed into the shades. Nothing had ever been the same since Charles James Fox died, and beautiful Georgiana Devonshire, who had so loved him despite his pot-belly and dirty linen and unshaven jaw. Nobody like that was left any more except Prinny: everything else was humdrum, and one's brother Ralph's girl was here again for her second season. A gifted young woman, no doubt, but heavy on the hand and, as always, a trifle too pleased with herself: she got it from her mother, no doubt. As Lady Caro said, for once rightly, there were few possibilities in a combined talent for mathematics and a bad figure. However Annabella Milbanke's figure was not, her aunt decided, as bad as all that, if perhaps a little too narrow in the shoulders; but Lady Caro, a fairy herself, compared with every other female unfavourably in her own estimation and in that of dear William. However it was in any case becoming difficult to find a husband for Ralph's mathematical daughter, and Annabella had got herself, by rejecting several eligible suitors last year, the unfortunate name of The Icicle. That was depressing, and reflected on her habit of dwelling aloud on her unbending and everlasting principles. Mercer Elphinstone, who had refused even more proposals than Annabella, was merely known as the Fops' Despair, an infinitely more alluring title inviting even more proposals. However Mercer was very rich, Annabella herself only moderately so. One need not take too much trouble to ensure that the latter young lady did not fall into the hands of some fortune-hunter; Annabella was cautious enough to take great care, on her own account, of that and everything else.

60

Well, one's brother's child was the least of the responsibilities which loomed large this evening. At least William, her own eldest surviving son, was Member for Leominster; it gave one a certain standing which was welcomed, as things stood. Dear William, with his comically knitted eyebrows and lethargic ways and fine brain! Nobody could help loving William: surely not even his wife. They had been passionately in love with one another, certainly, at the time of the honeymoon, so much so that it had earlier been thought by Caro's family—and her mother Harriet Bessborough was hardly a model of all the virtues herself—that it was advisable, in view of everything, to let Lady Caro marry slightly below her station; after all, the Lambs were nobody except by reason of talent, being merely descended from an attorney. Dear Melbourne himself no doubt acknowledged this, and had always, at least after poor Peniston's birth, let her, Betsy, have her influential lovers and her Whig politics and go her own way, which of course included being a good mother to all her children, especially William and Emily.

Lady Caro drifted downstairs at that moment in a diaphanous garment, her fair curls cropped becomingly as usual, her great eyes wide and, as by custom, somewhat vague. Seeing her thus, with parted cherry lips, it was easy to understand why William loved her and endured as much from her as he did. Despite her tantrums Caro was enchanting, an elfin creature. She began to wander here and there among the silver and flowers and glasses, disarranging everything while waiting for the guests. Lady Melbourne quietly set the moved-about pieces to rights again; after all, it was Caro's evening. Everybody of note would be here who remained in town; she herself had sent an invitation to this young Lord Byron who was meantime the rage of London, thinking he might divert William's Caro for the time. Caro appreciated literature; she even wrote little things herself, as well as being able to draw with some talent, as a rule in mockery.

Lord Melbourne stumped in presently; he took little interest in events and never had, but stood by his wife and daughter-in-law to receive the guests. Annabella Milbanke arrived punctually, as was her habit with everything. It was a pity, her aunt decided, that the young woman wore her bright brown hair, which was otherwise her best feature, in a stiffly curled fringe, hiding her intelligent forehead. Her ponderous manner was not too evident this evening, and Lady Melbourne, who liked to arrange matters in advance, wondered already if The Icicle would make a suitable wife for this young poet, who was said to be in financial straits and who probably, like all poets, needed steadying. It remained to be seen; she herself would think about it when there was time.

Meanwhile others were arriving who were received everywhere, including the Hollands, who had somehow contrived to be so despite the fact that Bess Holland had in her time been divorced and came from Jamaica. No doubt her clever conversation turned the tide, but she would order everybody like so many slaves, was dark in complexion and singularly eccentric. Prinny of course was not here tonight; his gout was too bad, and in any case he was enamoured at present of Isabella Hertford, a Tory who pretended piety. To counter such things, here was Mercer Elphinstone, as usual too elaborately dressed for an unmarried young woman. One had half expected an engagement to Byron *there*, after the gossip there had been about a recent visit to Tunbridge Wells; but it had not transpired; no doubt Miss Elphinstone had rejected Byron also, as was her way: doubtless she would end an old maid, for all her money.

Others arrived, the room becoming almost full; then a small pale magically handsome man with dark curling hair limped in. Byron was announced. Betsy saw Lady Caro pause from where she had been chattering to one of the guests, and widen her eyes, so that their gaze flew still further, intense for once and brilliant as jewels. *That beautiful pale face is my fate.*

*   *   *

The party wound on its course, as parties do; the champagne was drunk, the jellies and sweet meats consumed, the glasses refilled and emptied again, with liveried servants coming and going silently in their powder and braid, and old Lord Melbourne taking himself off early to bed, his duty done. Mercer Elphinstone flirted here and there as was her habit, but without heart; she had seen at once what was happening. *The most absurd, perplexing, dangerous, fascinating little being alive ... all the regular beauties pale before her.* That was what he would write and not to her.

It was as though the two, Caro and Byron, had been pulled together by a magnet. Mercer dispiritedly offered to share a carriage home at last with the staid young woman in the brown fringe, who had been made known last year as Lady Melbourne's niece from Yorkshire. It was a question of *faute de mieux*: Mercer did not feel inclined for a solitary drive home. Annabella Milbanke would be better than nobody.

*   *   *

The two young ladies did not however take to one another on the journey. Staring ahead beyond the carriage lamps into a Piccadilly still crowded at that hour, they made forced conversation that entertained neither party. Annabella wrote later on that Miss Mercer

64

Elphinstone's manner had been 'very roughly agreeable' to her. She added that no doubt the constant and unfortunate encouragement accorded her made the heiress somewhat pretentious. Mercer's own opinion was not recorded. She had a remembrance far clearer in her mind than that of the self-satisfied young woman seated now on the opposite cushions; the sight of Byron staring at Lady Caroline Lamb, as though enchanted, like Thomas the Rhymer with the Queen of Elfland: would the enchantment likewise last seven years?

CHAPTER FIVE

Gout notwithstanding, in his dressing-room on the upper floor of Carlton House George Augustus, Prince of Wales and—since his royal father's evident lapse into a permanent state of insanity two years ago—Regent of Great Britain, the dominions remaining beyond seas and, by hallowed tradition if not actually, France, sat being laced most painfully into his stays. This done, and the royal cheeks duly rouged, his valet placed the famous high curled nut-brown wig from Truefitt's carefully on Prinny's head. The First Gentleman of Europe adjusted it fastidiously for himself. It had detachable side-burns which he did not choose to wear today.

The face he beheld in the glass had once been handsome; so handsome that they called him, in his youth, Prince Florizel. By now, wrecked as his body was by self-indulgence over the years, he could still be more charming than anyone: his manners were said to be perfection itself and as a host, he left nothing to be desired. However the Florizel tradition had in a way been unfortunate. At the time of his wedding—that was, his official one—eighteen years back, the bride had been told, before leaving Germany, that she was to wed the handsomest prince in Europe, but when she set eyes on George in England complained at once that he was too fat. As for *his* complaints about *her* they were legion: at the present moment he preferred not to think either of Caroline or of them.

He cast his mind forwards instead of back. This evening certain plans would, he had already determined, come to fruition: he would cement the projected alliance between his only daughter Charlotte and the Hereditary Prince of the Netherlands, Slender Billy, so called because of his extremely thin legs. The young man had been reared, during his parents' exile following Bonaparte's annexation of Holland, at Westminster School and Oxford for that very purpose; as far as his attendants would allow, he was to all intents by this time an Englishman, and had since then seen good service in the Peninsula with Nosy.

Charlotte—the young pair had been prevented from meeting one another since early childhood—must be given no opportunity to display her unfortunate stubbornness. He had without doubt not been firm enough with her at the beginning, though by now everything was tightened up in true military fashion: after all he was Colonel of the 10th Hussars. Physical punishment he however abhorred; he and his brother Fred York—Prinny grimaced even now at the recollection—had been whipped into outward conformity as boys by their father's orders, and had naturally made up for it as soon as they became young men. However Charlotte, though never thus chastised, displayed a certain habitual awkwardness of temper which could only have come from her mother.

The Regent shuddered away once more from the recollection of his wife, but in the end could not. Apart from her unwashed odour and pert manners, which had disgusted him too greatly to permit him to continue living with her, Caroline of Brunswick had constantly tried to do harm in the matter of their only daughter and by the end, especially as the King could no longer put in a word to the contrary, he himself, as Regent, had cut down the girl's visits to the Princess of Wales to an hour a month, and even that never alone. To separate mother and daughter completely would have given a handle to his enemies; and those were legion.

George Augustus sighed a little, gazing in the glass. If the Regency had happened after the King's earlier attack twenty-odd years ago, he himself would have been young, fit and able: Charlie Fox would have been alive; Maria was there: and everything would have been different. As it was, one must make the best of things; and this plan for the Dutch marriage was at least the forerunner of hope. If Caroline, his loathed wife, were as she constantly threatened to go abroad, it would give him, George, an excuse to divorce her and remarry, perhaps get a son; it was surely not too late, he was hardly more than fifty. For all that to happen, though, it was necessary to keep Charlotte out of the public eye; she was popular with the common people, who cheered her and in their ignorance—of course they were encouraged by certain politicians— shouted at her not to desert her mother. They knew, of course, very little about it, and were deliberately misled by the newspapers.

Charlotte herself had been conceived when he himself was too far gone with brandy to remember the event. Nevertheless he had at no time denied that she was his daughter. Her courage on horseback, and driving her greys at a spanking pace at Windsor, proved it apart from all else; and she was musical, which her damned mother wasn't, though Caroline herself evidently thought otherwise, singing her squalling duets with those Italians, whoever they were, in Bayswater. He himself played the 'cello fairly creditably. He also shared with Charlotte an interest in the arts, though there seemed scant leisure to discuss such matters. He found her, in fact, difficult to talk to; half in the sulks, as he had put it to his mother. 'If you knew Charlotte, she would delight you,' that perspicacious lady had replied.

An alliance with the Netherlands was however desirable for other reasons. Boney had placed his youngest brother Louis, and the latter's unwilling wife Hortense, Josephine's daughter, a blonde with, they said, certain appetites, on the Dutch throne: formerly the country had been a republic. The House of Orange should in proper course replace these upstarts, regaining its unique place with the ruler as Stadtholder, not King. Charlotte should live conveniently abroad, at The Hague, with her husband. Why, on two occasions lately he, George, had been embarrassed by her very existence; the first when they had cheered her, not himself, on the procession back from his own very first speech to open Parliament, being then newly made Regent; an occasion which should have been strictly his own. He had prevented Charlotte's presence accordingly later on in St George's Chapel, Windsor, when he entered it in state; she had sulked at that, and had written imprudent letters to Miss Mercer and no doubt elsewhere. It would certainly be better to have her out of the way despite his occasional affection for her: as time passed, she would be forgotten, like much else: out of sight, out of mind.

Forgotten. How many women truly were so? The Regent's hand, puffed with gout, strayed to where a hard object lay under his shirt. He wore the object constantly against his heart. It was a miniature, framed in diamonds, of his true wife, Maria Fitzherbert, married long before Caroline of Brunswick was brought to England as a condition of paying his debts. He seldom thought now of Maria herself—she had turned out to have the devil of a temper, not to mention false teeth—but the miniature would be buried with him. It hadn't been possible, as Maria was a Catholic, to admit to the marriage at the time; it would have lost him the throne. How he had loved her then, loving him also as she had done in the end, with her fine eyes and white skin, silver-gilt hair, and a profile like a goddess! He had regretted that necessary denial later on of the secret marriage in Parliament; there was no choice, however: that had been Fox who pointed it out, sly old Charlie. Maria had been furious, saying the pair of them had rolled her in the kennel like a whore. She had forgiven him then, however, and again after the Brunswick marriage, made after all of necessity to pay his creditors, who were pressing. He sat now in the great house

70

that had mostly caused the debts: he was forever adding to it, importing and buying strange and beautiful objects with which to embellish it; Oriental vases, Egyptian tables, a clock fashioned like the turbanned head of a negress that rolled its eyes to tell the time and the hours, the everlasting hours when he dared not be alone.

Well, it was time to go; the Dutch alliance was waiting to be cemented. He would see to it that Charlotte conformed to his wishes; a daughter must after all obey her father.

He rose, and with the assistance of the waiting valet, struggled into his precisely tailored coat. The stays chafed as always; but it was necessary to wear them, his weight continued to increase despite bouts of dieting. Moving with dignity, the First Gentleman made his ceremonious way down the Grand Staircase, with its fanciful wrought-iron twisted balustrades, to the waiting company below in the Corinthian Room. The company included a small thin young man with protruding teeth, who smiled rather too often; the Prince of Orange. The Regent set himself, using all of his persuasive charm, to make the poor boy feel at home. They talked affably on the Regent's part, shyly on the young man's, of Wellington's war in the Peninsula, until it should be time for Princess Charlotte's carriage to draw up before the famous Carlton portico from Warwick House, her nearby

71

dilapidated residence. She was late.

*   *   *

At Warwick House itself, guarded as it was outside by two not overly attentive sentries, the Princess Charlotte of Wales had been surveying the gowns laid out for her choice to wear that night by Louisa Louis, her remaining dresser. After some thought—she did not want to appear too greatly decked out to meet this Dutchman—the Princess selected the last of dear Mrs Gagarin's made-up confections, violet satin trimmed with black lace. It set off Charlotte's white skin to advantage and showed her graceful arms and bright golden-brown hair, but on the other hand did not appear unduly frivolous or hopeful. Mercer Elphinstone, whom Charlotte liked to call her dearest Margarite, using a first name seldom remembered, had taught her to be particular about clothes; but Mercer after all had plenty of them, while she, Charlotte, had to make do with an allowance of £800 a year. While Mrs Gagarin had been alive it had been possible to permit ends to meet, more or less; but Mrs Gagarin had died of a wasting disease only this summer. She had been married to a Russian who proved to have a wife already, which was unfortunate; but she had been devoted to oneself. So, of course, was Mrs Louis, who laced one's plump young body now into the

72

violet gown, making small cooing noises as she performed this necessary duty. All her servants, in fact, were devoted to the Princess, who was unfailingly kind to them.

Charlotte surveyed herself at last in the glass. The violet was certainly a trifle sober, but her long white neck and mature bosom rose above; and the new way Mercer had induced her to do her hair, with fullness at the sides, was becoming. It was a pity her eyelashes were light, but there was nothing to be done; Papa and the old Queen, her grandmother at Windsor, would never permit cosmetics. However this Dutch prince might not prove at all to one's taste, although Mercer had seen him coming off a gilded barge at Portsmouth not long since and had said he behaved with decorum. Whatever he was like, this evening was to be decisive; Papa had said she must make up her mind one way or the other, and that thereafter it could not be changed.

The long blue Brunswick eyes stared in the glass rebelliously, and Charlotte's full young bosom swelled again with resentment. To marry somebody was after all a solemn undertaking, and required time for both parties to reflect after meeting one another, and conversing on several subjects. Papa himself had suffered from not having any time at all to reflect on the unsuitable bride they had brought him long ago from Brunswick, who had become her own mother, by now almost a stranger. 'They disliked one another from the start, I believe,' thought the heiress-presumptive without emotion; she had been accustomed to her parents' separation from her early childhood, and always remembered her mother, the Princess of Wales, as living somewhere else, with a horde of strange adopted children. By now, the old Princess, as Caroline was called, had grown very odd. Charlotte disengaged her own mind from the memory of the brief love affair with Captain Hesse, which her mother had certainly encouraged; it hadn't, luckily, come to anything; Charlotte realised now that it had been a fortunate escape. Since the discovery of all that, she had been permitted to see her mother only rarely. As for Papa, long ago when she was small he had used to have her brought to him daily at breakfast, but that had stopped as she grew older and, no doubt, more troublesome. He was still at times kind to her: he had given her her Broadwood pianoforte and had once tried to teach her the Highland Fling at Oatlands, which attempt had snapped a tendon in his foot. One could never predict such things, and though he was said to be fond of children she herself had never had the confidence of Minny Seymour, Mrs Fitz's ward, supposed to be Papa's daughter, who had perched on his knee on one occasion and said, 'I'm Minny. You're Prinny,' and since then nobody had called him anything else.

Poor Maria Fitz would have been kind to her, Charlotte, also, but the papers had reviled Maria in cartoons which tried to pretend that she was teaching the heiress-presumptive to use a rosary, an assumption totally untrue. 'I would not have permitted it,' Charlotte told herself; the Bishop of Salisbury had made her a staunch Anglican in the same manner as Papa had made her a staunch Whig: it was a pity about that recent change of government.

On the whole, there seemed no sane advice nowadays—the old Queen was stuffy, and most of the aunts, though not all, sly—from anybody except Mercer. How grateful she, Charlotte, was to her dearest Margarite, so confident in knowledge of the world! She herself would certainly relate, in a letter this very night, all that should have passed regarding the Prince of Orange.

'It's time, ma'am dear,' said Louisa Louis. How young the child still seemed, never mind being well-developed about the bust like all the ladies of her family! That dress was too old for her; best say nothing. She'd had a hard time, the young Princess, between that mother and that father, and the old Queen with her strict notions and the King stark staring mad. The Princess wasn't wearing jewels tonight, not even the little diamond arrow made like Prince of Wales feathers she liked to wear in her pretty hair on occasions. *That* had come out of a belt the Prince Regent had had sent to him by the

Sultan of Turkey, and by some means it had gone round George's vast middle. They said that Lady Hertford had had her eye on the diamonds in it, but for once he'd given it to his daughter and, bless her, the Princess had had it made up into ornaments at once. Some had gone into the arrow, and some to that Mercer Elphinstone, who didn't need them if anyone did. Again, it was best to keep quiet.

Princess Charlotte laced on her slippers, which she liked to do for herself; and draped her shawl over one shoulder and arm in the elegant manner Mercer had shown her. It was after all December, and as well not to grow chilled; she knew she caught cold easily. Her nerves already felt taut; it wasn't only the prospect of this important meeting with the Prince of Orange, she was always like this when about to confront her father. It was necessary to say and do exactly the right things, or else he became angry, perhaps because he thought she was becoming like her mother, whose manners were certainly extraordinary and who quite openly refused to wash.

Well, she was nevertheless herself, Charlotte, the Hope of England, and no other. She descended the stairs, and entered the waiting carriage; she must be careful not to show her drawers as she emerged, the way they said she usually did: but so did the Duchess of Bedford, and hers were trimmed with lace. It seemed absurd, in any case, to have to drive the short distance to Carlton House, where Charlotte rode most days in the garden; but appearances must be preserved. At least if she liked the Prince of Orange enough to fall in love with him, the protection of a husband would ensure her some relief from Papa's supervision and, also, the attentions of her uncle Sussex's son, Augustus d'Este, who followed her everywhere in an embarrassing manner with his eyes and then pretended he hadn't been looking. Also, there were persons like Hesse, whose acquaintance Charlotte now greatly regretted having made; no doubt Mercer would get the imprudent letters back that she, Charlotte, had written him at the time she thought she was in love.

There it all was, and one would see what happened tonight. The coachman had whipped up the horses, but the pillared portico of Carlton House came in sight almost as soon as he had done so, and the carriage slowed to a halt with a grinding of its wheels, and the footman flung wide the door for Charlotte to emerge.

*   *   *

William, Hereditary Prince of Orange, heard with some trepidation the sounds announcing Her Royal Highness's arrival. He knew only too well that, since his own escape to England as a small boy of three and a half with his

77

parents, all of them fleeing from the depredations of the Corsican Monster who had annexed Holland for his own arbitrary purposes, he, William, had been subtly groomed as a possible bridegroom for this same Princess Charlotte. He knew nothing more of her directly than a faint memory he still managed to retain concerning their last and only meeting at Shooters' Hill, when he had been four and Charlotte not quite two. He remembered her golden curls—they would have darkened by now, no doubt—and her staring, and already critical, long blue eyes. She had been too young to walk safely alone, and had been led about by a pair of scarlet reins fastened securely round her small body. All that was very well; but since then the Princess's reputation had become, if not truly blown on, at least talked about; and Slender Billy retained the thinking of a Dutchman as regarded females and their submissive status. Charlotte seemed to have a preference for military gentlemen, and although William himself had seen distinguished service as far as it went under old Nosy in Spain, he had at the same time been exposed to the same gossip as any other fellow in the regiment. It sounded as if Charlotte resembled her family, and that in itself was not an edifying thought. William of Orange would have preferred to marry some less tomboyish bride, perhaps a Prussian like his mother; or better still like his mother's sister, his aunt Frederica, Duchess of York. However she, for one, spoke well of Princess Charlotte and was evidently kind to her: that was encouraging.

There came into the room then, with a somewhat hearty stride, a very young girl in a violet satin gown trimmed with black lace. She was exceedingly pale, and looked as frightened as he himself felt. It made William, already, sympathetic to her.

They were made known to one another by the Regent, who as usual overpowered the company and thereafter made informed talk. William could not afterwards remember what were the first words he had exchanged with Princess Charlotte, only that her mouth was beautiful and so were her teeth; a point he himself envied, as his own stuck out. He felt more greatly at ease with her than he would have expected, partly because she was evidently shy; had she been bold, he would no doubt have been prepared to believe the worst.

They went in to dinner in the Gothic Dining-Room, but the glories of Carlton House were forever lost on William of Orange. Dinner over—and he could not afterwards remember what subtle glories, created by Carême, they had eaten and drunk—the Regent came to take his daughter on one arm and the Prince on the other, for the customary walk up and down the famous fan-vaulted conservatory. By now, the Hereditary Prince was more than reconciled to the thought of his marriage. It did not signify that Charlotte was heiress-presumptive; he knew he would have wanted to marry her had she been a goose-girl. The future seemed indeed pleasant. When the Monster was defeated, as was already happening in Spain, he, William, would return to his native land, with his charming young bride on his arm. Together they would rebuild a constitutional Holland. It would be a relief to be at home again, little as he himself remembered of it; but England was a raffish country, where everyone drank too much, including, at times, as he well knew, himself. He had been careful not to succumb to temptation in such a way tonight; there were better distractions for once. Beyond the Regent's portly form walked William's heart's desire. He knew he would never alter as long as he lived; whatever befell, he would always be faithful to the remembrance of Charlotte of England.

*　　　*　　　*

Charlotte herself likewise walked slowly on her father's arm, having respect to the Regent's gout and the terrible memory she still retained of his breaking the tendon in his foot at Oatlands that time while trying to teach her the Highland Fling: it had taken him weeks to recover. So far, everything had gone pleasantly enough; she allowed herself to admire the

Gothic vaulting which had been copied from Henry VII's chapel in Westminster Abbey. She had decided that she did not dislike the young Prince of Orange; he seemed pleasant and well informed, if not precisely handsome. Nevertheless when her father came to her afterwards and said persuasively 'Well, I suppose it will not do?' Charlotte defended the young man by saying that she did not find him in the least objectionable. Nobody could have foreseen what happened next; it had been the wrong answer. The Regent, beaming all over his rouged and still comely face, instantly called the pair together and blessed them amid the congratulations of the company, which included Lord Liverpool, the Prime Minister.

Writing to Mercer afterwards, the Princess admitted that she certainly hadn't meant to engage herself to the P. of O., as she styled poor William, quite yet if at all. Apart from national complications which Charlotte had enough shrewdness to begin to perceive, William's teeth were not as good as they had been described to her, and he was much too thin, with legs, come to think of it, like a spider's. She was glad that, when all of this was first mooted, she had begun to play off her elderly cousin Gloucester, known generally as Slice, against this other prospective bridegroom, with the result that her aunt Mary, who had regarded Slice as her own particular beau for years, had advised Charlotte sourly that it was in her best interest to marry elsewhere as soon as possible. Poor Mary, like the other Old Girls, as Charlotte called them, had had to wait far too long to be married themselves: the King, as long as he had authority, had forbidden it on behalf of all his daughters except Royal, the eldest, whom George III regretted having seen married at all and who was now in Germany, calling herself Queen of Württemberg by grace of Boney.

Well, there it partly was; and Mercer and Lord Grey would advise if there was anything to be done. Perhaps, knowing her father, there was nothing. Charlotte began to be fearful; whom, besides Mercer, could she trust? What, now, was to happen?

*　　　*　　　*

'The trouble,' said Mercer some time later, seated in Portman Square, to which Lord Grey had with his usual unwillingness paid a hasty visit—it took four days each way by coach—from his beloved family at Howick, 'is that the Prince of Orange may well expect to take the Princess out of England.'

'He cannot, and neither can the Regent force his daughter to marry against her inclinations,' replied Charles Grey firmly. 'The heir to the throne may not by law be taken out of the country. It was partly for that reason that poor Prinny himself was not permitted to go to

82

Germany to select—and, God knows, inspect—his bride in person. Had he so been, he would surely have chosen the other possibility, Louisa of Mecklenburg, with happier results for this nation. The Queen of Prussia's widower mourns her still, and visits her tomb daily. She was a beautiful and courageous woman who would have made a better consort by far for Prinny than poor eccentric Caroline.'

Mercer was not thinking of Prussia's heroic Queen Luise, but of the handsome man before her, whose views influenced her profoundly but with whom she was not, and had never been, in love. It was almost incredible that this by now highly moral Whig politician, regarded everywhere as a pillar of the virtues and most happily married to a Ponsonby bride who had borne him a large family, should in his time have been numbered among beautiful Georgiana Devonshire's lovers and have fathered at least a daughter on her, born in France, whom kind Mary Grey had adopted alongside all her own. Perhaps also—few breathed this—the present young Duke, himself in love with Princess Charlotte, was Grey's son by the late Duchess. Mercer's sharp-witted friend Hary-O Granville, Dearest Hart's sister, had confided this possibility in closest secrecy. There was also the recurrently whispered possibility that Dearest Hart was Bess Foster's son. Hary-O herself was no stranger to such situations, her husband of four years now, the elderly Granville Leveson Gower, having after all by the time of their wedding fathered two children on Caro Lamb's obliging mother, the bride's own aunt, Lady Bessborough. At thought of Caro, Mercer felt a stab of pain in the heart. Byron remained enchanted, William Lamb complaisant. Society accepted the situation.

She returned to safer topics than those in her mind. 'The young Princess is versed in law,' she ventured. 'It was a part of her education, which the Regent did not neglect. This open jealousy of his has only manifested itself of late: in his way, he is fond of her, although she resembles her mother in certain physical respects and others: her impulsiveness, for instance.'

She knew, in fact, why the Regent was angered and obstinate at present: the lines *Weep, daughter!* had appeared again, this time with Byron's name openly beneath. The Regent they said was hurt rather than angry; but the Princess would not be permitted to see Byron again, and one's former plans were ashes.

'The people still cheer her, and tell her not to abandon her mother,' said Grey. 'Did they know how much harmful gossip the old Princess purveys, they would think otherwise.'

'It is the Tories,' said Mercer, who blamed the rival party for everything.

Her blue eyes regarded Charles Grey

steadily. He was still spoken of as the handsomest man in England, and she knew well enough that she herself was called the Grey Mare. It mattered nothing. Grey's happy marriage had produced a horde of happy children, whom Mercer recalled seeing on the sands at Howick when she visited there; the boys had been riding a donkey, the girls playing at housekeeping in the little seaside cottage set aside by their parents for their sole use, and Eliza Courtney, as Duchess Georgiana's girl was named, was with them all, being of course a little older. It must be pleasant to have so happy a childhood to remember. Mercer's own had been somewhat solitary, aunts and cousins having treated her with excessive respect because she was so great an heiress.

She twisted her foot sideways to survey the fashionable Athenian boot beneath the gown's short hem. Skirts were becoming increasingly skimpy, revealing the ankle and, very nearly, the calf; the young Princess's bouncing walk showed more than it should. 'Were the Princess of Wales to take herself abroad, as she desires, being ignored by all except the lower orders in England, it would make it easier for the Regent to divorce her for imprudent conduct, as almost happened in 1806,' Mercer said. 'A remarriage, and a male heir, would dispossess Princess Charlotte. Her mother does not think of that, but we do. To have her out of the way of the public eye in Holland would suit the Regent very well; out of sight, out of mind, by the time all is done concerning a divorce.'

'You are a perspicacious young woman: I agree with you profoundly,' said Grey. 'It is essential that the Prince of Orange must be brought to a declaration that he will not remove his wife to The Hague even briefly; a short stay could become a long one, especially if the Princess gives birth to a child by the marriage.'

'Slender Billy seems biddable,' Mercer said, 'if a trifle unsteady in his cups. He was after all reared as an Englishman, no doubt for this very purpose.'

'The Dutch are a stubborn nation, with an heroic history of their own,' Grey replied. 'They may not relish the thought of their Hereditary Prince as his wife's English lackey.'

'Well, we must see to it,' said Mercer firmly. 'Cornelia Knight—you know she was formerly the old Queen's reader there—tells me matters are difficult, in any case, with Windsor. The Queen dislikes anyone Prussian, and Slender Billy's mother is of that nation. Strangely, Queen Charlotte is spoken of by everybody here as favouring the marriage; she is frequently misjudged, being seldom seen nowadays.'

'Well, the Orange engagement has not yet been formally announced, and perhaps never will be. Meantime you must advise the

Princess; you are in a position to do so.'

'She is more likely to take a dislike to the Prince, with or without my advice, if once she sees him drunk,' remarked Mercer prophetically.

*   *   *

In fact, William of Orange had already dug his own grave, with the best of intent; honesty was his undoing. On his first formal visit with the Regent to Warwick House, he and Charlotte were permitted to sit regarding one another in the privacy of an alcove, still chaperoned by the solid, nearby presence of Prinny, not to mention that of Cornelia Knight, to whom the Regent chatted most affably, having got his own way or, at least, believing he had; under the circumstances nobody could be more delightful. As for Notte, as the Princess called her, she was an ageing maiden lady, daughter of a naval officer, with a certain talent for making pen-and-ink drawings of Italian scenery; she had published a folio of these in her youth. She had been present in Naples when Mercer Elphinstone's father the Admiral, at that time in command of the Mediterranean Fleet, had fallen out with Lord Nelson over the matter of Minorca. Notte knew less about that than what she remembered directly about her own journey home, with Nelson and Lady Hamilton, after the death of her own excessively demanding widowed mother. '*She* danced a tarantella for us by request at a German inn,' Notte murmured, tactfully refraining from any mention of the amplitude of Lady Hamilton's proportions revealed in course of that process. They had in any case continued to captivate Nelson.

Prinny was pleased; the old thing was an entertaining enough companion; she hadn't been at all happy as reader to his old mother. As for Notte, she greatly preferred her own present situation and endured its inconveniences cheerfully. After the two visitors had gone she would be alone again with her beloved Princess, without Miss Mercer, who fancied herself too greatly and was besides almost constantly present; in Notte's opinion she was after the young Duke of Devonshire now, but had not much hope. A sudden outburst of sobbing from the alcove caused both Regent and companion to hurry forward, despite gout and protocol. 'What, is he leaving already?' remarked the Regent jovially.

Slender Billy looked crestfallen. It wasn't that; but he had felt it only honorable to make it clear to Charlotte that when she was his wife, they would have to live mostly—or, as he had put it to her, at least part of the time—at The Hague. The thought evidently distressed his beloved greatly.

Charlotte could not in fact contain her sobs.

This was exactly what Mercer had warned her of; how right her dearest Margarite always was! Now, she herself saw the whole thing clearly; it was all a plot to get her out of England. It was of no avail to say anything; she must have time to think, to consult Mercer, to make certain of her own rights as heiress-presumptive. She mopped her tears resolutely at last with a handkerchief, having explained nothing to anybody. That was to come.

Prince and Regent took their leave then, the Regent deciding that, after all, he knew young women; it was all of it a summer storm, Charlotte needed a firm hand and always had. He would instruct the young man accordingly. There could be no announcement made quite yet in the newspapers; certain formalities had to be observed first. The Regent murmured about it in soothing wise.

In her own mind, which was not without its perceptions, Charlotte was already working matters out for herself. She recalled that Philip II had not been allowed, by the laws of England, to take Queen Mary Tudor with him to Spain; not, Charlotte reflected pertly, that he would have wanted to. She would consult Mercer, also her own uncles York and Kent and Sussex. They would protect her against her father and this Dutchman. Tarry Breeks would be of no help: he was a fool, and as for her uncle Cumberland, she dreaded him. Above all, she must help herself.

From then on, there was very little Slender Billy could do that did not incur the growing dislike of his young unofficial fiancée.

CHAPTER SIX

Mercer, her thoughts relatively far from the Princess for the time, was gazing at herself again in the glass. She saw a face less trustful, harder in the mouth, than that of the young woman who had ridden beside Byron on donkey-back at Tunbridge Wells over a year ago now. Since then too much had gone amiss to consider him as a bridegroom; less the affair with Caro Lamb, about which all London had talked, than the *Weep, daughter!* lines, admitted to in print on the second occasion, which had put the poet firmly out of royal favour for all time. She herself must forget Byron; and as his coronach—Mercer was after all a Scot—she had a further plan.

She had gone to a chest where certain shining things lay, and had taken them out. They made up the rainbow-hued costume from Albania, worn by Byron himself in his portrait by Phillips. He had sent them to Mercer saying he had only had them on a half-hour, and she might care to wear them at some masquerade. She had demurred at accepting such a gift, but of course had done so; and here it was, gleaming with silver and gold threads. Mercer wound the turban round her head; it hid her hair; she might have been any woman of the East, an odalisque, an houri. The short bodice, stiff with its metal embroidery, disguised her full bosom; and the long camesa—'or Kilt, to speak Scottishly' he had written—she hadn't cut to the knee, as he said they did in that far country, and in Scotland as well. There were greaves for the legs, and a knife, and ataghan 'wherewith to cut your fingers if you don't take care'. The words sounded as if spoken in Byron's deep and remarkable voice; he might have been in the room. Mercer held the folds of the camesa against her cheek, then let them go.

It would never happen now that he would become a noted politician, climbing by means of her money. He and Lady Caro Lamb had for a time seemed like god and goddess together, caught up in the clouds and everywhere else of note: by now, the pace had slackened; they said—she hadn't seen it for herself—that Caro Lamb waited for Byron by custom outside houses to which he had been invited and she had not. That behaviour would weary any lover; Lady Caro was a fool: he had once cared enough to ask her not to waltz, because he could not bear to see another's arms around her. Meantime, they said—how much they always said about Byron!—that Lady Melbourne had suggested The Icicle, her own niece Annabella Milbanke, to him as a wife, and he had duly proposed, but The Icicle had turned him down. Well, it would be good for his vanity; ah, Byron! But she must not allow her heart to break, let alone stab herself with the ataghan; that was not her way, and never would be.

She herself had lately also rejected a further suitor, Colonel Cadogan; Papa was becoming increasingly impatient. However she, Mercer, wanted a husband of matchless distinction, and an ambition blazing like her own; who now would serve? Coolly, Mercer had already thought over the eligibles of town; there was one, overtly dismissed like herself, who could not be called a fortune-hunter because his fortune was even greater than her own and with whom she might make common cause: Dearest Hart, sixth Duke of Devonshire, perhaps Grey's son by Duchess Georgiana or perhaps otherwise Bess Foster's by the old Duke: it did not signify, the title was there, and she herself could bring enough ancient blood to such a marriage to suffice them both.

Hart was, of course, in love with the Princess; Charlotte's wedding, to Slender Billy or another, would settle that matter, though no doubt Hart would remain devoted to her as was his way. *Your Grace will please to recollect the difference between you and my daughter.* So they said, rightly or wrongly, the Regent had addressed the Duke after the cartoon last year called The Devonshire Minuet, with the

Princess's skirts held gracefully and with correctness and Hart looking affectionate and carrying his *chapeau-bras*: the pair danced well together. Why was it so unthinkable for royalty to marry a commoner? It had been done, God knew, by both the younger brothers of George III; perhaps that was not the best argument, one of the brides having they said been a former rag-and-bone hawker in Holborn. Dearest Hart would have been a better bargain: but she would try for him herself. Old Cornelia Knight would spy, of course, and pass comments: that troubled nobody.

A figure had appeared in the doorway; Queeney, returned from driving out, still stripping off her gloves. Her expression was cold, as always; the pale eyes stared at Mercer's twisted oriental turban.

'What are you doing? It was indelicate to accept that gift; it should be returned. There is in any case unceasing gossip about Lord Byron.'

'Not at all; I was thinking of having my portrait taken in it, by Saunders; it will give him some employment. He is still not so popular at full-lengths, he was better off as a miniaturist.' Mercer spoke slowly and somewhat insolently, determined to pass the moment over; she objected to being come upon suddenly in such a manner by anyone, let alone being ordered as a stepmother thought fit.

'Nobody can prevent you, but such a portrait will not hang in my drawing-room; you should be ashamed to show it. We would also prefer, your father and I, to know when to expect you to dinner, or else not; you seldom trouble to tell anyone in the house whether you are coming or going, let alone where.'

She swept off, and Mercer was left with the reflection that Byron himself was not now welcome in Lady Keith's select drawing-room. There had been too much scandal for strict propriety according to the tenets of Streatham.

Mercer slowly divested herself of the Albanian garb. She knew exactly the pose she would choose to adopt for such a portrait; that of Byron's Oriental slave. Despite everything, she knew that she would never love again in quite such a way, though it was true that there might, again, be love. In any case she would never forget Byron. The poor young Princess would not, of course, be permitted to meet him again. 'I have seen a *great deal* of Lord Byron lately!' The passionate echo was still among Mercer's letters. The Princess and he had probably discussed politics rather than poetry, although Charlotte bought every epic of Byron's straight from the printer. When she became Queen, she would no doubt encourage poets; but in the meantime they must both marry elsewhere: one's carefully laid plans had come to nothing.

The thought brought Mercer back to

recollection of this projected Dutch marriage. It was certainly inadvisable, and must not take place. It would be most inconvenient if Charlotte was taken out of the country by anyone at all. Fortunately, by now it was not only possible to cause her to find constant fault with her present unfortunate fiancé, but to look elsewhere on her own account. In fact, Charlotte had fallen in love again, this time perhaps more suitably than with Captain Hesse. Her new passion evidently was for a Prussian prince she called F. Meantime, Slender Billy had not only been seen, drunk as a fiddler, on top of a London coach, but had undoubtedly been so while in Charlotte's presence, a thing she would not soon forgive; and, worse, he still appeared at parties to which she was not invited. Perhaps it was the way they behaved to their women in Holland; well, let William of Orange go back there, and find some other wife.

* * *

Charlotte had in any case already betrayed Slender Billy by an unfaithfulness of the mind, committed at the very moment he had chosen in which to admire her appearance in a silver-and-white gown, again at Carlton House; the Regent's unmistakable presence hovered in the near distance, among distinguished company from Russia.

'You are in great beauty this evening,' had remarked poor William.

Charlotte smiled, brilliantly but absently. 'You know I must do you credit now!' she replied, but the blue gaze had already fixed itself on a spectacular male figure in gleaming Prussian uniform; F., at a great enough distance to avoid immediate knowledge of his chief social drawback, an appalling breath. It was whispered that even Madame Récamier herself did not seem to mind it, such was the Prince's charm. By the time Charlotte came close enough to notice, love had conquered all. Meantime Slender Billy was gazing at her in adoration; how beautiful her teeth were, with the tiny space between the two in front! He felt that he could look at her for the rest of his life, especially when she smiled. It did not occur to him that this seldom happened in his presence. He himself liked to smile a great deal. It was the best way to make friends. Had he known, his constant indulgence in the exercise of smiling was one of the things which were beginning to irritate the heiress-presumptive almost as greatly as the sight of his too-thin legs, like those, she thought once again, of a spider. 'That nasty ugly spider-legged little Duchman,' she was soon to misspell to Mercer. At the beginning, it was true that she had found Slender Billy pleasant enough; but the ground had been cut most unpardonably from under her feet. It was not an agreeable situation by now, but one of course remained polite. How handsome the Prince of Prussia was! He looked about thirty-five, and had bowed over her hand most charmingly.

Later, after conversation with a Russian beauty of loose morals named Madame Tatischeff, who told her a great deal more, Charlotte reflected that it was a pity, after all, that there had never been any question of marrying Devonshire at the time; at least he didn't grin incessantly. Had she herself been married to him by now, her emotions would of course have settled. It was not so long, after all, since royal persons had been permitted to marry subjects, and not always salubrious ones at that; look at Slice's mother and her rags and bones. That had, of course, been one reason for the old King's bringing in of the Royal Marriages Act: well, there it was. In any case she herself had never felt for Devonshire as he quite evidently felt for her, despite her having kept his portrait balanced on a chair that time so that Notte had had to say to someone that it was a likeness of the Pretender when young. That early cartoon of herself, dancing a minuet with the devoted Duke, had likewise expressed their separate feelings exactly, but had caused evident consternation in circles high and low. Nevertheless Dearest Hart would not have taken her out of the country, only as far as Chiswick and Chatsworth; that would have been pleasant.

She thought of Slice, her aunt Mary's beau, again. It might serve to delay matters regarding this Dutch marriage if she herself were to make it known that she preferred Gloucester, knock knees and all, to the Hereditary Prince. There had been bets laid in the clubs, Mercer had told her, at some point about the Cheese versus the Orange. Meantime, silence was golden; except of course with Mercer and Notte. Notte knew more about love than anyone realised, despite her faded appearance now; a pity the naval officer in Naples she had fancied long ago had not returned her sentiments. Unrequited love was extremely hard on the feelings. If only F. returned one's own!

CHAPTER SEVEN

Byron was drinking claret. He did not use the silver-rimmed skull kept for the purpose at Newstead Abbey; this was the Albany; *autres temps, autres moeurs*. He murmured the French to himself uncertainly, having learned it, by mouth only, long ago from his mother, who had it in turn from her grandmother of Jacobite times. Later he himself had, of course, read as much as he could, and in any case picked up languages easily; but in this particular instance lacked the basic grounding.

He gazed gloomily into the drinking glass,

presently refilling it. This Piccadilly lodging he had at first taken pleasure in, its proportions being graceful and its site prestigious, more so than the cramped rooms in Bennet Street he had occupied on first coming to London. However several matters were spoiling his present enjoyment of the green view across to the Park.

Firstly, that damned Caro Lamb was liable to reappear at any minute, dressed as a page according the piquant fancy, as he had at first thought, which had enthralled him; but by now, the fascination he had initially felt was turning to alarm and loathing. It was not merely that she had told him, at an early stage in their relations, that her cynical and worldly husband William Lamb had initiated her into certain perversions which suited her boy's dress; that would not have shocked Byron in itself, being as he himself had long by inclination been since before the Eastern travels, in fact as early as Harrow, where everyone indulged. They had done so, he and she, in both sorts of lovemaking; it occurred to Byron that William Lamb might well have been cautious in such a way in order to avoid having further children by Caro, their one surviving son being an imbecile. The thought increased his pity for her and, perhaps, at the same time removed a little of the allure. Also, there seemed no extremes to which Lady Caro would not go; waiting outside houses for him in the public street, getting herself talked about, to Byron's embarrassment, was only one. Anything she contrived merely sated physical passion, then rendered it wearisome; lately she had sent him a sample of her pubic hair. That trick was no doubt copied from the other Caroline, Princess of Wales, during the so-called Delicate Investigation of 1806; they had found such a sample then, said to be hers, in a box on board Admiral Sir Sydney Smith's ship. Byron's mind roved from Caro Lamb to the young Princess, only child of so disastrous a royal marriage. Charlotte was beautiful, gifted, intelligent and smelled clean. Her father would have given orders regarding her upbringing in such ways; Prinny was notably fastidious, and his wife's education had been neglected in Germany.

Byron thought briefly of the odours of women. Certain men, though never Prinny, found Caroline of Brunswick herself alluring: they included Sydney Smith, of course, also Lawrence the painter. The last-named was however sexually odd, owing to certain deprivations in youth: and having oneself met Caroline, it was possible to separate the natural endowment from the unwashed state which in itself had so repelled Prinny. On the other hand the Regent liked the company of Dorothea Lieven, the Russian Ambassador's wife, who stank like a civet. Dorothea was witty, however; no doubt the gossip that she occupied the Regent's bed was unfounded. Prinny was doubtfully in a state of health, at present, to bed any woman. No doubt the young Princess would shortly be Queen, with improvement all round.

Byron gazed into the claret's depths. The mystery of women included one he could not yet fathom. He was troubled by this unusual aspect in, of all persons, Annabella Milbanke, Lady Melbourne's niece to whom he himself had at one point been induced to propose and who had, very properly, declined him with others. The refusal having brought Byron slight relief—it would have been, as he had said at the time, a cold supper—she had recently reopened correspondence, replete with the most elevated sentiments including the clearly expressed initial statement that she loved another. Her letters had, however, continued, in so puzzling and involved a way that at last he had written in despair to Augusta 'What does the woman want?' What Miss Milbanke wanted by now, it was increasingly evident, was for him to meet her parents formally. If, after all, she was reconsidering him as a husband, it would at least relieve one pressing necessity; money. He was in debt up to the ears; had been so, despite his mother's careful savings and Murray the publisher's advances (one could not, of course, keep those, Byron gave them away to needy friends), ever since his travels abroad. Fornication apart, a man could do nothing at all without incurring expense. To save Newstead, beloved Newstead of his ancestors, from a forced sale was now his most urgent need.

Newstead. He had loved the place ever since coming to it as a boy, when his great-uncle the Wicked Lord's army of crickets, the only creatures to have loved him, had marched out of the house upon his death. Newstead with its lake, and the ruined chapel and long stone passages and gloomy rooms redolent of abbots' ghosts! There was one such, likewise a curse laid on all of the name of Byron at the time of the Dissolution, when his own roystering forebears had drunk wine out of monks' skulls taken out of the rifled tombs. No son had since then ever inherited direct from a father. Would the Princess of Parallelograms, correct in every particular, bear him a son if he took her to wife? A cold collation; perhaps not, in the end. She had, at least, made the advance on this occasion.

Byron turned the emptying claret glass in his fingers, noting, as he always noted everything, that he still bit his nails. Mercer had used to tease him about that; by God, that was a fine woman, but by far too rich. Now, Caro was become too abject to tease him, which fact bored him in addition to everything else: also, he had a conscience concerning William Lamb, her husband. The man loved Caro, and would endure anything without complaint or harshness; but that was no reason to take advantage of his good-nature now that the magic was gone. Soon he himself would round on Caro, like a savage beast, no doubt in verse, if she came in here waving her satin-clad tail again. Her family spoke of taking her to Ireland; perhaps it would happen.

Miss Milbanke. A greater contrast to Caro could not be imagined; changes were lightsome, as the Scots put it. Byron doubted that possibility; prim, chilly, mathematical, stuffed with principle; at least such a wife would steady him. It would be refreshing, somewhat like a cold bath, perhaps, to be managed by such a woman.

Also, Annabella's dowry would stave off the creditors, at least for the time. He himself could go on writing in peace; he had already the notion of another epic, and a flicker of an idea for a fourth canto of the *Childe*. Later, free from worry, perhaps up at Newstead, that could commence, with his preceptress present somewhere to keep him in order. Meantime, he must go back to his accustomed diet of charcoal biscuits and soda water; too much claret caused him to put on weight. He smiled; perhaps if he did that, even Caro Lamb would lose interest; and it would at least stop her unwelcome visits if he had a wife.

Meantime, to consider broader matters, they had destroyed his poor little pagod, Napoleon, at Leipzig. Byron had always had three enduring loves; the Emperor, George Washington, and the labouring classes of Britain and Ireland who suffered under a selfish rule. When he had leisure from everything else, he must take up that penultimate cause again. Meantime, the Allied leaders were to come in consort to London, to pick at Napoleon's bones and send him off alive to Elba. Fat Louis would come down from Hartwell to be restored to a kingdom which doubtfully wanted him or his sour-faced Bourbon niece. Stupidity was about to prevail everywhere; the times were not inspiring. Well, he himself must continue to be his own inspiration; at least that faculty was still within.

He took up his pen, which had a lightly carved *repoussé* gold handle; and wrote a reply to Annabella Milbanke. It was pointless to wait for Augusta's answer to his earlier anguished question; she was always cheerfully vague about such things. If only brother and sister were permitted to marry as had after all of necessity taken place in Genesis, at the beginning of the world! *In Saturn's reign, such mixture was not termed a stain.*

Augusta.

CHAPTER EIGHT

Mrs Piozzi scanned her newspaper, registered the fact that the Princess Charlotte might or might not be engaged to the Prince of Orange, wished the pair happy if it were true—but the papers published a great deal of irresponsible nonsense, as she herself had cause to know—then read the rest of the news idly and without her usual avid interest in all that took place anywhere. She was too greatly occupied with her own unhappiness. Everything had gone wrong once more.

Firstly, there was the question of Streatham. The late Henry Thrale had left her, as his widow, the life interest, but lately the tenant—such a house was of course far too large for oneself to live in—had gone inconveniently bankrupt. It was extremely difficult to find anyone to replace him, although there had been a feeler the other day from Prince Lieven, the Russian Ambassador. He would have to occupy Streatham Park mainly by himself, no doubt, his sharp-nosed Princess being mostly elsewhere, supposedly in the beds of very high society indeed. Princess Lieven was certainly no beauty with her chicken's neck; it must be her conversation. In any case the rent should be forthcoming with such an elevated tenant.

Everything would however have been so

much simpler had only Queeney and her sisters agreed to buy the rights of the house from her, their own mother; but there was a united refusal. Neither Cecilia, after a pleasant visit made recently to her and the boys at Segroid, nor Queeney, advised no doubt by her chilly old Scot of a sailor husband, would agree. They knew, without question, that all they need do was wait for her, Hester Salusbury Thrale Piozzi, to die, then Streatham would be theirs by Thrale's will in any case. It was not a pleasant thought on the part of her girls, in especial as she herself had somehow heard again, after all these years, that Admiral Lord Keith had stated in a letter to Queeney that it soothed her mother from the recollection of her improper conduct to worry over Streatham 'which I daresay Ranckles her now and then, if Vanity would permit her to confess it'. What a thing to write to a daughter about her mother! The impudence of the man, merely because he held a title! Piozzi had been a gentleman; they could say what they liked, she knew better than anyone. If only he were here now to comfort and advise her! Like most Italians he had always understood the value of money, and respected it. He would never have allowed her to be driven to the pass she was in now, she, a poor widow with nobody to advise her; not that she usually needed, or heeded, advice from anyone else.

She moved restlessly, scratching the long-healed scar on her lip; it had come there after a fall long ago. It had been pointless to try to turn Johnny, dear Piozzi's nephew whom they had adopted together from Milan, into what she had herself described at the time as a scholar, a Christian and a gentleman. Hester had strained every nerve, and remaining social contact, lately to obtain for him entry to one of the better Oxford colleges, and had succeeded at last with Christ Church, which of course was not cheap. It had been satisfactory to think of Johnny as accepted among high-born young Englishmen, attired like them in a square scholar's cap and black gown, and ensconced in the comfortable, high-ceilinged rooms with their view of the quadrangles and within echoing sound of Old Tom. She had had that satisfaction, last year; that beholding the young man in such a way among the rest, who treated him in no way differently from themselves. Why should they, after all? His name, by now, was John Salusbury Piozzi Salusbury by law: the last a very old name she was still convinced came down from a mediaeval personage named Adam of Salzburg despite Queeney's expressed doubts. Salusbury itself had been Papa's name. Nevertheless Johnny had told her lately that he wanted to leave Oxford, having no interest in learning. It was indeed a pity; he had received gifts from so many of her friends to set him up, including china from Lady Kirkwall, and a handsome quarter's allowance from herself. At least he had not been as ruinously extravagant as Lord Byron, who at Cambridge had spent all his poor mother's careful hoardings on loose ways immediately. Sophia, his grandmother, would have had a good deal to say about that: but, like so many friends, she was dead. One missed her Cornish fancies, blurted out unexpectedly.

Byron. These romantic poets, as they were beginning to be called, would no doubt be but the fashion of a passing hour. Dr Johnson would have had no time whatever for them, would have said something to root them out of everyone's consciousness for all time and render them absurd. He also would have helped her over Streatham, no doubt, even only by telling her what to do. The girls had been so angry with her for cutting down the trees, but it was necessary to have money for the place's upkeep, and they were no help. It was all very well to sit waiting for her death before laying out a penny on the place themselves.

She returned to thoughts of Johnny, as being pleasanter by far. She could forgive him everything: his wanting to leave Oxford, his asking leave to live in future as a country squire at Brynbella, because he had fallen in love. The young lady—Hester Piozzi smiled, her rouged old face breaking into amiable wrinkles—was of good family, a blessing, after all. Her name was Harriet Pemberton. She would make a charming squire's lady in dear unforgotten Flintshire: of course one would make over Brynbella formally to the couple, which necessarily meant Johnny. They could be married next year; there was no reason for delay.

Mrs Piozzi returned to her paper. It looked as if Bonaparte's star was most certainly starting to decline. Things had never been the same for him since the dreadful French retreat from Moscow; but how he had earlier improved the roads in Italy! She and Piozzi had had smooth journeyings while Gabriel played his travelling harpsichord on their way. It was pleasant to remember: to remember.

CHAPTER NINE

Young Princess Charlotte had been in a state of increasing rebellion ever since catching first sight of F. in full glory. It was true that she and Notte hadn't been invited to dinner that night at the Regent's, merely to appear together afterwards to meet the guests: and beyond the elaborate centrepiece on the table portraying, of all people, her grandmother the Queen and her old mad husband, with Prinny himself, patronising the arts—it was true the King and Queen had once done so, collecting paintings,

109

but that was a long time ago—beyond all that, wilting anyway by then in the heat of the candles, and past the crumbs and débris left from the feast in the dining-room, had been F., infinitely to be desired, but unattainable while she herself was still attached to the ridiculous little 'Duchman'. Present also, however—she had evidently sat on the Regent's right—had been Princess Lieven, with her scrawny chicken's neck and oddly arranged thin dark hair, and even odder fascination as she certainly smelt: and, more importantly, beautiful Madame Tatischeff, who had since called at Warwick House to continue the conversation with oneself. Charlotte did not perceive that the Russians were using her for their own purposes and intended to try to break off the Dutch marriage to further these: she only knew that Madame talked to her again of F., and on leaving took away a gift Charlotte had already lovingly purchased for him, a talisman to pin in his tall uniform hat. She gave everyone gifts; Devonshire had had a gold watch-chain he always wore and always would, Saunders the painter a chair, Mercer a bracelet. Moreover, Madame Tatischeff's talk, of the glories of St Petersburg, built long ago on a marsh but by now full of gilded spires and coloured palaces and containing the incredibly handsome unmarried Grand Duke Nicholas, was accompanied by further aid: later she brought a return gift from F., which

110

Charlotte duly cherished; a small gold ring with a turquoise heart set in it. It strengthened her to turn it secretly on her finger while the kind little Duchess of York, herself a Prussian Princess and Charlotte's aunt, tried to put her off F., saying his breath was so horrible she herself had had to change her seat recently in a box at the theatre and sit beside somebody else. The whole thing was grossly exaggerated; Aunt Frederica had bad teeth herself, and after all didn't seem to mind the smells of the animals at Oatlands she slept with in her grotto, the Duke being by custom elsewhere, though that old scandal about his mistress Mary Anne Clarke and army preferments had been four or five years ago now, and he was back again as Commander-in-Chief of the army and very well liked indeed.

Other uncles had been helpful, though she hadn't mentioned F. openly. Her uncle Sussex in particular, who had had similar troubles of his own in youth, proposed to raise it in the Lords that she, Charlotte, must on no account be taken out of the country. Slender Billy meantime would give no such assurance, merely continuing to smile and smile, like Shakespeare's villain, and get drunk; and in the end Charlotte dispatched a letter to his lodgings on her own account saying firmly that their engagement was at an end and asking him to inform the Regent. In fact she was a little frightened of doing so.

William replied to her letter with hurt surprise and great dignity, and had the correctness to advise her to tell her father herself. As a result, fury broke out that spring. The newspapers published a memorable cartoon shortly, with an element of truth; Prinny, prancing with rage and wielding a broom, sweeping away Notte, Mercer, with an escaping Charlotte herself in the background, and poor Louisa Louis knocked to the floor and the Bishop of Salisbury standing nearby apostrophizing his own wig. In fact 'all those damned women', the Regent had said, must go; and Cornelia Knight, ejected the very same evening, and offered a room for the night instead in Carlton House out of compassion, replied with firmness that her father had served the King many years and that she herself could endure a night's inconvenience elsewhere. In fact she had hosts to whom to go. All of the ladies were to be replaced with new ones, who presumably would not influence the Princess against her father. Meantime, Charlotte did not know who they were to be: and was a prey to wild misgivings. How could she ever part with her dearest Margarite? How, without help from Margarite and others, could she now reach F.? It was true that he did not seem, so far, to echo her own enthusiasm; his letters were courteous, but lacking in any sign of passion, and he hadn't proposed. Worse, the person who, Charlotte was informed at last, was to replace dear old Notte was the stuffy Duchess of Leeds, a second wife: the first, who had been very beautiful, had run away long ago with Lord Byron's father Mad Jack and had then been divorced. There was no likelihood of the present Duchess's running away with anybody; and her daughter, Lady Catherine Osborne, was a spying snivelling little creature. Everything was becoming intolerable, and there was even word of sending *her*, Charlotte, to confinement at Windsor, no doubt to run mad there alone, like the King.

Suddenly, Charlotte herself was no longer to be found. It was by then high summer, and a distraught young lady, without her maid, was observed to be signalling at anguished intervals down the busy Haymarket towards Pall Mall. No driver worth his salt would stop, as such a young person must be very ill-advised and bad for custom. Both epithets were meantime true about the heiress-presumptive, whose worst enemy at present was herself. In a hastily donned bonnet and flung-on pelisse, she had somehow made her way unrecognised past the Warwick House sentries and was attempting to reach, of all persons, her mother.

*   *   *

Mercer had already been shaken out of her usual self-confidence and firm sense of direction. She had heard the Princess say she

113

would go to her mother's: Louisa Louis had seen her put on her bonnet and pelisse; well, the thing to do was follow. Mercer ordered her carriage, and on the way lapsed into black foreboding. Everything was going wrong. The papers had made her ridiculous in the cartoon showing the Regent prancing into Warwick House in a rage and sweeping her and the others out with a broom (in fact he had called there and scolded her notably about the breaking off of the Orange marriage, and for once in her life she had burst into tears) and, also, there had been a notice in the *Morning Post* connecting her name with that of Devonshire, and the Admiral, likewise furious, had written to deny any engagement to the Duke. There would be none, Mercer knew by then: Dearest Hart had made it clear, at one of his enormous champagne breakfasts at Chiswick House, that he would not marry her or anyone at all. Was it for the sake of his mother's memory and her affair with Grey? Was it because he was the son not even of Grey, but of Bess Foster? Was it because of Princess Charlotte? Mercer had been too miserable to ask, and now there was this flight of the Princess herself to be seen to; word had come that a courteous young Jewish art dealer in the Mall had helped Charlotte into a hackney and that she had herself directed it to Oxford Street; that meant Bayswater and the old Princess's house at Connaught Place, a most unfortunate haven to have chosen with regard to the young Princess's reputation.

Others were following, mostly in humble hackneys also, summoned in haste by the Regent, who would not go to his wife's house in person but, as originally intended, was present that evening at a card party. On arrival Mercer's uncle by marriage William Adam—he was of course there, he was everywhere, having become a Privy Councillor by means of an ear long kept to the ground—thrust his round anxious face in at her open carriage window, sweating slightly; the summer evening continued warm.

'They say the Princess of Wales is over at Blackheath, and has been sent for in haste. We had maybe best go in.'

His Scots voice soothed Mercer. He had been an aspiring young lawyer who had had the temerity to carry off, and marry, her not too young aunt Eleanora Elphinstone from among a mildly resisting posse of aristocratic relations. Since then he had continued to better himself, taking silk in England, becoming a member of Parliament and climbing steadily in the Regent's personal favour. It was as well to have him here among the rest.

She followed him, threading her way among the press of cabs and carriages that by now thronged Connaught Place, used as it was to being deserted by most society other than doubtful. Inside, they found the young

Princess in hysterical laughter; the thing was done, the news of her flight would soon be all over London. Her bonnet lay by her on the floor and Mercer picked it up; the curling gold-brown locks, which somebody had once compared to a mediaeval madonna's, were disarranged with haste. Charlotte had in fact never looked more beautiful; Mercer reflected, a little jealously, that Dearest Hart still wore the gold watch-chain the Princess had given him and said he always would; the poor Prince of Orange, dismissed, was likewise said never to take off her ring. As for F., God knew what she had sent *him*, besides letters; fortunately he did not seem at all ardent. It remained to be seen what would happen next; at present, nobody knew.

'My mother is out,' remarked Princess Charlotte with sudden flatness, adding that she herself had ordered dinner when she arrived.

Caroline of Brunswick's carriage drew in at last from Blackheath, and she made her unsavoury entrance, hardly embracing her daughter. She was unhelpful—nobody, Mercer decided, could have expected her to be otherwise—and over dinner firmly reiterated her intention of going abroad, in spite of everything. Her eyes did not, as usual, meet anyone else's. Charlotte had recommenced her brilliant laughter and talked with apparent ease; everyone said she was in good spirits, but there was tension in the room. It will not do for

116

her to spend the night at her mother's, Mercer was thinking; if she does, her character is gone.

Another carriage was making its way meantime towards Connaught House, summoned by an anguished note from Charlotte herself; inside sat her favourite uncle, the Duke of Sussex, by now an eccentric-seeming figure in a plain black skull-cap. He had once been a beefy, if athletic, young man who had scrambled nightly across attic roof-tops in Rome to make love to Lady Augusta Murray, whom he had wedded in good enough faith at an Anglican ceremony there and, later, at a second such in St George's, Hanover Square. However the King had thundered in with the Royal Marriages Act and had declared both ceremonies null and void. Poor Goosey—Sussex had discovered by then that Lady Augusta was a goose indeed—was left with the stigma of being a mother but no wife. It was their son Augustus who made eyes now at Charlotte to her constant embarrassment, and who was considered legitimate only in Ireland, where people thought differently. All this made the Duke sympathetic to irregular situations like the one arising at present. He was ushered inside, and saw the Princess alone downstairs.

Brougham, her mother's adviser and Caro George Lamb's beloved, who somewhat resembled an ambitious beagle, arrived also; and presently led Charlotte to the window.

There was to be an election next day and dawn was already breaking over Hyde Park. Blood would certainly flow if it were known that she had fled here, he assured her; and Charlotte knew in any case by then that the whole enterprise had been a miserable mistake. Notte had been dispatched back to Warwick House and had duly returned with her night-things, but she hadn't used them and after all would not. It would be best, she now knew, to return in a carriage of her father's: nobody could gossip then.

This came, at her own request, with much pomp of powdered lackeys; and once inside, Charlotte, her cheeks still wet with tears, recalled what might well be her last parting of all with Mercer: when would she and her dearest Margarite be allowed to meet again? Her father had earlier made it clear that the place to which she was to be sent was Cranbourn Lodge in Windsor, to see nobody but her grandmother the Queen; but even the company of Old Plugnose, who was not always as unsympathetic as everyone thought, would be better than that of the dull Duchess of Leeds and her spying daughter, Lady Catherine Osborne. Lady Catherine had in fact spied so constantly that Charlotte had lately locked her in the water-closet for a quarter of an hour, saying through the door that that must be where she wanted to be, she was in the room so often. Afterwards Lady Catherine had gone on

118

spying and listening to everything, whether it was said in English, French or German; lately the rest had tried Italian together, and the persistent young woman had got herself an Italian dictionary and had been seen poring over it studiously by the light of a candle. The whole situation was beyond belief, and beyond her own ability to deal longer with it.

At any rate, here they were at Carlton House, and the Princess was kept waiting in the carriage a full half-hour because nobody knew what etiquette to employ on her arrival, such a thing never having happened before in precisely the same manner.

Charlotte herself was in great trepidation at the thought of meeting her father; he would certainly be angry. The single consolation about the whole matter, if it was one, was that she knew now what it was like to ride in a hackney carriage, with its smell of humanity, dirt and damp straw. No other member of the royal family had ever done such a thing before herself. She had that to remember, at any rate.

CHAPTER TEN

Two days before Princess Charlotte's hackney-carriage adventure, a young man of surpassing dark good looks was seated in his Marylebone lodgings writing a letter. He was in shirt-sleeves, having discarded his tight and braided uniform coat: the resulting sight entranced the Abigail, briefly looking round the door armed with her duster and broom. Prince Leopold of Saxe-Coburg waved her away. He was aware, nevertheless, of the splendour of the uniform coat, a Russian general's, draped over the back of a chair. It gave him a sense of importance, a circumstance he had somewhat lacked from birth, being the youngest of his family. As he could never inherit the Duchy of Coburg, which would go irrevocably to his brother Ernest, he must look elsewhere; and this in any case accorded with his present inclinations.

He passed a hand over the dark locks which had fallen meantime over his eyes, and paused in the writing of his carefully phrased letter: it was necessary to frame every word with caution, as it could make or mar his suit. The Regent, to whom the letter was addressed, was notorious for his sudden petty dislikes; one must take pains not to incur anything of the kind. It was particularly important in the present instance, a delicate one indeed; in fact, a proposal that he, Leopold, Prince of Saxe-Coburg-Saalfeld, be considered as a husband for the Princess Charlotte of Wales, heir-presumptive of Great Britain.

Leopold laid down his quill, and took some moments to recall his few meetings with that same adorable personage. The first had been in Pulteney's Hotel, on the back stairs. This unlikely milieu had been made necessary by the presence among other officers of the Confederation, of Slender Billy himself in the foyer below, attendant like the rest on the celebrated Tsar Alexander. That had possibly been the reason why Charlotte had not been invited, as her aunts Mary and Elizabeth had been, to meet the imperial giant and his sister the Duchess of Oldenburg, who was said to have come over secretly hoping somehow to marry Prinny. Charlotte had contrived to meet them both nevertheless; and rather than thrust her way, with Notte, again through the crowds in the Park, preferred to wait and order a carriage at the rear of the building. He, Leopold, had of course offered his arm to so refreshing a young creature in her summer gown and bonnet; and had, for the first time in his cautious life, fallen in love.

It was not a state of mind to which he had expected to have to accustom himself; its very intensity troubled his precise and well-regulated nature. He was of course already fully educated in the amorous arts, his voluntary teacher having been a Prussian princess well versed in them; he himself had been eighteen at the time, and was now twenty-four. At the back of his recollection, not to be thought of further importance after the way matters in Europe had turned out, was a subsequent brief affair with Queen Hortense, Napoleon's fair-haired stepdaughter; she had fancied him briefly, but he had found himself replaced in permanent fashion by a gangling long-legged young French aide named Charles de Flahault de la Billarderie. It was more flattering to remember that the Emperor— Leopold having gone there to seek his fortune while things pointed that way in the first instance—had remarked to somebody that he, Leopold of Saxe-Coburg, was the handsomest man ever to set foot in the Tuileries. Now, with Saxony no longer under the Bonaparte heel, matters were different: he himself was an officer in the service of Tsar Alexander the Blessed. He had however made it clear in this letter now before him, knowing that the Duchess of Oldenburg had not found personal favour with the Regent, let alone he with her, that he was far from favouring the Russian Imperial family in any way personally. One of them, after all, the Grand Duke Constantine, had made a shocking husband to Leopold's elder sister Juliana; among other faults Julie maintained he was like an ape, and he certainly had tufts instead of eyebrows. The second sister Victoire's marriage, to the difficult old Duke of Leiningen, had been on the whole more successful; but that was of no immediate relevance.

Reading the finished letter over, the young man could see nothing wrong with it; it was complete with well-turned phrases in excellent French. He had made it tactfully clear, assuming her father's displeasure, that he himself had been mistaken in accepting the young Princess's impulsive invitation to visit her at Warwick House, which had of course happened. He admitted that he should decidedly have asked her father's permission first, but had assumed that in England such customs did not pertain; the Princess had after all implied that others were in the habit of making her such visits. He, Leopold, now realised his mistake, and apologised to Charlotte's still unknown father profusely. He also pointed out that as he himself had a cool and steady nature, aspirations which, as he would not yet formally state, might perhaps be possible for His Royal Highness to keep slightly in mind. After all—the letter did not say so, but everyone knew—it might not be too easy to find Princess Charlotte a suitable husband after the recent altercations with the House of Orange.

Leopold then sat back and thought of Charlotte herself. How attractive she was, with her white skin and beautiful hair, and her vivacity! The Duchess of Oldenburg had greatly approved of her. Charlotte's laughter had shown pretty teeth, with the narrow space between the two front ones poor Billy had liked. Leopold himself had trouble with his own teeth and seldom showed them. He also knew that his way of speaking in any language was deliberate and slow, showing, to the

123

assumed approbation of the listener, how he always thought before he spoke. The English did not by custom seem to do so. It was in fact impossible, he had already found, entirely to please that nation.

Leopold sealed the letter and sent it off; and thereafter recalled his own history, the uncertainty of his boyhood and his father's slow dying after chilly exposure overnight in a marsh when the upper castle was attacked; his own careful education by his grandmother, whose favourite he had been; the slow rise thereafter to promotion in the army, and the encounters, well enough fought, at Lutzen and Bautzen. The Tsar had embraced him at last when, after riding hard many versts in the snow, he had presented himself formally in the Russian camp and declared himself, with the rest of the confederation of Saxon princes, against their conqueror Bonaparte. Alexander had made him a general, but war was over by now, and he must look to the future; as was to be hoped, to an even higher position, that of future Consort of Great Britain. He was already persuaded that Charlotte herself would have no objection; she was known to fancy handsome young men. Their talk together had been easy, even flirtatious. He remembered every word.

What Prince Leopold could not have foreseen, for it was not in his nature to do so, was that the Regent summed him up at once and ever after referred to him as the Marquis Peu-à-Peu. As for Charlotte, on being informed of the gist of so smug an epistle from a jumped-up German nobody had heard of, she was furious. Whoever she would marry, if by now she was to marry anybody at all, it would not be the egregious Prince of Saxe-Coburg. She still burned uselessly for F.

CHAPTER ELEVEN

Lord Byron was surveying newspaper cartoons several months old, which from time to time he tore out by habit to amuse himself in retrospect. One was of the famous Warwick House débâcle, and he had kept it for the sight of Mercer Elphinstone in one of the coal-scuttle bonnets the Duchess of Oldenburg had then already made fashionable and which, by this time, all the women in England who had any money allowed them wore. The other was of Princess Charlotte in a buttoned-up driving coat she could not possibly have taken time to put on, and an obsequious cabman swearing to defend her with his life. At news of that episode, *The Times* had thundered out a leader about a father's rights and a daughter's disobedience. Remembering his own talks with that ardent royal creature, Byron hoped her family were not being too hard on her; very little had been heard of Charlotte since she had been removed to Cranbourn Lodge, though he had heard she had been seen out riding in Windsor Great Park. As for Mercer, he saw her so seldom now that it was not possible to ask her whether or not she had again been permitted to visit the Princess.

He himself had settled certain matters; he was engaged to marry Annabella Milbanke in the ensuing December. The prospect filled Byron with no undue excitement. He had duly been to visit her and her parents at their house of Seaham in Yorkshire, had decided that he could not endure her mother and that her father, Sir Ralph Milbanke, Betsy Melbourne's brother, though good-natured enough, became a pretentious bore over the port. There was likewise a jumped-up companion-housekeeper or such who regarded him with evident doubt, not that that mattered. In any case the thing was, more or less, done. Lady Melbourne was looking already for a house for them to rent in London after the marriage. Meantime Caro Lamb, thankfully removed to Ireland by her family, was said to be writing a novel; no doubt she would put him in it. He had heard, by way of someone or other, that she herself had been put into so damp an Irish house that she had marched in carrying two candles in the dark saying: 'Here comes the master,' and in ahead of her walked a toad.

That was the kind of thing one relished about Caro, but he was glad to have her out of the way; and meantime, while there was still freedom, had diverted himself with other women. Lady Oxford's autumnal charms had been restful after Caro's crazed persecution, though truth to tell he had loved best, and had written a poem on, her eleven-year-old daughter Ianthe. If only Ianthe were old enough for him to have married! An enchanting child; the times were always out of joint, and he had his cold collation waiting at Seaham. Perhaps Bell was however not so cold after all; she had flung her arms round his neck on arrival, but later in the visit had begged him to leave earlier than had been arranged, lest her feelings tend towards impropriety. Byron had left with a mixture of relief and mild amusement. Marriage might not be so dull.

Now, there was a little time of freedom left, only a little. Byron took up the gold *repoussé* pen and began to write. The sound of carriages passing beyond the courtyard did not disturb him. He would be sorry, despite the remembered incursions of Caro, to bid the Albany farewell.

*　　　*　　　*

The world was changing meantime, or perhaps rather going back to what it had been. Napoleon had escaped from Elba and had come back, as he had promised, with the violets; and Marshal Ney, the bravest of the brave, who had sworn to return him to the Bourbons in an iron cage, had instead done as hundreds of veterans had likewise done at sight of the small stout figure in the familiar grey overcoat, and had rushed towards him. Once again, there was war.

War. Byron knew very well that there was war likewise within his own mind, his heart; that that last would never belong in truth to anyone except Augusta. Augusta, his half-sister whom he had not met till he was a young man, and who, like him, had in her veins the wild blood of Mad Jack; Augusta, with her heedless laughter, the way they always understood one another without words and were perfectly at ease; Augusta, married to an unsatisfactory cousin near Newmarket, with her children, one of whom might well be his own: Medora, who unlike any reported child of incest had not turned out after all to be an ape. There had been that time they had been snowed up together at Newstead, he and Augusta, in the place of monks and ancestors, and had made love. It had been the most natural thing in the world, but society would make of it damnation, ostracism. His own early teachings in Scotland, the furtive handlings of his nurse May Gray, had convinced Byron early that he was in any case damned. Damnation meant delight, and so be damned to everything. He wouldn't dare see Augusta again until after the marriage; if he did, he knew that he would not marry. That would make a scandal second to none; he had best endure, and survive somehow, and pay his debts; the creditors were again pressing. Annabella, Princess of Parallelograms, would keep his thoughts from straying where they should not: she had a fine enough bosom on which to lay his head, once he was permitted to do so.

Augusta. She had been the sole surviving fruit of her father Mad Jack's elopement with the fair and frail marchioness, who had died by following Jack Byron too soon out to the hunt in France after the birth. After that there had been his own mother, poor soul. She had nursed the little Augusta when the child lay ill, then the grand Holdernesse relations had taken Augusta away to be brought up in circles far removed from his own, those being the third-rate lodgings in Aberdeen, the poverty and constant unedifying scenes. If they had met in childhood, they would have grown up together as brother and sister, not lovers under a dark star. Having met her for the first time much later, not soon enough, he had known at once that there could be no other outcome, in the end.

Augusta. He himself was after all to become a husband in December. That would settle it; he would become at the same time a

129

respectable citizen, like Sir Ralph over the port. Lady Milbanke had leg-bones that bowed forwards: the new short hems showed at once when a woman's legs were not what they ought to be. Augusta had graceful limbs, a long neck, freckles; she was lovable, never cold, never correct, never after all knew everything, damned like himself, like him, damned, forever damned, a Byron, a Byron.

   Augusta.

             *   *   *

Waterloo was fought three months before Byron was married. Among those fighting on the side of the Allies was Leopold of Saxe-Coburg. He was close in correspondence by then with Mercer Elphinstone, who however gave him small encouragement in his suit: the Princess, she assured him, wanted to be troubled by nobody for the present. This happened to be the truth. She had been disillusioned about F. by those who knew: and being young, suffered greatly.

CHAPTER TWELVE

A fat blowsy woman in a black wig sat on deck, clutching to her a boy of unintelligent aspect, as the *Jason* ploughed through the August

Channel seas. Caroline of Brunswick, Princess of Wales, was leaving England at last to do as she liked. In fact she had always done so, which was part of the trouble: the English, apart from the common folk, had kept their noses in the air from the beginning. Even the Tsar— Caroline's mouth drooped over her late grievances—even he, who had confessed to a curiosity to visit her, had been officially prevented from doing so, and she had sat waiting, dressed up, all day to no purpose. That was after all only one more insult; the rest were too many to count, unless one began at the outset.

No doubt her unspeakable husband—he was in fact Mrs Fitzherbert's, as Caroline had once been heard to remark—was glad to be rid of her; no doubt going away was the only pleasure she had ever given George Augustus. As for *him*, he had given her none at all, despite everything she had been led to expect. Long ago they had come to her in Brunswick, when she was in love with dear Captain Tobingen, and liked to call him her husband and herself his wife and to pretend to go into labour on the beds: and had told her she was to marry the handsomest prince in Europe instead. It was a lie. She had made her disillusionment clear on first setting eyes on George, and he likewise; he had at once, in her hearing and everyone else's, asked Lord Malmesbury, who had told her in Brunswick that she ought at least to buy a toothbrush, to fetch him a glass of brandy as he felt unwell. That had been most uncivil. If she, Caroline, had been permitted to remain in the becoming striped dress in which she had travelled, and the wide-brimmed black hat which showed off her golden hair, then her best feature, it might have been different; Madame Harzfeldt, her father's mistress, had herself chosen the hat and gown, and that one knew how to dress. However the bridegroom's quite evident mistress likewise, an old grandmother named Lady Jersey, who was in attendance, had made her, Caroline, change instead into a white gown which was too tight, and a concealing white turban. It had made her look like nobody and nothing, and had been done on purpose; and the English talked unendingly of baths, which it was too much trouble to take. Now, as for the past few years since separating from Mrs Fitzherbert's husband, she, Caroline, was free to do as she chose in such matters, not to wash herself or her stockings and linen if she preferred to wear them as they were. Why should not everyone live as they chose? It was a waste to keep washing linen: she had said so often.

That woman, Lady Jersey, had almost certainly put Epsom salts in her, Caroline's, food shortly before the wedding night. That no doubt was what had made her conceive as quickly, but it was unkind and inconvenient: and as for the bridegroom, he had been so

132

drunk he had spent most of the night afterwards in the grate where he had fallen. Somehow, Charlotte had been fashioned between them; Caroline had less affection for her than for Willikin, who was here with her now. She liked to tell everyone that she had given birth to him also, in fact was beginning to believe it herself. 'Prove it, and he shall be your King!' she had told them. It was true that Willikin was not very bright, but neither was George III, who had reigned for many years over the English without their complaining of the fact. He had been kind enough to her at the first: after all, he was her mother's brother. It was the Old Begum, his wife and George's mother, who had stopped the King's being kind, and had also stopped her, Caroline, from seeing her own daughter. They had called the whole matter at that time the Delicate Investigation. The rest of the family, come to that, would hardly bear investigating; there was a scandal about every single one, and she herself had done her best to spread it: after all they were doing the same for her. Only Gloucester, egged on by many and fearful of what she, Caroline, *could* say, if she chose, had even lately escorted her everywhere, including Vauxhall.

No, it had not been an advisable marriage; she would have been happier by far left behind in Brunswick with Tobingen. It was useless to repine now; she and Mrs Fitz were alike discarded and she herself forbidden to appear at Court. Well, it was no loss. She had her own friends. After moving to Kensington and, later, Bayswater she had used to wander freely about the lanes, chatting to ordinary, kindly folk; the ones they called the common people. The common people liked her and hated fat George. Brougham had advised her to make it clear to everyone how seldom she was allowed to see her daughter Princess Charlotte. In truth she had not greatly missed seeing Charlotte; there were the adopted children, hordes of them, instead at her own house in Blackheath. Charlotte was the property of Carlton House, and one had therefore done one's best to compromise her, first with the Fitzclarence boy and later on with dear Captain Hesse; but the plan had not worked out, though she had herself locked the pair more than once into her bedroom at Kensington. Well, all of that was water under the bridge. The last she had seen of Charlotte was when they took her away from Connaught House lately in her father's carriage. It had been awkward of her to arrive there in the first place.

Charlotte. They had tried to persuade her, Caroline, lately that for her daughter's sake, she should stay on in England. As it was suddenly of such importance for her to stay, she had gone. They had ignored her for long enough while they had her there; now, they could do very well by themselves till she chose

134

to return. That would be as soon as fat George was king, and could hardly refuse to admit her, Caroline, as his queen. Queen of England, like the Old Begum was now; they wouldn't be able to ignore her any longer then. It would be high time to come back. Meanwhile, they would be happy together, she and Willikin; there would be sunshine and official welcomes from Bonaparte's Italian brother-in-law; festivities, carriage-drives and grape harvests, perhaps even a journey to the East. It was a long way already from the constant spite of the Old Begum, who had resented her, Caroline, from the beginning because she had wanted her own Mecklenburg niece to be the chosen royal bride.

The Princess of Wales passed her tongue round her neglected teeth. She still hadn't obeyed Malmesbury and bought a toothbrush; who was he to order her? She would twist her own dirty stockings any way she liked. She would wear none at all, perhaps, in hot weather, in the beckoning south: certainly no drawers.

The ship ploughed on. Over one shoulder could be seen a grey land which was France, ruled over again by the stiff unwelcoming Bourbons; she would certainly not go there. She would go instead to Geneva, and Italy, and Egypt, and wherever else she chose, wherever there was laughter and freedom.

Willikin squirmed suddenly in her arms;

despite the smooth voyage, he was about to be sick. Caroline let him go; he was not in time, the dear child, to reach the side. He was like herself, unsuccessful at everything; that was perhaps why she loved him so. 'Prove it, and he shall be your King!'

Well, she was rid of tiresome young Charlotte, and Brougham and his everlasting advice, and the Old Begum and all of them could go to the bottom of the Thames, and she, Caroline, would drive beside the Arno soon in an open carriage in flesh-pink tights or none, and would go to some fancy dress ball as Venus, wearing as little as possible: that would show them; it would all go back to England, and so, at the right moment, most certainly, would she.

CHAPTER THIRTEEN

A year later, after many things happened in Europe, Mercer Elphinstone and her cousin Clementine, who had lately been married to Lord Gwydyr, a loquacious and loose-lipped young Whig hopeful, were seated together in a carriage on its way to an informal evening in Portman Square. Mary Grey had indicated, in a letter to Mercer enclosed with her card of invitation, that there would be a newly arrived French officer present to whom they

136

themselves were glad to extend hospitality. It was inferred that he had fought at Waterloo; no doubt not all houses in England would be willing so to receive him. Regret at the fall of Napoleon was not openly condoned here: many felt it in Whig circles, however.

Mercer switched her mind back to young Lady Gwydyr's consequential talk. Clementine had always had a good opinion of herself since the days when her adoring mother used to write poetry about her, being the only surviving child, at Drummond Castle, where the two girls had shared a governess in Mercer's own youth. Clementine was the last of the old Jacobite line of the attained Earls, formerly Dukes, of Perth. One benefit from that long-ago association, apart from the constant friendship now in London, was that both young women spoke excellent French; they had shared a Mademoiselle, an *émigrée*. The accomplishment was not common these days in England, France having been closed for so long and Boney remaining the great enemy. Nor, for the same reason, had there been any Grand Tour for young noblemen, to broaden their minds. 'We are becoming more insular,' Mercer thought. It would be interesting to meet the young Frenchman. She had said nothing of today's visit to Papa, who had been in charge of the fleet spread out like a net to prevent the Emperor's escape after Waterloo, and had likewise had charge of the arrangements to send him to St Helena.

She drifted away from what Clementine was saying and thought again of the Byron marriage; they said it was not faring too well, but that might be gossip: it was in any case to be expected. She had encountered the couple once or twice, and Byron had seemed attentive enough to his wife, bending over Annabella's chair to point out the notables to her; but Caro George Lamb had said Caro William—of course, that was to be expected also—had made a most malicious drawing of the pair, taking off perfectly the proprietary air of a full-bosomed Annabella (they said she was pregnant) entering with a small and miserable Byron on her arm. Also, it was said the couple never entertained and dined separately at home; that was not a good sign: Queeney and Papa would never have done without their *tête-à-tête* dinners as a means of fostering their marriage both in the early days, and now. However perhaps Byron, with his strange preferred diet of charcoal biscuits and soda-water between undisciplined bursts of brandy and claret, preferred to eat alone. He had once remarked that women should in any case be seen eating nothing except lobster salad; it was on a par with his remembered comments to herself about the fair sex's always being given the wing of the chicken, which he would have liked for himself. A strange mixture of a man, still in ways a child! She herself, she was convinced, could have managed him. The secret, she remembered, was to make him laugh. 'Augusta always does,' he had once said to her. Mrs Leigh seemed of importance to him; he had once hurried down to meet her on the Sussex coast in the old days, like a lover to his mistress. It had perhaps been a mistake for the newlywed couple themselves to visit her, as one heard they had done, towards the end of the honeymoon—the treacle-moon, Byron had called it. The bride should have established her own hold firmly first. Well, oneself could do nothing, except to wish them well. Clementine was still talking, by this time about what everyone knew who read the papers.

'They say the Regent still tries, after all this time, to press his daughter into the Orange marriage, or one of them; he suggested the young brother Prince Frederick. Gwydyr says an alliance with Holland would embroil Britain in Continental troubles, and that those will soon begin under the oppressive rule of the Bourbons and Metternich.' Clementine, sounding as though she repeated a lesson, patted her side-curls beneath the fashionable hat she wore. She was so pleased with herself and with Gwydyr—they said she always had to be the centre of attention in any group of persons—that it evidently did not occur to her that Mercer might know more about the Orange matter than she did.

Mercer forbore to comment on the

139

Princess's situation, which was still very unhappy; Charlotte longed for F., and was unwell, with a pain in her side and a troublesome knee like her young aunt Amelia, who had died of consumption. She wanted to get away to the seaside, and the delay in giving permission seemed unreasonable; suspicion still, evidently, attached to everything Charlotte did or wanted.

'He would not even permit her to be present long ago at St George's Chapel, Windsor, in the procession,' Mercer reminded herself. Things had come to such a pass that the handsome Grand Duke Nicholas, whose miniature Charlotte had greatly admired when shown it by the Tsar's sister the Duchess of Oldenburg, she of the coal-scuttle bonnets, had been sent a message by Lord Castlereagh not on any account to come to Britain with the rest of the Russian suite. Two of them, Counts Pahlen and Naryshkin, had courted Mercer herself at the time, and would have carried her off most willingly to St Petersburg; but the wonders of the marsh-founded city did not attract her, though Devonshire spoke of a great desire to visit them himself.

'You are silent today,' said Clementine, noticing for once. 'How tedious the journey is with this press of carriages! We could have walked by now.'

'This is not Scotland. Nobody walks here.'

Hearing her own dour reply, Mercer

remembered her Scottish blood and her Scots grandmother, after whom Clem had been called. Clementina Fleming had been married at sixteen, had borne her husband twelve children including the Admiral, and then had suddenly elected to come down to London to live in a house in the Marylebone Road. Without Grandmama's chaperonage, oneself would not have come upon the social scene so early: but Grandmama had died soon.

They found themselves at last within sight of the trees of Portman Square, with carriages already halted about the Greys' town door; it was seldom husband and wife were in residence here together and away from their beloved Howick. Waiting inside would be a warm welcome from Grey and dear Mary, with her fine-boned face and elegant Irish manners and warm charity. Mercer emerged from the carriage behind Clementine, who as a married woman preceded her.

Once up the steps, a man's tenor voice, singing agreeably in French, sounded already from the salon. Perhaps, notwithstanding Waterloo, the Frenchman would be welcome at other houses with such a voice; it roused a chord in Mercer, who was not, as a rule, musical. They went in: and for the first time, she set eyes on Charles de Flahault de la Billarderie.

CHAPTER FOURTEEN

Princess Charlotte did not find unofficial detention at Cranbourn Lodge as bad as she had expected. The air was fresher than at Lower Lodge, where she usually stayed and which depressed her with its damp and for some other reason she could not name. Despite the pain in her knee which again began to trouble her—she had always had it at times, and tended to stand sideways accordingly— she felt, on the whole, better than for some months, especially as she was early permitted to ride. The old Queen was reasonable when she called, and was not, after all, as ordained, Charlotte's only visitor; there were the two younger aunts, Mary and Sophia. The elder two princesses remained about their separate business at Windsor and were nowise missed.

Left alone afterwards, Charlotte would enumerate the whole family of what she had used to call in childhood the Bulls and the Cows. The youngest of all, fair-haired and romantic Princess Amelia, had died only three years ago; how much longer it seemed! They said she had dragged the King down with her death into madness, as he had loved her particularly. 'He would have gone mad anyway,' the Princess thought with the hard clear logic of the young. She could remember

142

George III, a kindly old man in a white wig, taking her on his knee as a child and saying: 'What? What?' but never listening to the answer. By now, he was kept at Windsor in a place by himself; nobody but her kindly uncle of York, his favourite, visited him; the Queen was afraid. They said the King was blind now and almost deaf, but he still played the organ; its thin sound came sometimes on the wind when she herself was out riding.

Yes, he had been kind, her grandfather; but not to Amelia, despite loving her so: he would not permit her or any of her sisters to marry after the eldest, Royal, had done so in the year following that of Charlotte's own birth. Royal's wedding procession, wickedly drawn by the cartoonists as both she and the Württemberg bridegroom were by then very fat, had happened to be the only time Charlotte's own parents had been portrayed together; her mother had looked small and harmless in Court feathers, and her father, his wife on his arm, had his nose in the air. Since then, Bonaparte had made Royal's husband King of Württemberg, and Royal herself, overweening somewhat no doubt by reason of her palace with a new gilt crown on top, had dared to write a letter to her mother, Queen Charlotte, addressing her as Dearest Sister. The old lady had been much enraged; but that could not be the only reason for the continued spinsterhood of all the remaining daughters.

143

Gossip—in other words, Charlotte's own mother the Princess of Wales—said that they were nothing of the kind and all had their own affairs, even secret marriages, and Princess Sophia had certainly had a baby. Well, Sophia was sweet, and a friend; Charlotte liked and trusted her better than Mary, who tattled to the Queen. So did Princess Elizabeth, snipping away up at the Castle at silhouettes made out of black paper. She was likewise fat and discontented, desperate to be married, and middle-aged long ago. Princess Augusta—they said she was privately the wife of General Brent Spencer who lived over at Lea—must have been handsome in youth, but was now merely fashionable, especially her hats. That had been made easier since the Regent had arranged for all the princesses to have money of their own instead of depending wholly on the Queen. Again, Old Plugnose had been furious; but it served her right, as before that she had made all her daughters miserable and had yearly, on her birthday, insisted that they each do something different with the same old dress. Charlotte admitted that it had been kind of her father to persuade Parliament about the money; he could after all think of others.

Marriage. It was not a subject on which Charlotte desired at the moment to dwell; but rather than sit thinking of F. and the way he did not write to her often enough, she thought again of the royals. Mary was the beauty of the family, and had always assumed that Slice, her cousin the Duke of Gloucester, was her particular cavalier; and appeared now to have forgiven Charlotte for using him as the Cheese against the Orange, but one never knew. At any rate, the Regent had been exercised enough over the whole matter to send a request that she, Charlotte, change places from where she had been sitting once beside Slice and his sister on a sofa at Carlton House. She had got up and gone out of the room, but returned later on to make renewed friends with the couple. Slice himself was stupid and had noticed nothing, but his sister, another Sophia, was pleasant and everyone liked her, so it had been worth coming back.

Charlotte turned the ring which she still always wore on her finger. It was a gift from F.—they had after all exchanged those gifts— and contained the small turquoise in the shape of a heart she so loved. The ring was worth far more to her than its value; if she ever lost the stone, it would mean bad luck. She had seen Mary—one never called the younger princesses aunt—staring at it the other day. Perhaps after all *she* was relieved, because of the Gloucester situation, if Charlotte was wearing somebody else's ring. Gloucester— everyone called him Silly Billy as well as Slice— and she were in fact welcome to one another; that matter had merely been a feint, like fencing. Anyone—except, of course, the

Orange or his younger brother, whom she, Charlotte, would never countenance—was better than the smug though handsome Coburg prince who had written that overtly sneaking letter to her father.

Princess Sophia's past was a mystery. She must have been very beautiful, more so, if one thought of it, than Mary. She was too thin now. It was without doubt that she had borne a child, about a dozen years ago. That was known among the family and probably outside, though of course never openly spoken of. It was allowed to be thought that old General Garth, who had been an equerry for years and had a large purple birth-mark on his face, had been Sophia's lover; but that was difficult to credit. No young woman could have fallen in love with anyone as old and ugly; and if the General had seduced Sophia he would not any longer be in favour, whereas he was very much so here, fetching and carrying and forever making a fuss. There must be some other explanation; but one did not, naturally, ask. Sophy was a dear; she was often ill, but when she was well enough came here to Cranbourn Lodge, and never criticised or pried or offered advice, merely listened; it was restful. She wore a wedding ring which she preferred not to have noticed, sitting as a rule with her small slender hands twisted so that the ring could not be seen. Perhaps General Garth—it was the kind of order he would obey—had been made to marry her to save appearances.

*   *   *

At that same moment, back at the Castle, Princess Sophia herself sat alone as she often did, the other sisters being engaged in their duties about the Queen. It was true that her genuine ill-health was often stressed by her a little; at least she was free of the necessity of handing the royal snuff-box, unlike poor Elizabeth, whose task it was. Sophia was used by now to solitude. She could hear the wind lift and lay the thin matting the King had ordered long ago to line the corridors in his spartan way of treating them all: it kept nobody warm. Her own sight was beginning to be bad; perhaps she, like her father, would become blind. It didn't matter; she still had her memory, and would remember. She gave her little crooked smile.

During her youth, and that of her brothers—dear impulsive Ernest had been at home then, not with the army, not yet so cruelly wounded in the face as he had become, turning one eye forever sightless outwards—during that time, she and her sisters had been allowed to meet very few young men. If they danced, and there was often music in the evenings, it was with their brothers; Royal had once lost her shoe going down the dance too violently with dear George. Royal's marriage had been arranged very late, and was the only one their father would ever allow; for some reason, despite his own extremely fertile marriage, he refused to countenance married love and children for his daughters. His sons were different; but poor George's marriage had of course turned out a failure, and York's pleasant little Prussian wife continued barren. The centre of all their lives was George, whom the King for some reason hated; there was no disguising it; but of them all, their mother loved him alone and when he was born, had had a wax image made of him as a baby; it was still to be seen lying below the glass top of the Queen's dressing-table, for her to gaze on daily.

That apart, they all, every one, had Hanoverian blood; and that could not be expected to remain cool always, especially when one was young. The King did not allow himself to understand this, but their mother understood well enough; oh, well enough. She had never said anything; but Augusta and her Irish general had remained discreet, only she, Sophia, had not. Later on, the sight of poor young Amelia, lying on a sofa with a seton in her leg, a dying invalid, hoping in vain to live to be twenty-five and petition Parliament to let her marry her chilly but adored Charles Fitzroy, was enough. Oneself had not waited to become like that, or to die young at all.

There was, after all, a remembrance, a gift of love; love so delicious that its stolen instants would be enough to sustain Sophia till she was old and blind, shredding paper between her fingers to stuff pillows for the poor. She knew now that that might come, as she also knew that it was necessary to wear General Garth's wedding ring after that forced ceremony for the sake of appearances, Garth being of better birth than the man she, Sophia, had chosen. *He* had been young and personable; the only young man not to be noted as he stood, unnoticed by anyone who came and went, outside her door night after night, forever present yet forgotten, taken for granted; a footman.

What had made her think of him sooner or later as a man, with feelings? He hadn't been like Papendiek, the great bear of a creature who was a page belowstairs and had married a young girl who disliked him and later became the Queen's reader. However it had happened, she, Sophia, had begun to know that *he* was aware of her night after night, and she of him. They both knew; and knew that they knew, without words spoken that might be overheard. She, Sophia, had sidled out one night in her flimsy shift, her hair combed out like a fair veil about her shoulders, her soft slim breasts brushing against him where he stood, stiff in his livery. She had seen the glow of hot male desire rise in his eyes, sensed it in his

149

aroused young body; and had taken him by the hand and led him in. They had loved then, briefly but in such a way as could never be forgotten; however long she lived she would never forget. If heaven was like the sweet rush of fulfilment that had come, she would be glad to see God; and God would not be angry.

He had been taken away, of course; somebody had tattled, probably Elizabeth. One day he had simply been no longer there. She had passed the days in anguish so intense that she hadn't noticed, for a long time, that things were not as they should properly be with herself: then she had known, but still concealed matters as long as she might. It was however difficult to deceive the prominent pale-blue gaze of her father; he watched them all, all the daughters, constantly, missing no smallest detail.

One day the Queen had sent for Sophia. She had gone in fear and trembling, knowing she was no longer slender by then. The small indomitable figure, its hair piled high above a velvet cushion, had been seated alone; that in itself was significant, there was usually someone in attendance on the Queen.

'Princess Sophia, you are about to have a child. Who is the man?'

The voice, with its very faint trace by now of a German accent—the Queen had learnt English thoroughly, as she did everything— was cold. So were the strange slitted eyes, fixed gimlet-sharp on one's body beneath the gown. 'I have told the King you are ill with dropsy,' the Queen continued. 'You must take to your bed and not be seen until after the birth. Arrangements will then be made. Now go; go straight to your room.'

She hadn't answered, of course, to give the name; whoever it had been, anyone at all, would have been considered unsuitable; the matter had simply not occurred. She had obeyed thereafter in every particular, including the private marriage to the ugly old soldier with the purple birth-mark; it didn't matter, except that it seemed that, once, Garth had happened to occupy rooms below hers and could be blamed, if questions were asked. They were not, except by the King, who kept enquiring as to how Sophia was, if she was ill today or well. He was told she was ill; worse today than yesterday; then, at last, after the birth, that she had been cured by roast beef. 'It is a singular thing,' he went about repeating to everyone. 'My daughter Sophia was swollen with dropsy, and has been cured by roast beef.'

The child had been born with the new century, privately at Weymouth. Sophia did not now recall the pain; one forgot pain, except in the mind. She had hardly seen her son's fair head before he was bundled off to godparents, a working tailor and his wife in the seaside town. Later, when her brother Ernest was at home, they stood together looking down at the

151

child in his cradle in the tailor's house: she wasn't allowed to show any feelings. Ernest knew, of course. They had always been close to one another. She had wept when she heard of the wound he had taken in battle, though Augusta spoke of it heartlessly as their little bit of glory from the war. Augusta would have made a good soldier's wife; a pity she was never allowed to acknowledge General Spencer.

The child. He had been taken away and given Garth's own name, Thomas, and reared by Garth at his house in the country. He would be sent to Harrow shortly in the autumn; she was quietly kept informed. Since the King's confinement matters had become a little less severe, and she was allowed to see her son for herself more often. Tommy was a handsome child. It was difficult to know what to say to him; their meetings were formal, like those of two strangers: kindly questions and polite answers, and then he would be taken away.

It was sad indeed about the poor King. He and she, both blind; but herself surely never, never mad. She had no illusions, no defences left. She was fond of young Charlotte, and hoped she at least would marry where she loved. At least the girl had had the courage to stand out against a marriage she disliked: but she had after all never had to hide her feelings like all of one's own generation; Royal, Augusta, Elizabeth, Mary, Amelia, poor Sophy: herself, poor Sophy.

CHAPTER FIFTEEN

'I take it very ill that any daughter of mine should have her name coupled with one of Bonny's French officers. The Devonshire business in the *Morning Post* was bad enough, and before that there was that poet, not but what ye are well rid of *him*; they say bailiffs are at his door along the street. Ye have refused many a good offer which would have kept your position in society, Margaret. This Frenchman is not received in the best houses. Seek less unsuitable company in the future.'

'He will certainly not be received here,' put in Queeney, from where she sat as by custom. They were all four alone in the Piccadilly drawing-room; it was fairly early in the day.

Mercer looked down her strong nose; it was a way of hiding her feelings. The Admiral, whose Scots accent had grown pronounced as it always did when he was angry, stood erect and handsome despite his increasing mid-sixties, wig immaculately powdered in the fashion of last century still, shoulders back as if standing on the quarter-deck; in fact a model of what his men had mutinied against being forced to go on looking like at the Nore years back. Georgy, aged six, sat round-eyed at this altercation—there had been several by now—between Papa, Mama, and Mercer, of all three

153

of whom she was fond. They did not appear to be resolving their differences on this occasion more than on any of the others.

Mercer tried persuasion. Besides having been given the unwelcome task, in which she herself had signally failed, of trying to retrieve Princess Charlotte's imprudent letters written long ago to the rascal Hesse, her father had been justly infuriated by having to deny the officious, and unjustified, recent notice of her own engagement to the Duke of Devonshire in the *Morning Post*; some mischievous person must have inserted it. It had no doubt made the Admiral feel as foolish as any other father would have done, and she herself had perhaps pursued Dearest Hart somewhat too openly to have avoided speculation. In fact, the Duke's gentle and affectionate nature had attracted her; she had almost fallen in love with him, but in no way in the fierce manner she now felt enduring love for Charles de Flahault. Dearest Hart and she remained friends, and that matter was ended; but Charles by now filled Mercer's mind, her heart, her ambition. She had plans for him, in the same way as she had once had plans for Byron: but the visit to Tunbridge Wells was long ago, in another country, though the man was by no means dead. One seldom however saw Byron nowadays, except in the distance at Drury Lane of which he had been made one of the managers. Otherwise, he was stated in private to be distinctly at odds with his wife of only a year and to have shot belowstairs at soda-water bottles while Annabella lay in childbed of their newborn daughter. A memory rose in Mercer's mind; Byron had always taken a poker to knock the heads off bottles; that must be it, and society had that matter the wrong way round also. Well, it was no longer her affair; her present business was to placate Papa concerning Charles, but with Queeney seated forever present in her queenliness it was more difficult than it might have been in earlier years.

Whether the Admiral was placated or not, Charles de Flahault was the man she herself would marry. Mercer had determined on it; this time things should not be allowed to go wrong. She could do a great deal for Charles, could become a wife who would drive him on and up: left to himself he was, perhaps, a trifle inclined to let matters slide, and in his present situation that would never do; she and no other must carve out a place for him. He had the great advantage of charming manners, a handsome presence, a voice, and the blood of ancient France. She herself had the advantage both of blood and money. She could bargain with those in the way the French understood; Charles's mother in Paris, as she already knew, approved. Mercer set the thought of him aside meantime and returned to the hardly charitable picture in her hindmost mind of young Lady Byron in the act of giving birth.

Surely even Annabella's complacency had deserted her for moments. Everyone seemed to be producing daughters: perhaps she and Charles would break the curse of Aldie together one day, and have a son. The thought of it brought a slow flush to Mercer's cheeks, and the Admiral's jaw set obstinately, mistaking her reasons.

'It is of no avail to play the innocent and blushing miss,' he said. 'Ye are twenty-eight years of age, Margaret; it is high time ye were settled, but in decency, not with a penniless Frenchman who fought against us two years since, and who has no money, the great long feckless lump, save what his mother sends him. Bonny used to ca' him daddy-long-legs.' Lord Keith had lapsed increasingly into the Scots vernacular of his boyhood as his rage increased. Queeney looked pained.

'They even turned him down to go off with Bonny to St Helena,' finished the Admiral triumphantly. 'A pity they didna send him. He would have troubled fewer folk.'

'Papa, this is completely unjust,' Mercer said. 'Most of his former aides applied to go into exile with the Emperor, and only two were taken. You cannot judge of a person you have consistently refused to meet.'

'Emperor, is it?' roared the Admiral. 'What sort of a traitor to her country has he turned my daughter into? I dislike all foreigners, in especial all Frenchmen, and that one is the

156

worst of any.'

Mercer held her ground. 'The Comte de Flahault is not only presentable, but has seen service you of all persons, Papa, should by no means despise. He was not only at Waterloo, but survived the terrible Russian retreat of 1812. Any man who did that does not deserve your scorn.'

'It was his luck, damn him,' said the Admiral unfairly. 'Better men died in the snow. As for Waterloo, he arrived late for it, and saved his skin again. He has no right even to the title of Comte, let alone a surname. The world knows who his real father is; Talleyrand, as slippery a fish as ever took priestly vows and then dishonoured 'em. In diplomacy, at cards, in murder—mind the Duc d'Enghien in '04—it's all the same, and with women, like his son. I didna think ye were a fool, Margaret.' He returned to the theme of Talleyrand, for the time not yet resident in the embassy at Portland Place. 'Anyone would think so old a man was in the springtime of life still; he was the lover of du Barry, and now his nephew's wife is his latest mistress; that's Talley for ye. His son will be another such. I doubt not; have no more to do with him.'

'Georgy, go upstairs to the nursery,' put in Queeney. The extra-marital relations of the erstwhile Bishop of Autun and Adélaïde de Flahault, at that time the young wife of an elderly and complaisant nobleman who had

157

ended commendably enough on the guillotine, were not suitable subjects for the ears of a child. Georgy went unwillingly; the talk had begun to be interesting, but she had been trained to obey.

The Admiral barked on, having many injured feelings to relieve; Mercer's name was being bandied, once again, all over town. He proceeded to castigate Charles's mother, who after the Revolution had forgotten herself enough to become a milliner in Hamburg and had then written a novel, then another, then had married a damned Portuguee. 'It's *his* money, no doubt, that she sends to this precious son of hers to enable him to cut some kind of a figure in society here, in as far as it will accept him. They say it's a pittance, and all he has; mark that, for your own sake, Margaret. A fortune-hunter! His mother, they tell me, is even in correspondence with the widow of the Pretender, who in *her* time ran off with a poet.' He spat out the latter word; Margaret—he always thought of Mercer by her first name when he was angry with her—seemed to have an unaccountable penchant for such folk. The wrath of the entire British Fleet poured itself out in scalding fashion on Mercer's head; but unlike the time the Regent had scolded her at Connaught House, she remained dry-eyed.

'You pronounce Prince Talleyrand's name in the trisyllabic form, Papa,' she replied coldly. 'Most Britons mistakenly do.
158

Correctly, it should be *taille et rang*, the ladder and the rung. Charles told me.' She knew such a remark would infuriate her father and it did; under the continued stream of ready naval vocabulary she turned at last and went out, finding herself at last trembling as she seldom did. It should never be at all necessary to have such scenes. She thought again of Charles, to calm herself; and of how he had told her of his old first stepfather the Count's kindness to him, allowing him, another man's son, to use his ancient name and also, his family crest of the de Flahault blackbirds. Charles should certainly meet Papa at the Portuguese Ambassador's shortly, and an encounter must not be avoided. She hoped Queeney, who despised such affairs as no doubt lacking in any conversation worthy of Dr Johnson, would not come. If she did, one could perhaps play one's last card; Adélaïde de Souza herself, Charles's absent mother, was said to be a daughter of old King Louis XV by way of that monarch's visits to the Parc aux Cerfs. The fact might not add to the respectability of Charles's family, but it perhaps added to its lustre. Soon, she hoped to meet him again at Woburn, also at Twickenham where the still exiled Orléans family resided; her own horizons were widening in interesting ways, and she looked forward to making a diplomat of Talleyrand's son, after the manner of his father, politics in a husband being no longer in question. There was no more prospect for Charles in the army meantime either, or as yet in France.

* * *

Mercer had by now begun to allow Prince Leopold of Saxe-Coburg a little encouragement in his steadily persisting suit. It was after all not going to be easy to find the Princess a husband; the elusive F. had not made any proposal, and Charlotte had lately been much afflicted by the loss of the turquoise heart from her beloved ring. Also, her aunt Mary had, no doubt intentionally, removed some of her niece's antipathy to Leopold by showing some slight interest in him herself; perhaps it was tit for tat over the now reclaimed Slice. Charlotte was beginning to say again, as she had done at the early stages of the Orange engagement, that perhaps love could come after marriage. Marriage certainly had its advantages; the Regent had, most unjustifiably, refused on her behalf the Tsar's recent offer to her of the Order of St Catherine, saying it was only for married women, which everyone knew to be untrue. Altogether, 'the Leo' as Charlotte began to call him, might be better than nobody; and nobody much in Europe now seemed inclined to risk incurring the fate of poor Slender Billy. That unfortunate young man was about to be married, as it turned out unhappily, to a sister of the Tsar, which land-locked autocrat had long had an eye on the ports and possibilities of Holland, like his ancestor Peter the Great. It showed, as Princess Charlotte's father could have pointed out to her, the duplicity of Alexander the Blessed, damn him, and his platter-faced sister of Oldenburg; both had been out for as much as they could get, including possibly even himself. The thought chilled Prinny, remembering how in any case the pair had been cheered everywhere they went, which he, most unfairly, never was. Also, he suspected that the Duchess had intended to marry him if he could by some means (God knew at present what) be rid of Caroline: to divorce her would increase his unpopularity. As the Duchess, although elegant, had a face like a dinner-plate—they said her father the mad Tsar Paul had been almost noseless with inherited pox—and had announced that music made her vomit, it would not have done at all. He himself must proceed cautiously in such matters; so cautiously that it might well never happen; he didn't want another unseen bride, and the ones he saw continued insufferable. He began to think almost affectionately again of Charlotte, for the time.

*   *   *

Leopold of Saxe-Coburg showed no undue haste to return to England, deeply in love as he undoubtedly still was. The caution of so young a man was extraordinary; the Prince would go far in whichever direction he went, and for the present without doubt deserved the name Prinny had earlier bestowed on him of the Marquis Peu-à-Peu.

As for Charlotte, she had at last achieved her wish of being allowed to go to the seaside, though summer was by then well past. She was greeted by a peal of joy-bells and much cheering when she stopped overnight at an inn near Salisbury; the Regent, when he heard, was again affronted.

*   *   *

However Weymouth did Charlotte good; it was the place where her grandfather George III had long ago undergone the then newly fashionable process of sea-bathing for his already precarious health, and every time he emerged from the machine and was duly dipped in the sea a band had played *God Save the King*. Charlotte wanted no such accolade, nor did she bathe; but her knee grew so much better that she was able to climb dexterously up a ship's rope to be made welcome by the crew, also to visit a nearby monastery and wander alone among its shadows.

CHAPTER SIXTEEN

In an upper room in a large well-maintained house in Leicestershire, a young woman was lying on the floor, writhing and crying and beating her fists against the boards. Her long brown hair had shaken loose from its pins, and was dishevelled, lying anyhow about her narrow shoulders. The maid Fletcher had looked in for moments, then had gone, unwilling to be a party to it all. It would have been hard to recognise, in this half-crazed maenad, the self-contained Miss Annabella Milbanke who had accompanied Mercer Elphinstone with strong disapproval home in a shared carriage from Lady Caroline Lamb's party more than three years since, and had later married the coveted Lord Byron. Still later—although not by much, just over a year—she had left him, taking their infant daughter Ada with her. The Byron Separation was already rocking London.

The polite world would talk of nothing else for some time, even Princess Charlotte's rumoured engagement to some young German prince without a shilling of his own. They would speculate and mull over what they only half knew. Caro Lamb was dropping hints, but nobody believed her; that novel she had written, *Glenarvon*, with everyone satirised in

163

it, had put her firmly beyond the pale. Nobody however knew the full truth but Annabella herself; and Byron's poem, which he should never have published openly, about their parting—

Fare thee well, and if for ever,
*Then for ever **fare thee well!***

—went only to prove what she, Annabella, had for some time privately thought, that if he were not judged insane by his doctors, in which case he was naturally an object of compassion, she must never, never return to him. While she was with him he had been, often and unpredictably, cruel. The worst time of all was perhaps the one when, in Augusta's presence, he had flung himself down on his knees and begged her, his wife, to forgive him all wrongs done; and she, with Christian forbearance, had replied 'Byron, all is forgiven,' whereupon he had leapt to his feet, folded his arms across his chest and burst out laughing. Such treatment was surely unendurable, unless Byron were mad.

She loved him: in spite of everything, perhaps even because of everything. It was tearing her heart out not to go back, though at times she had feared for her life. However it was true that her principles had always guided her, and since that talk alone with Mama and Papa—how unfortunate, come to think, that Papa's own financial embarrassments had prevented any relief to Byron himself during the course of their marriage!—there had been a bailiff sitting in the house at the time of the birth, a sad brute—since then, it had been made clear, by her parents, the lawyer, and dear Mrs Clermont, that she herself had been amply justified in coming home; home to this grand new house of Kirkby Mallory, recently made available by the terms of a relation's will. Byron had expected to follow her and the child here shortly; well, now he must never come.

The pretentious rented house in Piccadilly had cost too much. Her aunt Lady Melbourne had exceeded her authority in settling on it for them both: something smaller would have been best, and yet, and yet it would have made no difference; at times it had seemed as if he hated her: she had almost feared for her own reason at such times.

It was not even the matter of his half-sister Augusta. That had been hard enough to endure, although Augusta herself had been kind. Augusta would be the excuse, if any were needed, that Annabella Byron would give to the gaping curious world over the years; the sterile years that would follow now, alone. She could never, never reveal the real reason behind her parents' prohibition, and Lushington the lawyer's, against any return to such a husband. Despite her marriage vows, made at Seaham just over a year ago, she must forsake him, the beloved and cruel, the damned, as he himself had so often said; the damned forever, with no hope of salvation. Mad, bad, and dangerous to know; that had been Caro Lamb's phrase, and Caro had been Byron's mistress, as everyone knew. He had had many women. He had even taken a Drury Lane actress during her own pregnancy; oh, she knew that also, well enough.

Mad. Could it possibly be—one did not of course mention such things—the pox? Byron had admitted that he had once had it, that time he had shown her his 'little foot'. Most gentlemen, except of course Papa, contracted pox at some time, and in certain cases it went, she understood, to the brain. If all of that were indeed so, one could again forgive; but after what Mama and Papa had told her, having been more greatly shocked by her confidences than ever before in their decent, predictable lives, one's own principles came to the rescue, as always. As for Mama, she had already caused a green curtain to be drawn across Byron's newly hung portrait, saying Ada must not be permitted to see it till she was twenty-one. Ada was still at the breast. That was like Mama, precise and unyielding; a little like one's own self, perhaps, and yet she, Annabella, had without doubt yielded much too often in all ways over the past year; even on their last parting. Had she been firmer with her husband, as Mama was with hers, the outcome might have been different; but ever since the

166

wedding-journey to Halnaby, when Byron had scowled at the sound of joy-bells rung for them in the town as they drove by, things had gone wrong. There had been silence on the journey, and he had left her, on arrival at last, to go up the steps by herself to the waiting servants, turning away alone. Later, on the sofa before dinner, he had suddenly taken her, as might have happened with a housemaid. Later still, in their bed together in the small hours: 'Good God, I am surely in hell!' What bride would have endured all of it without a withering at the heart?

She hadn't fallen pregnant immediately. That had happened later on, at Six Mile Bottom, Augusta's husband's house near Newmarket. Colonel Leigh had not seemed to put in any appearance. They themselves should never have gone there, or not as soon; not during the honeymoon, but it had after all been her own suggestion. 'Augusta always makes me laugh,' he had told her; and she had been anxious to please him. If she had foreseen!

Augusta. He had been growing fond enough of *her*, his wife, after a day or two at Halnaby. She had looked over his shoulder on one occasion when he was writing a letter to a friend in London and it had said: 'Bell and I rub along tolerably well together.' He had always called her that or, later, Pip because he said her cheeks were like a rosy apple, a pippin. There had been affection, after all, at times.

167

They had clambered among the rocks one day and had been greatly at ease. It had been a mistake to end all of that to journey to Newmarket. However apart from pleasing Byron, she had wanted to analyse the situation she had briefly observed before their marriage, long ago at Lady Glenbervie's, when Augusta Leigh had been present and Byron had seemed notably affectionate and playful, more so than one would expect between a brother and his half-sister. She, Annabella, had resolved, perhaps even then, in her own mind, to intervene.

It had been useless. Byron and Augusta Leigh had sat up night after night together after she, the bride, had been dismissed to bed. 'We don't want *you*, my charmer.' How callously cruel he could be! He would come up to her afterwards and make love, of a kind; it had been then that the child had been conceived. Byron had already told her, as if he enjoyed shocking her, that Augusta's youngest child, Medora, was his. He had looked down at the tiny mysterious dark-haired creature with a tenderness he had never shown to her, his wife.

What was one to think, then or now? She had made a resolve at the time and had gone down again, only once, to confront them in the room together. As a rule she had walked the floor, up and down, up and down, till he came. A floor. By now, she was lying on one, abandoned and alone.

168

It was when he knew she was pregnant that it had begun to happen, the unspeakable thing she hadn't fully understood then; to safeguard the baby, he had told her, they would make love from now on the way they did it in the East. She, Annabella, had been too innocent to know that it was wrong, the worst possible sin; buggery, the lawyer had called it quite openly, although in private. He had also said they should make Ada a ward in Chancery, as her father was no proper guardian for her. Papa and Mama had agreed.

She hadn't known, hadn't understood at the time what it had signified. She could never, never mention it to anyone; others could think and say what they liked, for the rest of her life. It was, evidently, what unnatural men did with one another. If it was known, it put them outside society. Byron, lover of his half-sister; Byron, who practised unnatural vice with his wife; Byron, with his pale enchanting face and the sudden, matchless and entertaining things he said when he had stopped hating her, his wife, even for moments. Byron, whom she would never see again; she herself had determined on it.

Fare thee well.

He had always spoken of himself as damned. It was the truth.

Annabella turned her cheek against the unyielding floor, beating the boards with her

169

fists, uttering great sobbing breaths. How easy it would be not to stand out against his by now pleading letters, to return to him with the child, pretending nothing had ever been wrong between them! However one could not, knowing everything, do so: not now. It was of no use to recall homely things; the way he called her Pip and she him Duck: the way, when they were seated together, and the parrot had bitten her foot—Byron had parrots, dogs, all manner of animals always—he had thrown it angrily in its cage out of the window, and a servant had picked it up later on and brought it in unhurt saying 'Johnny'. All that must be put firmly to the back of one's mind, there to remain.

Byron. There must be a separation, Papa had said, for her sake and Ada's. *He* had called their daughter Ada after an ancestress; had mentioned her in the *Farewell* poem. *Are her lineaments mine?* They were so; every turn of the child's head reminded one unbearably of its father. Ada—like Medora—had his dark hair. Perhaps for both reasons one had left her, apart from feeding, a great deal with the nurses for the present. One must endeavour, when all of this was over, to bring her up suitably, giving the Byron blood no opportunity to prevail. It might otherwise betray Ada into indiscretion in the future. One's whole life must be given up to that, perhaps also to deserving charities, and certainly to the sustaining of principle.

For now, though, there was only desolation; she was after all still a young woman. Annabella sobbed on; and presently a door creaked open and a second female presence, a servant superior to the maid Ann Fletcher and in any case less suspect as not being married to Byron's valet, entered the room. This was Mrs Clermont, of anomalous position in the Milbanke (by now prestigiously the Noel) household. She was neither housekeeper, companion nor governess, but a mixture of all three, and trusted with private commissions as well; she had been sent alone to London to investigate the facts of the marriage. She had in fact come up from the kitchens at Seaham, and had been present all of one's youth; a pillar to which to cling. She knelt down, the familiar smell of soap and soda coming close; and took Annabella in her arms.

'There now, my darling. There now. Don't you fret over that bad man. You are never to go back to him. You will stay here, with me and with your Mama and Papa; we know how to love you and use you well. Don't fret now, dearie, don't fret. When you went to him you were like a flower, in your pretty dove-coloured dress with the white fur trimming on the little cape. After you come back with him from Halnaby, I could see for myself you didn't care what happened to you. He wasn't good to you; he is good to nobody except himself. If you'd heard what I heard about

171

him, at Mivart's Hotel in London, while I was there, you wouldn't believe, and I wouldn't ever tell you. You stay here; Mama and old Mrs C. will have a care to you and the little love. It isn't her fault. We'll be happy together, all of us, you'll see. You stay here at home; don't ever go back to him.'

The hands, worn and forever shiny with long use of harsh soap in early days, caressed Annabella. Gradually the young woman's shuddering sobs ceased and she allowed herself to be comforted. It was beginning to be uncertain which was truth and which lies. She contrived a wan, prim smile.

'You are right, Clermont,' she said. 'I am resolved not to return. The marriage was inadvisable, after all. Pay no heed to my wild fit; it was for a moment only. I am fully myself again.'

She was to remain herself, unceasingly, implacably, for many years. She lived to be old.

CHAPTER SEVENTEEN

The polite world had as already stated been so greatly taken up with the Byron Separation—how could *she* have borne not to return to him after those heart-rending lines *Fare thee well?*—that it almost failed to notice Princess Charlotte's formal engagement in February

172

1816 after the arrival, at last, of her Leo. On meeting him again the Princess was so greatly impressed with his undoubted dignity of bearing, not to mention his looks, that she referred to him thereafter, in the few remaining letters she was ever to write to Mercer Elphinstone, as 'Cobourg'. At Brighton, where they had leisure to talk, she began to find herself—she and 'Cobourg' agreed after all in most things—subtly put against the man in whom her dearest Margarite was evidently very much interested, one 'Flahaud'. In her occasionally phonetic spelling of words she had not read, the Princess warned Mercer of what she had been told; the Frenchman was a womaniser. Mercer took no heed of the warning; anything Charles might be, or have been, merely added to his fascinations now; and the chance was taken to drive a wedge between the friends. 'Cobourg' did not in any case intend that anyone should influence his future wife but himself; and he had a score to settle with Mercer Elphinstone for her early discouragement of his suit. Also, though he did not of course mention the matter, he and 'Flahaud' had shared a mistress at the Tuileries, none other than the former Emperor's stepdaughter, Empress Josephine's daughter Queen Hortense: it would be most improper if they must now repeatedly meet as man to man.

The cartoons meantime portrayed Leopold

173

as inoffensive enough. One showed him begging his way into the saloon at Windsor cap in hand, with the old Queen, who not having been seen lately was represented as still slender and fashionable in long coloured gloves, and Charlotte holding a skipping-rope and saying she would have preferred an English bridegroom, facing him without enthusiasm. Charlotte's escape from the Dutch alliance was unforgotten and, until the knot was tied, nobody could be entirely certain that it would be so. The Prince of Saxe-Coburg had in any case never been heard of before.

The wedding was meantime postponed, but not through any fault of Charlotte's; the Regent was unwell, but gave out untruly that his daughter had suffered a bilious attack. It was said among those who knew that Prinny had tried, again, to bribe whoever married Charlotte to keep her out of the country; but the Marquis Peu-à-Peu was in England at last, and there he would stay. Prinny temporised, and hid his pique.

A house was rented and hastily furnished for the couple in Camelford Place. It was not all it ought to have been, though convenient to Piccadilly. Soon, however, a pleasanter abode was in prospect, in the country but convenient to town; Lord Clive's former estate of Claremont near Esher, which Charlotte had once herself visited in company with her aunt of York. It was said to be a pretty house, though the estate had been neglected.

Early in May, the wedding morning dawned at last. The Princess sat for her nuptial portrait, and while doing so thought of various matters not directly connected with her bridegroom, who did not yet totally occupy her mind. She was puzzled by the Regent's gift, made only two days ago, of an ornate silver salver to General Garth, in stated gratitude for the General's care of herself on the occasion of her recent visit to Weymouth. Such a gesture was, to say the least, both mysterious and unnecessary. Garth had made himself obnoxious to her at that time, thrusting poor Sophia's boy, due to go off to Harrow, under her nose constantly; everyone had remarked on it. The family was certainly under some sort of obligation to Garth. The less said the better, perhaps, as the Regent was at least now amiably disposed towards herself; had been increasingly so ever since her confession to him of the long-ago Hesse affair and the way her mother had encouraged it to a degree that might well have compromised Charlotte irretrievably. 'Providence must have preserved you, my dear child!' Prinny had said, and had burst into tears. Charlotte herself had cried also. It had been a relief to bring the matter into the open, at least as far as her father was concerned. Mercer's Papa had not contrived, after all, to obtain her own letters from Hesse, despite having sent that personage a questionnaire in twenty-six parts which had probably done more harm than good. All Hesse would say was that he would give the box of letters to a good friend who in the event of his own demise in battle would sink it to the bottom of the Thames. That was no comfort: the Thames gave up its secrets at every random tide, and any mudlark might retrieve the box to his undoubted profit. It did not bear thinking of, but at any rate the Regent now knew all.

As a sign of daughterly affection Charlotte had pinned in her hair today the little arrow of Prince of Wales feathers made from the Sultan's diamonds. It would go very well with her silver lamé and Brussels lace wedding gown. It was almost time to put the latter on; how time flew! Meanwhile, the artist had drawn her with features that looked too narrow, and the small veil over her head made her seem married already. Charlotte preferred the sketch that the Frenchman, Alfred Chalon, had already made, to be completed later on. It showed her in a pearl-coloured shawl and matching slippers, with a striped dress she liked, and a wreath of fresh roses in her hair, firmly pinned to a little cap of black net tied with ribbon. She could adopt the fashion this coming summer, when there would be plenty of roses.

The thought itself made her remember Kew, where the old King's mother and Lord Bute had begun a notable garden last century.

Charlotte's least favourite uncle, the Duke of Cumberland—she called him Prince Wiskerandos, knowing very well that his luxuriant Germanic moustaches had been grown to hide his scarred face—had brought his bride there. For reasons not stated the old Queen had banned the new Duchess of Cumberland, who after all was her own niece, from Court. Frederica of Salms-Braunfels had been married twice before, but that was nothing to the point; she and Wiskerandos were said to be much in love. It was odd to think of anybody loving Cumberland; his language had always been extremely coarse, but that no doubt was with being so constantly in the army. 'He is the only member of the family, except for Sophy, who is not in the least inclined to fat,' Charlotte thought; she herself had been warned that she had her mother's figure and could expect to lose it. Well, the Wiskerandos couple were said to be expecting a child, and no doubt she herself would have children in due course by Leopold. It was curious that she could not feel any desire for these. Perhaps it was because her own childhood had been lacking in secure love from her own parents. Leo, however—how soon she found herself calling him that again!—had assured her that he loved her and had from the beginning, and would cherish her. He had looked handsomer than ever as he said it. Perhaps they would be happy.

*   *   *

The ceremony took place in early May in the
Crimson Drawing-Room at Carlton House, lit
by chandeliers. There was much murmuring
because of the presence of Lady Hertford, the
Regent's current favourite, who many said
should not have been invited. However there
she was, and it might well be true that she and
Papa did nothing but read the Bible together
on the ground floor at Manchester Square.
Mercer was not present; she was said to be
unwell. Charlotte had taken time that day to
write her a brief note, and would do so again
tomorrow from Oatlands, where they were to
spend the honeymoon. Poor Lord Byron had
called his a treacle-moon; Charlotte hoped her
own would be different. Oatlands was never
free from the smells of pet animals, monkeys,
dogs, birds, all kept in the house and in aunt
York's grotto. She would take Leopold to visit
the grotto; it would be a subject of
conversation. He would perhaps grow
accustomed to the vagaries of her family in
time; his own did not sound nearly as odd.

Charlotte walked down the short distance
between the rows of standing guests, on her
father's arm. Prinny was magnificent in a
scarlet coat, gleaming with orders and braid.
More orders glittered on a handsome figure
waiting at the end; bridegroom Leo, copiously
decorated in the Tsar's service during the late

war. Charlotte felt herself handed over, and heard herself take the vows. It would be restful, after all, to obey.

At the end, Prinny suddenly gave her a great hug, like any other father. It heartened Charlotte greatly. Perhaps he had some affection for her, after all.

CHAPTER EIGHTEEN

Mercer was indeed unwell on the Princess's wedding day, her nerves taut as fiddler's catgut.

Her plans had collapsed like a house of cards: once again. It was clear already what would happen, and by now she was powerless to prevent it. If she could have foreseen what her recent encouragement of Leopold's suit would come to mean! But she had not known the truth in time, and now it was too late.

That was not all. The Admiral had stated recently that he would disinherit her formally if she married Charles de Flahault. That meant forfeiting an expected income of twenty-three thousand pounds a year on Lord Keith's demise. Mercer did not regret the prospect of such loss for her own sake—there was still her own money from her mother, also the Keith title remained hers in course by law—but she had hoped, in the ruinous world of diplomacy, to finance without stint the man she was to marry and cause him thereby, even by bribes right and left, to reach the top of any available tree. That, aided by the Princess's friendship when Charlotte should become queen, ought to have been certain, after all one's care and effort. Now, nothing was so any more; one must start again from the beginning.

The only certainty was that she herself loved Charles de Flahault. He did not love her; evidently she must be difficult to love, but she would win his affection in time. His father Talleyrand was close-fisted, and would not help with money; he had no doubt learned to respect it as a result of his own enforced exile during the Revolution, when he had worked with his hands in the United States of America, dragging his club-foot (how constantly club-feet pursued one!) through uncultivated swamp, selling real estate as and when he could in packets: one could not help but admire the man, a member, as Talleyrand was, of so aristocratic a family that physical work had probably never been heard of among them before. By now, having returned to France at the rise of Napoleon, the erstwhile Bishop of Autun—he had been forced into a soutane at twelve years old, without explanation, Charles said, and the title given to his younger brother, who had both feet like other people—had to support a wife he regretted marrying and who he by now paid to stay away. At the time the

First Consul, about to become Emperor and anxious for an appearance of morality, had decreed that all men of position must either marry their mistresses or else discard them.

Madame Grand—that had been her name—would not at the time be discarded, and had thereafter changed from being an adorable mistress to become a fat, disagreeable and embarrassing wife. 'He never now sees her,' Charles had said. 'He sends his lawyer once a year to enquire for her health.' It had been one more inadvisable marriage; how many there were, and now Papa said she was about to make one herself! But Mercer knew she would never embarrass Charles. Everything she could still do for him should be done. His mother, whom he had, of course, consulted, approved of the match—as well she might, thought Mercer wryly—and had communicated news of it already to the Pretender's widow in Florence, the lady who called herself Madame d'Albanie and had finally left the impossible old drunkard an unkind fate had foisted on her in order to embark on a sustained love affair with an Italian poet; now Alfieri was dead Madame d'Albanie was having another with a French painter, Fabre. Perhaps, when Charles was again accepted on the Continent—at present old Louis XVIII, restored a second time, refused to readmit him to France, but she herself would pull the necessary strings in time—well, perhaps she and Madame d'Albanie would one day meet; also, of course, Charles's mother, Madame de Souza, in her tall house in Paris with its rose-garden. One must work towards that; this present black hour would pass, but in the meantime it had to be faced, along with its reasons.

To have agreed to part with the prospect of so large a fortune as Papa could deny her was, no doubt, incredible to the thrifty French. Charles had looked at her with amazement and, at last, heartfelt gratitude; he knew, now, that she, Mercer, truly loved him. He had opened his hitherto closed heart as a result, telling her of the young woman he had loved long ago in Warsaw, on campaign; Anna Potocka was married, that was not a difficulty. Then—

The one he had named then was the danger, still; Napoleon's stepdaughter, Hortense Beauharnais, herself the daughter of Josephine with Josephine's charm, and wife to the Emperor's youngest brother Louis, most unhappily matched; late Queen of Holland; how Holland recurred! Queen Hortense herself was now in exile in Switzerland, separated from her husband.

Charles did not love Hortense, he admitted, but felt himself bound to her by ties it was hard to break. Her marriage had been wretched; she had been forced into it by her mother, who was afraid at the time of being divorced and abandoned by Napoleon, as had later

182

happened in any case. Now, Charles was still prepared to marry Hortense, who had long been his mistress, if she would obtain a divorce from Louis Bonaparte. 'She will not do it, because she says it would compromise the position of her two young sons,' Charles had said, his handsome face thoughtful and compassionate. Mercer had been roused to resentment; how could this unknown woman expect to keep Charles and yet give up nothing at all for his sake? She herself was different, as was lately proved. She used all her persuasion; and watched Charles weaken by degrees. It was to his better advantage, after all, to marry herself rather than a divorced Bonapartist. There was no bar, not even that of religion; although a formal Catholic, Madame de Souza was herself a disciple of Voltaire and had reared her son accordingly. Papa's inevitable gibes about papists were not in question; the matter could be settled in such ways with ease and understanding.

However the disclosure that Charles had not been Hortense's only lover was disturbing, and might well be true. It explained the Princess's continuing advice against 'Flahaud' since her own betrothal, since the very time when she and 'Cobourg' began to agree about all subjects under the sun. Leopold had visited the Tuileries while it suited him to do so; and as usual had made the most of his stay. Two men who had shared a mistress were like dogs over the same bone; and the Prince of Saxe-Coburg would not, as time went on, encourage continuing friendship between his royal wife and a woman who had married his erstwhile, and altogether more successful, rival. Mercer saw everything clearly now; much too clearly.

*   *   *

A note had been brought round by hand that morning from the Princess, describing how she was dressed and how she felt. One's presence was still missed, evidently. Later on, Mercer heard the cheering of the crowds as the newlyweds drove away together in their carriage, drawn by grey horses—poor Slender Billy had procured greys for Charlotte in his time as well—to the honeymoon at Oatlands. On the following day, a further note came from the bride made wife. The Prince, Charlotte wrote, was the perfection of a lover, though she could not yet feel comfortable in his presence. That would come, Mercer reflected. It would not be long before Charlotte was a submissive wife, pliable as wax in her German husband's hands. Well, at least one was prepared. Papa, in his naval battles—how she had followed them with close interest and pride as a girl, and had even made those careful paintings of some of them on china, with the characters dressed as ancient Greeks! That was long ago now— Papa had often had to alter course and commands at the last minute, depending on the tactics of the enemy. She herself would do the same. The Admiral might, in his dour unspoken way, be fond of her still; but she would marry Charles de Flahault de la Billarderie, come what might, and take him with her meantime to Scotland.

* * *

Other matters crowded into her mind, making it like an overfilled box whose lid would not shut. It was only a fortnight since Byron had left England for ever: and before that, she herself had been the only person of standing prepared to speak to him in public after the scandal of the Separation and the growing rumours about his relations with his half-sister. Caro George Lamb, with her mousy propriety, had seen fit to cut Augusta Leigh at a ball given by Lady Jersey to try to induce society to accept a situation of which, after all, it was not fully cognisant. The ball had been a disaster; skirts had been drawn aside and every lady present, except Mercer herself and a few gaping onlookers, had withdrawn to a further room to avoid Byron's by now leprous presence. He had stood defiantly alone, and Mercer's quick compassion had blazed up in her; after all, she had loved him, and who in any case could judge anyone else and throw the first stone? She had hastened to Byron, and remembering their shared laughter at Tunbridge Wells had rallied him in her own way.

'You should have married me,' she had told him roundly. 'I would have managed you better.'

The remark was noted, of course; and ascribed to Miss Mercer Elphinstone, mistakenly described by one unacquainted witness as having red hair; generations to come would describe Mercer's hair as the wrong colour accordingly. Byron had smiled; and on leaving England, had sent her a letter and a book with an affectionate inscription; it was Lord Brook's *Life of Sir Philip Sidney*. More even than that, Mercer valued a phrase in his subsequent letter to Scrope Davies, who had delivered the package to her as asked. *Tell her that had I been fortunate enough to marry a woman like her, I should not now be obliged to exile myself from my country.*

He had gone; the creditors had almost seized his travelling-carriage on the quay. Mercer stared down at his letter to her which had come with the book. *I cannot conclude without wishing you a much happier destiny . . .*

Destiny. She had once tried to forge it for them both; then again for herself, with Devonshire. The Duke was now in St Petersburg, having developed a close friendship with the Grand Duke Nicholas after the latter's much-delayed visit to England.

Charlotte had incautiously pronounced the Grand Duke's miniature, which had been shown her, as so handsome that she had said she would marry no one else until she met him, as a result of which he had not been permitted for some time to enter the country. Well, Leopold was no doubt equally handsome; and, it seemed, the perfection of a lover.

* * *

Lord Byron's carriage, modelled on that found abandoned by the Emperor Napoleon at a farmhouse near Waterloo, bowled some time afterwards along the good roads the Emperor himself had caused to be made long ago in Italy. Their surface scarcely jarred the special pole built under the coach-body to soften any shocks. There were none; the carriage had lately crossed the Alps, leaving the Shelleys and, thank God, Claire Clairmont behind. She had pursued him first in England, just before departure. He did not, at the moment, want to think of her or the child she had borne him. He preferred to remember England itself, even now, where the ways were execrable; England, for which his heart still ached; isle of beauty, where the bailiffs had almost seized this very carriage as he prepared to embark. Certainly the carriage was not paid for, but was essential to him, perhaps more so than the other things which had of necessity gone; his library,

187

including the eight-volume Virgil old Lord Keith had bought. Byron himself had nevertheless a few books here with him now, his dog at his feet, a folding table on which to write; an extension on which to stretch his legs if he felt so inclined, and a *nécessaire*. All this the Emperor had personally designed in his own version. The original carriage, having been looted by the Prussians, had been brought across to England almost after the fashion of the Elgin Marbles, to be exhibited last year as one of the spoils of war at the Egyptian Hall in Piccadilly, where Byron had seen it and had ordered Baxter's the coachbuilders to copy it for his use.

Piccadilly! How the name itself brought memories both of success and damnation! The centre of fashion, London's very heart, where hostesses held the drawing-rooms to which he had once been welcome, but was no longer invited now; not now. Piccadilly, where old Betsy Melbourne had, no doubt with the best of intentions, hired a damned expensive house in which to live with a wife who would no longer cohabit with him, whose flight after a year had meant his social ruin.

It was her mother, of course, the old beldame with the bowsprit legs. Judith Milbanke, lately by inheritance Lady Noel—it amused Byron to be able to sign himself N.B.—had never been at all sure of him, catch as he was, nor had he been able to endure her, though they had maintained the civilities. It was like her to have hung a green curtain in front of his Albanian portrait, as she said to protect it from smoke at Kirkby Mallory. Disapproving also had been that companion creature, Clermont. Byron would not have remembered her name but for its likeness to the other, Claire. He would send for their child when he was settled at last in Venice: Allegra should atone for the lack of Ada. Allegra, oddly, resembled Bell, of all people. That Clermont woman would be brooding over Bell now.

Born in the garret, in the kitchen bred,
Promoted thence to deck her mistress' head,

So it went on, vitriolic enough. *Dines off the dishes that she used to wash.* A memory came to Byron of his own boyhood in the shabby lodgings in Aberdeen; that hadn't been much better, come to think of it: better not think.

Faugh! What did such things matter in the end? One lived for the present. Yet he had tried, had almost managed at times, to love his wife, except that her total lack of humour drove him as mad as her unexpected subservience; she hadn't ordered him, as he had hoped, but had expected him to order her. For as long as he lived, though, he would cherish the thought of their daughter Ada. By now, Ada must be walking and talking, deliciously, unattainably.

189

He had hardly had the chance to set eyes on her blue gaze after it had opened; he would be allowed to know nothing of her except in occasional formal letters, or she of him. Ada. He had found the name long ago in family archives at Newstead; it had been that of a twelfth-century ancestress, mother of kings. Ada Byron. Whatever else they denied her or himself, they could not take her name away, drain his blood out of her veins. *Ada, sole daughter of my house and heart*. Later he would send for a portrait of her, to study her child's features as they must by now have become.

All he had to study now, unless he opened a book, were the fast-moving rumps of the four horses needed to draw the equipage; the fresh smell of their sweat came to Byron as they galloped onwards in the sun's heat. So must Napoleon himself often have sat, perched at this height in order to miss no jot of what took place ahead. That man would miss no single detail. A commander was, after his fashion, a poet. Byron stared at the backs of the two postilions. He was travelling in style to Venice; no need there to creep in by the back door, he had already hired a palazzo. Word would have spread among the canals of the pending arrival of the wicked English milord. The lagoons beckoned, the islands, and all manner of shadowy delights. He would disgrace himself in Venice as he chose. They said—Byron had heard this on his earlier travels—that if the city disliked anyone, a dead cat would be seen by them sooner or later floating in the canal. He would swim out near the islands tomorrow to find out. After the pain of ostracism in London, a dead cat would nowise disconcert him: nothing now could.

He remembered, again, the one being who hadn't publicly disowned him: Mercer Elphinstone. That was a courageous and generous creature whom he should no doubt after all have married: the fact of her fortune had deterred him, whereas the fact of Annabella's—he would certainly not have married Bell had she been penniless—had, most unfortunately, decided him. Had it been made evident that the financial difficulties of old Sir Ralpho, as Byron called his father-in-law behind his back, would prevent access to any money whatever, there would have been no second proposal, perhaps not even a first. As it was, the latter state was even worse than the earlier had been. So the world went; and Bell, yielding as she had seemed to be to him, had become a hard and implacable woman now; she had even refused poor Ann Fletcher a reference, and Byron had written to protest. It was his wife's damned principles again; best to be totally unprincipled. One lived long enough to find out as much. That earlier time at Seaham, it was laughable to remember, she had requested him to leave early lest she give way to impropriety too soon. Byron smiled

191

bitterly in the shadow of the carriage. Annabella never gave way in truth: not in her heart.

It was pleasanter to think of Mercer again, and others, though not all. Two of Mercer's cousins who were in the army had been taken prisoner by the Emperor and treated kindly. He had heard—was it from Mercer herself? Surely not; there had not been leisure—that the two had sent the captive on St Helena, that island sedulously pronounced in the wrong fashion by the British, a carved ivory chess-set to while away the dreary hours. One hoped General Bonaparte, as they called him now, would be allowed access to it; one heard that his imprisonment was so rigorous that his gaoler, Sir Hudson Lowe, even attempted to view him in his bath. Perhaps the prisoner remembered this carriage in which he had at the time bowled freely along his own roads, a small man in a grey overcoat and unmistakable hat. Like oneself, but not that time out of boredom, the Emperor had consummated his second marriage with an archduchess without too much further ceremony. They, the vultures in charge of the Congress of Vienna, had never forgiven him that, or the marriage; and they would never let him see his son again, the boy would be brought up as an Austrian. That made a bond between oneself and the fallen eagle; both were denied their legitimate children.

That honeymoon! The treacle-moon! The bed-curtains had flickered red with the firelight beyond, for it was winter; and he had wakened and said aloud that he must surely be in hell, with Proserpine asleep beside him. From a statement Bell had made to the lawyers, it was clear she hadn't been asleep. There was, after all, something devious about her. She had lied to him at the beginning of the renewed correspondence she herself had started, saying her heart was given to another; and she had lately opened a trunk of his private letters and read them. He wished her joy; they were all from women.

He had tried not to dislike her more ponderous aspects, had even tried to be playful; that had usually succeeded. Her eating habits he could not however endure to watch; coming from Yorkshire, Bell ate heartily. They had taken to dining separately; the beginning of the end, perhaps, but then there had been no sign of it, or any sign at all till after she had gone.

Well, now they were separated in all ways, England had disowned him and France would only permit him to enter on a limited passport subject to control, so he had not gone there. There had been Belgium instead, and the place of skulls. They said Prinny had persuaded himself that he had been in command at Waterloo; poor Prinny, denied military advancement by his father until it was too late!

193

His many gifts had been squandered, not entirely through his own fault: but Ireland suffered, and the poor of England, still.

Byron closed his eyes. For Prinny, life had become a matter of liaisons, of taking one woman after another and betraying most. Fresh loves waited for himself, no doubt, in Italy and wherever he might go; possibly he might even love a man again. Young De la Warr at Harrow, young Edleston who had drowned at Cambridge, he had loved, without consummating either desire physically. The losses had broken his heart on each occasion; but hearts mended, as his own was mending now. Ah, but he would miss the London friends, the company and laughter, Cam Hobhouse who had shared his travels, Murray the publisher, Kinnaird, Tom Moore with his lovable Irish wit!

General Bonaparte, as they called him, must miss his usual acquaintance also, on that solitary rock. Had he won Waterloo, England by now would have been better governed; would have ended with roads like these, and fairer laws. Soon now they would be in Venice, and the fabled city would rise above the sea-mist like a lovely ghost. Tomorrow he himself would dive into the Grand Canal from the house he had hired close by it. Dead cats. He wouldn't trouble with them, or with anything again except that, on leaving England, he had perforce had to leave Augusta. Would she have the courage to come out with the children and join him, leaving the unsatisfactory Leigh to his debts and his racing, leaving her appointment in St James's? The thought that he himself might never set eyes on Augusta again was not to be borne. Deprived of wife, child, home, country, sister, nothing otherwise remained to fill the empty place in his heart unless some cause presented itself; but what? At the moment, his heart was too sick to embrace causes. His farewell letter to Mercer Elphinstone and the book he had sent had closed a chapter forever; what must befall now was foreordained, as usual for his damnation; he, Byron, need not let the past trouble him further.

Dead cats.

CHAPTER NINETEEN

Princess Charlotte had by now long forgotten F., once the occasion of much heartburning in the days of her confinement at Cranbourn Lodge; he had been convincingly proved from hearsay to be a roué, also to have no affection to speak of in return for her former consuming passion. She was increasingly happy with her Leo. Not only was lovemaking delightful, but he won her heart by being now and again in poor health. The Princess had a compassionate nature; years ago she had carried the dying Mrs Gagarin, her dresser, about in her arms. Now, when as so often Leo had an attack of neuralgia—he said also there was a constant noise like a waterfall inside his head—she tended him, as at present, seated by his bedside reading *The Giaour*.

She had always sent for Byron's poems hot from the press. This—one could not help but notice—contained several instances of what society thought particularly shocking, but her mother had of course told her of a similar instance in the family years ago, which was never mentioned by any of the rest: Wiskerandos' seduction of Sophy. It was no doubt partly the reason why most persons, including herself, so greatly disliked the Duke of Cumberland; certainly the fact that he was a Tory counted also. Leopold however had advised her not to take sides in politics: how wise he was! She glanced at the dark head lying, slightly tousled, on its pillow, then returned to her reading. Byron's lines always stirred her; nobody could write like him. One had heard various stories about his improper conduct abroad, in Switzerland and, by now, Italy. The whole thing was very sad, if secretly diverting.

She returned to thoughts of Princess Sophia and her son. There was no doubt, her mother had told her, of whom the father had been; the Queen, Old Plugnose (Caroline called her the Begum) had long forbidden Prince Ernest, as he was then, access to his sisters' rooms, where he had too often been found prying by the door. 'He was sent off early to Germany, to the university and the army, and kept there,' Charlotte recalled Caroline's guttural voice explaining, with triumph at the back of it: there was no doubt that her mother relished any gossip that was hurtful to her estranged husband's family. Well, poor Sophy's situation was as sad as that of Lord Byron, and nothing was too bad for Prince Wiskerandos, though it was unfortunate that his Duchess had miscarried last year. Incest was not, of course, a subject to be mentioned to dearest Leo; it would shock his sense of propriety. She, Charlotte, was often reproved by him in any case for the thoughtless things she said, but so lovingly she liked the reproof. If they had any disagreement, he and she would make it up at the end of each day, and that was delightful also; he called it their *Missverständniss*. Charlotte's own German had always been fairly good; when they went to the theatre together she was able to explain the programme to Leopold, his English not yet being fully able to comprehend everything contained in it. They had sat side by side in the box lately at Drury Lane—they had arrived late and had been hissed, Charlotte remembered absently, as Kean had been in the middle of one of his tragic passages—and she herself had worn her favourite fashion of a headdress of fresh roses, and they had been sketched thus together by Dawe, who would undoubtedly take more portraits of them both when they were finally settled at Claremont.

There would be music there, too; her own Broadwood pianoforte, the present from Papa, would be in position already. They would sing together in the evening after walking in the grounds, planning changes and improvements; how greatly she looked forward to it all! There would only be invited visitors there, and perhaps Papa would not be as difficult over these as he had been when she had ventured lately to ask the Duke of Wellington to Camelford House to dinner; it would no longer be possible for the Regent to keep quite so strict an eye. She would, in any case, to show her affection for him, often wear the sapphire he had given her on the day, two years ago now, that they had opened Charles I's coffin at Windsor. It had been found to be quite incorrupt, the body, with one eye still open, but that had shut with the admission of air. Papa had stood behind Notte, who had been with her then at Carlton House, and had demonstrated on her stringy neck the precise manner in which Charles's head had been chopped off at the time. He had then given the sapphire to Charlotte; it blazed with history, and had evidently been returned by way of the late Cardinal King, having, they said, been smuggled out of England by the latter's grandfather James II in the heel of one of his shoes. Before that, it had crowned the ancient kings of Scotland. Now, it might well be in her own crown when the time came, Leopold had said; but it was unkind to think of Papa's demise, and in any case the old King himself was not yet dead, though it would undoubtedly be better for him to be so as soon as possible.

Leopold groaned a little and Charlotte leaned forward hastily, setting *The Giaour* aside, to bathe her husband's temples with lavender-water. He seized her white fingers afterwards and kissed them. How happy they were, and how seldom she now thought of other persons, even old friends! Both Notte and Mercer had called, separately of course as they had never got on, and had had in each case to be turned away; in one instance because of this recurrent neuralgia, and in the other because she and Leo were just about to go out driving. It had been unfortunate, but in any case Mercer was being obstinate about that unsuitable Frenchman; she had been repeatedly warned to have nothing more to do with him, but would not take advice.

Leopold, refreshed, turned his head now and regarded her. How truly handsome he was, exactly as Dawe had shown in that drawing at the theatre, with his long-lashed dark-blue eyes filled truly with love! His locks had tumbled meantime over his brow and Charlotte smoothed them. When they were

199

at Claremont, she would, she had decided, fold his linen for him like any housewife; they would be like a squire and his lady, with no interruptions such as had taken place on the honeymoon, when Papa had, most unaccountably, driven down to Oatlands on the second day and had sat for two mortal hours discussing the minutiae of uniforms. There had also been Stockmar, the young German physician in attendance on Leo; Charlotte knew her own free-and-easy manners still disturbed Stocky a little, but he would accustom himself.

'What are you reading, *mein Herz?*' asked Leopold, as a husband should.

On hearing that it was *The Giaour*, he frowned and said: 'Lord Byron is abroad for debt and other reasons, and his wife has left him. I would wish you to read more improving things, my Charlotte.'

He is still a fine poet whatever he has done, she thought a little rebelliously; but closed the book obediently and set it aside. 'I used to meet him often, and liked him greatly,' she remarked. At the time, it had been particularly exciting; she had seen few other visitors.

'He is not a suitable person for you ever to have known.'

'Neither was my mother, no doubt,' something made Charlotte reply. She went to the window and looked out. There had been no letters from abroad lately; no one had informed the old Princess officially of her wedding, or of the fact that, already and within the month, she herself had been reported pregnant, but there had been a miscarriage, not serious. The peace of Claremont would improve such things.

'Come away from the window, *mein liebling*; it is not proper for you to be seen from the street.'

It was another *Missverständniss*, to be put right later. Charlotte obeyed, and left the sight of passing carriages down in the street, dusty as they were with summer.

CHAPTER TWENTY

Formerly, when she had had any leisure, Mercer would occupy it in writing, in her strong, regular and not always comprehensible hand, duplicates of every single letter she had ever formerly written regarding the breaking off of the Orange marriage, for her own protection if it should be required. It had appeared till quite lately, long after most had supposed the intention forgotten, that the Regent was still determined to press the marriage with the Princess, if not for Slender Billy then for his younger brother Frederick. Now that Leopold had married Princess Charlotte himself the danger should be past that she, the baneful adviser, might be put out of favour; and yet it seemed that Leopold, who after all had every reason to be grateful to her for promoting his suit, was deliberately alienating the Princess, or at least keeping Charlotte to himself. What had become of what had once been so close a friendship, with almost daily letters from Warwick House? It was like the separation which had been enforced for a time between them when Prinny was angry about the débâcle there and in Bayswater and, again, the jettisoning of the unfortunate Orange. As for Slice, he was shortly to be married to the Princess Mary at last; one could not but feel sorry for that lady, intriguer as she no doubt was.

It was also just possible to be sorry for oneself. This was a new sensation for Mercer, yielded to as she had been almost from birth, her every wish met instantly: prevented in having her own way in nothing, first by adoring aunts at Elphinstone Tower near Stirling and, later on, by her grandmother and London society. Now, looking as so often in the glass, she fancied herself even older in appearance than the young woman in the turban whose likeness by Saunders now hung firmly on the wall. Nobody, after all, displayed great anxiety to marry her; Papa had long been impatient quite apart from the matter of Charles. Devonshire wrote in friendly fashion from St Petersburg, where he was now sojourning, driving out, as he described it, in a sleigh drawn by four fast horses alongside one which did not take any weight, and was merely attached by a loose rein to the side and known as a *furieux*. Devonshire's was spotted, like the carriage dogs which had become the mode last century in England. What a pity after all that he had not been allowed to aspire to the Princess's hand! What harm would there have been in her marrying a commoner of such high blood and immense wealth? Hart loved Charlotte; he always wore the gold watch-chain she had given him in her impulsive fashion long ago. Perhaps, for her sake, he would indeed never marry; and Hary-O, the sister who had herself married Lord Granville, had again lately referred to the well-worn tale that Hart had been born in Paris not to Duchess Georgiana at all, but delivered to Bess Foster by a man-midwife named Richard Crofts. Bess was now the Dowager Duchess, and inclined to give herself airs Hart would not tolerate. It was all very mysterious, but no doubt one mystery that would never be resolved. 'Bess appeared at the theatre about then, thin as a vegetable,' Hary-O had admitted. There was nothing wrong with Dearest Hart in the physical sense; like most men, he kept a mistress privately.

Papa did not: possibly he never had done. He continued unbending in every other detail; so much so that he had been barely civil to

Charles de Flahault when they had met at last, *malgré lui*, that evening some time since at the Portuguese Embassy. 'Don't like the feller and never will, too damned smooth, like all Frenchmen,' the Admiral had said afterwards. There was no doubt that to the rugged old Scot, French manners were effeminate despite the Auld Alliance. Mercer told herself once more, and with truth, that Charles's were exquisite; he himself, in time, with money, would make the perfect ambassador.

He had finally agreed to break with Queen Hortense; or, as he chivalrously put it, Hortense had agreed at last to release him. Mercer said little about the absent lady and talked, instead, about the exiled Emperor himself, to whom Charles had been personally devoted and had, as she already knew, been thoroughly downcast when he was not chosen to go to St Helena with the selected few.

'You will be of more use to him here, among those who may aid him in the end,' Mercer said; privately she did not think it would happen. Napoleon, it was known, hoped that when the Princess came to the throne his rigorous imprisonment might be ended; he had heard of Charlotte as a liberal. However Mercer herself had heard the Princess say that Boney's imprisonment ought to be made even stricter than it was. Her youth at times made her inconsiderate.

Charles was still murmuring about the rights

of the tiresome Hortense's sons. 'The Emperor has a son of his own,' Mercer reminded him, thinking of the little fair-haired child now in Vienna: Hart had seen him there, driving in a carriage with his tutor.

'Metternich will never set L'Aiglon free,' replied Charles gravely. 'He will be a prisoner all his life. He last saw his father when he was three; how can a child of that age resist all that will be put into his mind against Napoleon? Had the Empress been a different woman there might have been hope.' He turned away bitterly. Marie Louise had already, while the Emperor was on Elba, become the mistress of a one-eyed Austrian officer and had borne him a child; Metternich had arranged all of that without delay. 'They say the little King of Rome clung to the door-handles at the Tuileries, and had to be dragged away by force into exile,' Charles said sadly. 'He used to love more than anything to watch the guard turn out to parade, and the guard was crazy for him when he appeared in his little uniform. He will make a soldier, no doubt, but not for France.'

'Nobody knows what will happen,' Mercer murmured. She turned eagerly then to talk of their future together: now that he was free to marry her she would give him children of his own, as well as fortune, security and devoted love. She made no mention of the anger of her family. Charles would lead her into a fresh life, after all. The Orléans clan were friendly; they themselves might be permitted to return to France in time. Mercer reflected on how things and people were connected in odd ways: Marie-Amélie, Louis Philippe's wife, had been a Bourbon princess of the Two Sicilies, and Papa had known her parents, the weak King Bomba and his termagant wife, Maria Carolina, sister of the luckless Marie Antoinette, in Naples. Cornelia Knight had been in Naples with her mother then also, and had fallen in love with one of Papa's officers, but the love had not been returned. Poor Cornelia—it was difficult to think of her as young—had travelled home in the end with Lord Nelson and Lady Hamilton, with her tarantella amply danced for them at the German inn. It would be interesting to hear of more such doings and to meet the people who did them.

First, though, they must go to Scotland. The wedding itself was to be in Edinburgh, and Clem Gwydyr had offered Drummond Castle for the honeymoon. It would remind one of old times; she would show Charles the sundial, and the tower she and Clem had used to climb as children. Soon thereafter, they would go together to Meikleour to await possible events in the south: it would be a mistake to become completely out of touch with London.

*　　*　　*

Mercer and Charles de Flahault de la Billarderie were married in the George Street drawing-room of an old kinswoman who remembered the Porteous Riots and also, being lifted up by a Highland soldier to see the young man she called The Pretender. 'You must call him the Prince,' the soldier had said gently, and the old voice related it yet again: but Kitty Murray of Henderland was by far more exercised by the bride's choice of green gloves and green ribbons, fluttering from Mercer's bonnet and her gown. Green brought no luck to a bride, Mercer was twenty-nine, and in any event this mixed marriage—a Scots minister from St Andrews in this very street had performed it, but there would have to be a papist ceremony as well—this marriage was not at all advisable; it was very well to say it was for love, but Mercer Elphinstone's father had cut her off and would leave everything he could to his younger daughter. The bride herself had an obstinate chin, however; the groom was handsome enough, no doubt, but Mercer would always be the better man of the two: that was well seen. Mrs Murray saw the pair off in their carriage, but shook her old capped head to herself at the lack of kin attending the ceremony. Still, there had been a handsome carved marriage-coffer sent in a gift by somebody; was it the Princess Charlotte? It was known that she and Miss Mercer had been close friends, among the grand folk to be found in London.

CHAPTER TWENTY-ONE

'We will not, I think, use the famous, the *berühmt* sapphire for this portrait by Lawrence. The stone is of so deep a colour that it makes even your eyes look pale, *mein liebchen*. When you are crowned it will be different; it will shine, like yourself, amongst all the rest.'

Leopold set the great Stuart sapphire aside to be returned to his wife's jewel-case. As always now, Charlotte watched his face, forgetting everything but how greatly she loved him. She had lately been heard to say to someone that if Leopold could not wear the crown beside her as England's king, she would live in a cottage in submission to him. It was a far cry from the rebellious young woman of the old days. Recently, here at Claremont when they were so happy, she had caused the centrepiece to be removed one night from the dinner-table where they had company, because it blocked her view of her husband's face. By now, it gave her pleasure to tie Leopold's cravats, fold his linen as foreseen, comb his dark hair when he came back from a day's shooting on the estate. Lately, since she had grown heavy with this latest pregnancy—

thank God, as there had been a second miscarriage during the year, but this time it should come to term—since that had happened, she no longer walked daily with him, but drove out instead in a low calèche in the grounds. She missed their shared walks; she and he had planned improvements everywhere, some of which had already been begun; a grotto was rising in the woods, to be precisely like the one at Oatlands, place of the honeymoon. 'It will remind future generations of our contentment,' Leopold had said in his ponderous German way. She loved this also; it was a part of him, he always thought most carefully before he spoke, dear Leo.

However, the Regent would have been pleased had she worn the sapphire in which to be painted by Lawrence; no matter, she would wear a dark dress and filmy drifting scarf instead. The child sat so well forward in her that she could no longer wear fascinating clothes such as the outfit in which Miss Charlotte Jones, who had made a crayon drawing of her each year since childhood, had portrayed her early in the marriage: in a Regency cap of velvet with double ostrich feathers, her arms and neck wreathed with pearls. However it was so delicious to be married to Leo that clothes after all did not matter. Lawrence was to make a companion portrait of him when her own was completed. Charlotte had the sudden, desperate certainty that she would never see it. Why that, when there was such happiness? It must be an echo of the black days, when she had felt herself abandoned by all the world and loved by none. Now, she was loved indeed; now, they were happy. Guests were few, only invited on such occasions as the one lately when, half in jest, she and Leo had been presented by the local people with a flitch of bacon in imitation of the famous one at Dunmow for praiseworthy married couples. It was known everywhere what an ideal couple they themselves made. In fact, it had become necessary to preserve their privacy; so many came to gaze at them at morning service in Esher church, which they had at first attended regularly each Sunday, that by now they had the chaplain read this privately in the drawing-room at Claremont instead. Likewise, when she and Leo sang together in the evenings, she accompanying him on the Broadwood, they would stop at once if anyone came in; it was only for themselves, with the sound of their voices in harmony like all the rest, all of the marriage, every aspect of it.

Charlotte frowned a little, feeling her customary headache assail her. These had become frequent now, but then she had been restricted, by Sir Richard Crofts who after all had much experience of women in her state, to a diet of tea and toast only. She felt tired, accordingly, but a lowering diet was always prescribed and one must endure it; as soon as the birth was over she could eat again as before. She tried not to think of the mutton chop she had formerly preferred for breakfast. Such things were forbidden, and blooding was necessary as well. It was all very tiresome, and her veins were small.

Crofts. She thought of him again, recalling that he had, long ago, delivered Duchess Georgiana (or had it been Bess Foster after all?) of Devonshire, sixth of the title, in Paris. One could hardly enquire as to the real truth of that old tale, interesting as such truth would be. One did not question Crofts, any more than Stocky, who anyhow would take nothing to do with her case. That was no doubt prudent, but she would sooner have had him, her husband's physician, than anybody. He had come to be her great friend after at first, as she was aware, disapproving of her slightly. He had come into the Oatlands drawing-room the morning after her wedding hesitantly, obeying her '*Aha! monsieur le docteur, entrez*' to find her standing before the fire, hands behind her back. Later on he had met with her walking, alone for once, in Claremont grounds, the summer wind blowing her light lawn sleeves beneath the Russian-style bodice. Charlotte knew by then that she had conquered his formality. If only he would give some advice!

Briefly, for the first time in a long while, she remembered Mercer. That young lady would have been copious with it, but one no longer

211

saw her. She had been present, with others, at the flitch of bacon ceremony, but without her husband, as Leo would not have welcomed Charles de Flahault to Claremont. Since the visit, when they had chatted together amicably enough, Leo had revealed certain things; Mercer's early discouragement of his suit, certain remarks she had made behind his back which had evidently been repeated to him. Charlotte had written accordingly to her former friend to say that she could no longer be received. It was true that the idea of the Lawrence portrait had come from Mercer, as she had recently had herself painted by him. 'Dress your hair simply,' she had advised Charlotte, and that piece of advice was the last that would be taken; the Princess's hair was twisted up in a plain tight knot on top of her head, which made her neck look even longer, and set off the disadvantage of having, meantime, so distorted a body under the dark dress.

Her hand strayed uncertainly to where the child lay in her. If only this birth was over, and she and Leo could return to lovemaking again! However as it was, she still knew contentment, as he had phrased it; assurance of being protected, cherished as he had promised her she should be; and, as she had also promised at their marriage, she would obey.

* * *

212

Leopold had reason to remember the Lawrence portrait after Charlotte was dead. She had had these fits of depression, due no doubt to her state, in course of the painting; and at its completion had hurried out of the room to where he waited and had cast her arms about his neck, weeping; she would not live, she told him, to see his matching likeness. He had comforted her; but at the same time remembered, as he remembered long afterwards, that she took no interest in their coming child, had not thought of names, made no effort as most women did to concern herself with baby-clothes. It was perhaps because her own childhood had been unfortunate. He would atone, once the child was born. They would continue in their present happiness, surely increased because there was an heir for England. Later, when Charlotte's father was dead—neither he nor the old unseen King could surely live much longer—he, Leopold, would govern prudently on behalf of his wife and son. It must be a son, if not this time then the next. He knew himself most capable of government; he could think already of many ways in which the British constitution could be improved.

Meantime, the Lawrence portrait of his dear Charlotte was superb, the best that had ever been painted of her. It showed a fulfilled and happy young wife, piled hair shining softly, eyes and mouth smiling with cool amusement;

213

a different creature from the tense girl he had married eighteen months earlier. Leopold had guessed then what he did not know, using all his native shrewdness. He had won her heart; and he knew even now that he himself had never known such happiness, and never would again.

Why had a poet already written to Charlotte of death?

She went into labour some time after the expected date. In fact neither of them had been certain of this. Sir Richard Crofts did not appear to be alarmed; one must contrive to have every confidence in him. But Charlotte's labour seemed shockingly long, thirty hours by the end. She never once cried out; she had given her word to some waiting-woman not to do so, but it might have relieved her; Leopold thought afterwards of that. He stayed with her day and night, lying at times on the bed beside her, when she would run her fingers through his hair. By the second day he was too exhausted to stay awake any longer, and Stockmar gave him a sedative and said he must rest. He stumbled away to sleep, God knew for how long; and was awakened shortly by Stockmar's shaking him, his face grim.

The young German doctor had reason. From the beginning he had had doubts; and now did not tell his master that the Princess was already dead, merely that matters were very grave. He saw Leopold hasten into the

214

death-chamber and when he saw her, with the dead child nearby, fall on his knees and begin kissing Charlotte's hands and arms. Stockmar's cold mind—he had affection only for his master, and lately also for the dead Princess—assessed what he knew of Crofts. The man was not even a qualified practitioner, it turned out, merely a male midwife recommended by some English society lady. Any knowledgeable person would have turned the child long ago: it was misplaced, a cross-birth. It had been thought risky to use forceps. The fool had then—Stockmar ascertained this later—finally killed the Princess by letting her bleed to death, giving hot fomentations instead of an ice-pack. The dead child was a boy, said to resemble the King greatly; but its head had been crushed in the unspeakably prolonged labour.

Stockmar closed his eyes. He had heard Charlotte's loud voice—she had been most lovable in such ways—calling out 'Stocky Stocky!' as she felt the ultimate agony come, and the death-rattle. He had gone in then, to find her knees drawn up and hands already growing cold. Immediately, he had gone for his master.

*   *   *

England mourned, the great bell of St Paul's tolling out in a November night in which fog

215

had lately dispersed. The Regent's carriage had brought him swiftly back from Lady Hertford's country residence at news of the onset of the labour, and he was in bed at Carlton House when they brought him the news of Charlotte's death. 'Great heavens! What will become of the poor man!' George exclaimed, in the way one does at first in intolerable shock, screening reality for the moment. Then he remembered Charlotte and the way he had never permitted himself to love her as fully as a father should have done; there was the constant likeness to Caroline to be overcome, but there had been differences, heartrending to think of now; Charlotte's gifts, so like his own, her courage on horseback and driving her greys—'Damme, she's my daughter, ain't she?'—the time he had given her the Sultan's belt and the sapphire; the time she had angered him so greatly about the Orange marriage; good God, if this had happened at The Hague he could not now visit her body! He rang for his valet, ordered himself to be dressed, and set out for Claremont. He must see her before they embalmed her, while she was still as she had been when she died, his girl.

On the journey, it occurred to him that there was now no heir for England. He himself had no heart to remarry after a divorce; not now. His brothers, even Clarence, must take brides, part with their mistresses: Dorothy Jordan had already gone, it was true. Kent had lived with his own choice respectably for twenty-four years, was it? Something of the kind: no matter. Poor Charlotte, poor Charlotte. He himself would not have the heart to attend the funeral with all its pomp; nothing, after all, brought the dead back to life. He would see her now, instead.

*   *   *

He saw her; and talked interminably thereafter to a grief-stricken Leopold in something of the same manner as he had related army minutiae to the young couple on their honeymoon. At the back of his mind was the thought that he did not want to see Isabella Hertford again. She and her damned reprobate of a son Yarmouth could shift for themselves and take the Bible with them.

Leopold heard little. He was obsessed with the cruelty, said by the doctors to be necessary, of removing the dead woman's intestines and brain for examination. He had gazed with her father down at Charlotte as she lay; her face, after the long silent agony there had been, looked peaceful. They should leave her as she was; but he himself realised bitterly that he had, after all, no power to forbid anything any more. He would have an impression taken of Charlotte's hand, and carry it with him everywhere; and there were the portraits. There had been several painted since their

217

marriage. One, majestic in a long dark cloak, showed Charlotte as if she were already Queen. There was another in ostrich feathers, white over her black dress. He had liked her to dress grandly. Now, there was nothing left. Presently, after the ghastly embalming was done, he would sit in a coach in her funeral cortège by night to Windsor, and pray there alone by her coffin at Lower Lodge, the place she had always hated. Then they would have the long service in the chapel, with himself and three of her uncles in procession: then at last her body, and the child's, would be lowered into the vault. The child's heart would be bestowed in a separate urn; he had seen that, and it seemed unusually large. Leopold fastened on this strange detail for comfort.

*　　*　　*

There were obituaries, epitaphs, orations: a memorial in bad taste raised in white marble at Windsor, a second, somewhat less so, in Esher church. Miss Charlotte Jones drew a final posthumous portrait of her Princess, bearing a martyr's crown and palm and gazing upwards. Perhaps Leopold's wife would have been taught to refrain from laughter at such things. There were jet-framed miniatures of her everywhere; Princess Mary sent the Regent a ring containing Charlotte's hair entwined with Amelia's. There were black bows over the shops; workmen wore black armbands. Slender Billy, hearing in Holland of the death of the girl he would always love, stumbled out of the dining-room alone. Byron abandoned his debauchery abroad to write feelingly of Charlotte in the final cantos of *Childe Harold*. His sentiments echoed those of Hart, Duke of Devonshire, who would never forget Charlotte either and for her sake, would never marry: he wore the Princess's gift of a gold watch-chain for the rest of his life. *Her charming ingenuous nature would have led her into a thousand dangers*, he wrote, remembering a bright-haired partner long ago in the minuet. He returned to Chatsworth, burying himself in plans for rebuilding, for improving the gardens. They would still be famous after he was dead.

Sir Richard Crofts—Prinny had written to him kindly—confronted with a similar outcome of a later case, took a pistol in the hall and blew his brains out. Near his body was found an open Shakespeare. *Where is the Princess?* a line on the page read. It might have been coincidence, or perhaps not.

Meantime, the royal stork race had begun. Tarry Breeks and Kent were married at about the same time. The bride in Kent's case was Leopold's newly widowed sister, the high-coloured and virtuous Duchess of Leiningen. There was no doubt of Victoire's fertility—she had a son and a daughter, with whom Prinny himself fell briefly later on in love to the alarm of all, by the first marriage—but her husband's elder brothers disliked her thoroughly. However there was no time to be lost, and Kent himself seemed pleased. Clarence's own German bride Adelaide was pleasant, but all her children would die. So, shortly, would Kent.

*　　*　　*

In the cottage at Kew he so loved, the Duke of Cumberland, poor Charlotte's Wiskerandos, was less concerned with the death of his niece, who he knew had never liked or trusted him, than with the delicate health of his adored wife Frederica. She had given birth to their stillborn daughter, in his opinion because of the distress caused her by the old Queen's unkind ban. To refuse to receive his Duchess at Court was on a par with the constant blackening of his own honour, which Cumberland prized above everything, among his countrymen here. A kind of obstinacy had made him return to England, a determination to show them he cared nothing; in fact, he cared deeply. He loved green Kew, the place of his boyhood, and everything English; he was a Protestant of Protestants, a High Tory. It had been cruel to send him abroad at fifteen and to keep him there, proud as he had nevertheless been of his career in the army: even his spoken English now bore the accents of Germany. That feller Byron had been caused to go abroad also. The whole thing reminded Cumberland of the matter of his own sister Sophia, things not however having gone as far as they had evidently done between the poet and Mrs Leigh. Sophy, last seen when she was a thin fair-haired child of ten, when he himself had been sent to Göttingen to the university, had become, on his own return eight years afterwards, an exquisite little creature, slender like he was himself. Both quick, clever and apt, they had taken to one another; nothing furtive or criminal about it, but it had been seized on, in the first place by the unspeakable Princess of Wales, George's wife, who had a mind like a cesspit; she had spread the slander about incest to her young daughter as well as to others. That feller Brougham, who supported her, hoping for the time when her daughter would be Queen, made it a political matter; it suited the Whigs well enough to blacken him, Supreme Master of the Orange Lodges and firmly opposed to Romish emancipation in Ireland or anywhere else. Why, his family had been called to the throne last century to forestall it, and would be betraying their oath if it was allowed! As and when he might, he would influence George; George was too greatly prone to influence in general, perhaps after all remembering the Fitzherbert affair. No matter; that was done with, and the Brunswick

221

marriage need never have happened either, with poor Charlotte, the only fruit of the sorry coupling, dead.

He himself had been elsewhere when Sophia's child was conceived. They hadn't taken the trouble to prove it, or to disprove, as he himself had done, other accusations by the way of the newspapers and the abominable versifier, Hood. *Galloping, dreary Duke.* He had been elsewhere, again, when two young women were jostled against a set of railings by some horseman or other: but as usual the blame rested with him, Cumberland, and after that set of verses always would.

No matter. He made himself think instead of Frederica, who was lying down; and his scarred face softened. How like an angel she was, with her child's features and bright hair curling beneath the upturned brim of the hat she wore for their walks! For her to love him in return, as she certainly did, was incredible; he with his ruined face and mended head—that damnable Sellis business had briefly exposed his brain—and the turned-out, blinded eye from the war. He had been handsome once; in youth. Frederica herself had been unhappy in her two previous marriages: both had been to scoundrels, neither of whom had been worthy of his angel or kind to her. He, her Ernst, would atone; had already perhaps done so, a little. Next time there might be a living child, a son.

'Princess Elizabeth, you may hand me my *Schnüpftabak.*'

A stout middle-aged woman rose sullenly in obedience to a little old one seated most regally, and went to a nearby table while a second daughter, no longer young either, looked on. They sat all three together in a badly-heated room at Windsor, their hands busy with knotting-shuttles; the Queen did not permit idleness even now, when they had financial independence at last. The old woman's eyes, which had never needed spectacles, glanced sharply as Princess Elizabeth took up the snuff-box from the small table and, as she had had to do now for a generation and more, handed it to her mother. Her Majesty opened the box, whose lid bore enamelled miniatures of her two dead sons, small boys at the time; inhaled a pinch of snuff into both broad nostrils, closed the box once more with a snap and handed it back to Princess Elizabeth. The whole process took place without smiles, thanks or talk; Augusta, the other princess present, was in disgrace and seldom spoken to since she had had the effrontery to produce, at breakfast some time ago now, that letter signed by all the unmarried daughters demanding more freedom of action and their own money. To think of it! Unmarried women to act so! They had cozened

George Augustus, naturally, to support them; he had a soft heart. Well, the thing was done, and passed through the Lords, so one could no longer prevent it; Mary had married Gloucester, after all the fuss, and much joy might she have of it: and Elizabeth, at her age, and despite the King's condition, had announced her intention also of accepting a marriage-proposal, naturally from Germany. Not even her mother's recent ill-health would turn Elizabeth's will; she had always been wilful, as well as fat. She fancied herself as an artist.

The Queen was herself grossly swollen with dropsy, her once slender body so distorted that nowadays, when she had her portrait painted, they had to disguise her stomach by placing a little dog upon it. She knew she had not long to live; it was as though the water was rising in her and would soon reach her heart. Then she would die. She, Charlotte Sophia of Mecklenburg-Strelitz, accepted the fact of death as she had accepted most things in life, unemotionally and with clarity. One had done one's duty always, and would go to God, there no doubt to meet again Alfred, Octavius and Amelia. The thought filled the Queen with no sentiment; she had never greatly cared for any of her fifteen children except the first, the matchless and beautiful George Augustus. She loved Prinny still, and since his appalling marriage, which she had from the first opposed, they had become friends and allies. He was, of course, too greatly occupied with the business of ruling on his father's behalf to come here to Windsor often; when he did, even the girls became less dull.

Charlotte Sophia raised a snuff-stained finger and scratched her head vaguely beneath where the velvet pad had used to be placed on top; her scalp needed scraping again. Fanny Burney had always read to her while this was done. In earlier days, long before Fanny came, she herself had had brown hair, soft and of a fine dark colour. A lock of it, being considered her best feature, had been sent long ago to the King of England in order that he might assess her as a possible bride. He had held the lock up against a candle's flame, pronounced the hair most suitable and proceedings had then been undertaken; he had not, however, seen Charlotte Sophia's portrait; there had not been time to have one painted till after the marriage. The court at Mecklenburg had been too humble for such things; the women mended their stockings in the evenings and the men were soldiers, generally away at war. However she, Charlotte, had accomplishments; she could play the harpsichord and sing Lutheran hymns, and was a fine and exact needlewoman. In all of her youth she had never been permitted to be idle, any more than she permitted it to her daughters now. In that long-dead time, she had found the leisure nevertheless to write a letter to the much-feared King of Prussia, Frederick the Great, begging him not to allow his armies to despoil her brother's little state of Mecklenburg, where everyone worked hard to avoid poverty. The letter had had consequences, for King George had heard of it in some fashion and as he needed a bride without delay—for reasons, *vor allem*, she herself did not learn them till later on—he approved of a young woman who could write such a letter. She herself was not informed of anything at all until the British envoy came to Mecklenburg and laid his leg formally beside her, Charlotte Sophia, in bed before everyone at Court. That signified marriage to the English King. She had then been despatched straight to England without more talk, except to be told that she was most fortunate to have secured a young, handsome and virtuous royal bridegroom. There was by then no further danger from the Papist Stuarts; the Protestant succession was safe, and it was part of Charlotte's duty to provide for it. She understood all of this and did not ask questions nobody would answer: there was no point.

It had been stormy on the way over and all of her ladies were sea-sick, even the beautiful Duchess of Hamilton who had been especially sent to instruct the new Queen in etiquette. The Duchess being however beyond speech for the time, Charlotte had left her and the other afflicted ladies and had gone up the ladder to where there was, on board, a harpsichord. She played and sang her Lutheran hymns all through the continuing storm. If one showed trust in God, God would deliver the ship safely; and to port it had duly come. On landing, to show she was married and the Queen, Charlotte had been put into a cap and furred mantle, then into an open carriage with three of the recovered ladies, and the curious crowds pressed close. They were well-behaved, Charlotte decided; one might perhaps have expected some cheering; as it was, only one man called out 'Poug! Poug!'

'Vat is poug?' Charlotte had enquired of the still pallid Duchess; her own English was not by then as perfect as it would shortly become.

Elizabeth Gunning, one of three beautiful sisters all of whom had made noble marriages, replied with commendable lack of expression. 'It means, God save Your Majesty.'

Later, Charlotte Sophia had found out what it did mean; and that she was thought comically ugly, with her pug's nose and strange slitted eyes. If the King thought her ugly also, he had given no sign. Her small figure had then been good in any case, and she had a long graceful neck. By now, this was sunk in her hunched shoulders; and her hair, after incessant pregnancies, had thinned so that for years now she had had to wear the formerly needed velvet cushion, having them comb the rest over the top. Lately, she had discarded the

227

cushion and had had her remaining hair, which was grey, dyed instead, and curled in a fashionable fringe on her forehead. That had perhaps been a mistake; but the King never saw her now. He never saw anyone or anything; he was both blind and mad. For the first time in her life Charlotte had been made afraid, that night he had come in and stared down at her intently from behind a lighted candle, between the curtains of their bed. His eyes, the prominent pale-blue eyes she knew so well, had stared as though she, the Queen, were a stranger; an unwelcome stranger, after so many years.

She must think again of fashions, at once. There were numberless gowns she never now wore. Everything was different; waists no longer at the waistline, skirts too short, not full enough, though she insisted on hoops at Court. She would not permit the princesses to wear the latest mode informally in her presence, even now they were supposedly independent. Only Augusta defied her, especially with regard to her hats; they were frivolous, there was no other word, it was improper while the King remained as he did. While he and she were together long ago at watering-places, she, the Queen, had often worn a short scarlet cloak and black bonnet, noticed by nobody. Lately, though, there had been too much notice taken; almost five years ago now, when she appeared briefly in London, they had stopped her sedan-chair in the streets and crowded round and hissed and spat at her, thinking it was she who was forcing on poor young Charlotte's loathed Dutch marriage. She, the Queen of England, who came of the blood of soldiers, had stood up in the chair unafraid. 'I have been in England sixty years, and I have never before been schpit on.' They had respected the tiny indomitable figure with its cold snake's eyes, and had left her in peace.

There had been mocking cartoons issued all of her married life. They had shown her always as having a wicked gap-toothed grin like a monkey, or else seated on a wooden side-saddle at the King's back, he dressed as a farmer. At Royal's wedding she had been shown as particularly hideous in a bonnet with blinds, at the King's side; always at his side. She had done her duty. Royal had been ungrateful for being dressed as a bride by her mother's own hands, and had had the impudence of addressing oneself as Dearest Sister—think of it!—after Napoleon had made her fat husband a puppet King. The King here had greatly regretted ever permitting his eldest girl to marry, even at well past thirty as she had been by then.

Farmer George: Jodely, the family had called him. He had made the boys, even young George Augustus, grow and harvest wheat and bake their own bread and live on it, and had whipped them too often, even York who was his favourite, so greatly arousing their resentment that they had turned away from what they should naturally have become, handsome and dutiful young men. Every one, except Ernest and Adolphus and the two who died young, had taken women and lived loosely in increasing scandal and debt. The debt was more shocking than the scandal; men were men, after all, but one should keep careful accounts. Even Ernest, who had bravely captured a French officer in the saddle and carried him back on his shoulders to the German lines, had scandalised her in the end, not by that evil nonsense spread by George's wife Caroline; there was no truth in *that*; but Ernest had married, in Waterloo year, one of her own nieces, who had been divorced—that was bad enough—and was almost certainly accessory to the murder of one of her husbands. Mary had told her of it. Naturally she, the Queen, had forbidden the new Duchess of Cumberland entry at Court; one had to remember the purity of the princesses. The King would have approved. He had always forbidden his daughters any access to such matters openly, go their secret ways as they might: of that he knew nothing: she, Charlotte, had seen to it.

The King. She had first set eyes on him at their wedding, on the evening of her arrival; a pale young man with a weak chin and the prominent unforgotten eyes, staring at her. She had of course played music to the company before they went to bed. He had seemed pleased with her playing and had said that later on, they must have concerts. This had happened; and there had of course been more cartoons, with the King nodding asleep and herself grinning widely, and beating time with her fan.

By then he was no longer pale; at times he had a skin rash. Once they were painted together with the first five children, and another starting: it didn't yet show, but she herself looked peevish. All of them wore costumes of the time of Charles the First. George Augustus was enchanting in blue satin, but the poor King did not suit his high lace collar; it showed up the pale stare, and the red rash, which was not left out of the painting.

That had not in any case been the first alarming sign: that had come soon after the wedding, and Charlotte Sophia never spoke of it. The King had seemed excessively violent and odd, but had after all got over it and appeared to be himself again: but one of the doctors had told her then that the King had been in love with Lady Sarah Lennox, who had been one of Charlotte's bridesmaids and had later disgraced herself by eloping from her first husband with a lover. 'Lord Gordon did penance for that sin by walking to Rome with no company but that of a large shaggy dog,' the Queen reminded herself out of the recesses of her mind. Lady Sarah had not been ugly. She was said to be the prettiest girl in England.

The Queen had interrupted her thoughts, perhaps deliberately; and took another breath of the snuff packing her nostrils. There had been an earlier tale still, that the King had been secretly married to a young Quaker and had had children by her, a son and a daughter. Her formidable mother-in-law, Augusta, Princess of Wales—Charlotte had never dared ask that lady concerning it—was said to have removed them both to South Africa so that they would be no more heard of. There was certainly—one had consulted the maps—a town there called George, and tales brought back, probably by Clarence while in the navy, of a young man named George Rex who had founded Knysna.

It was better not to know any more; and she had held her tongue as the King recovered. There was no help for the situation, as she was already pregnant with the glorious firstborn son. The wax model she had had made of George Augustus as a baby was still her chiefest treasure, lying always beneath the glass of her dressing-table. She would look at it daily as they dressed her hair, powdering, cushioning, scraping, and Fanny Burney's little awestruck voice going on reading, reading, before she retired after five years because of ill-health, playing cards with Schwellenberg each night having been too much for her.

The King had hated his eldest son. Was it because he himself, as a young man, had been offered an establishment and a separate income by his disgraceful old grandfather, George II, but had declined both and had begged to be allowed to remain with his mother? Then Prinny himself—that was what the world called him later, when the Fitzherbert business was almost over and done with—had demanded, from youth, exactly the same thing, had despite his father been granted it by a nation which then admired him as Prince Florizel; and had squandered it shamelessly on building Carlton House, which was still, even these days, eating up money unendingly. At one point George had dismissed all his servants and had shut it up, then later on had opened it again, with artificial rivers running down the dining-table full of fish, and coloured lights and all manner of extravagances. The Queen's House would have been readily available to him at the beginning; there had been no need for any of the rest, and it had led in the end, with the debts steadily increasing, to that heartbreaking marriage by national demand. Of all young women to have chosen, Caroline of Brunswick had been the worst; she herself had been against it from the beginning, but Caroline was the King's niece and so was preferred at the time to her own. They had not heard the last of Caroline yet; she was disgracing herself all over the Continent, and would certainly return to plague George Augustus as soon as the King was dead. What a Queen of England to follow oneself! George of course would never permit her actual coronation.

The King, at any rate, had hated George Augustus, had at one time, during the later mad attacks, pinned him to the wall by his collar. York, the second son, had however always been his father's favourite, and he and she and the little Prince of Wales had been painted early on by Zoffany, with herself in an elegant gown and her profile reflected in a mirror, and the two small boys dressed one as a Roman general, the other as a Turk. The Turk had disgraced himself also, had perhaps helped to overturn his father's reason as much as the death of Amelia two years later at twenty-six; there had been that unsavoury business of the supposed sale of army promotions by one of York's mistresses, a woman named Clarke. He had been forced to resign as Commander-in-Chief meantime, but had regained the appointment after the scandal died down. He was a good friend to his soldiers. If only he had been as kind to his wife, there might be heirs there by now; but his Prussian Duchess had borne no children. From Caroline, of course, there had been only poor Charlotte. It was all of it a sorry ending to her own unending devotion to duty; fifteen children, but no grandchildren except, copiously, from

Clarence in former days by that actress. Perhaps Clarence's bride, who seemed an amiable if not a robust creature, would fail to miscarry; the other, Kent's wife, was however, from the look of her, a more certain speculation. The pair of brides had knelt before Charlotte to be remarried in her presence, using crimson velvet faldstools. All one could do now was to hope and pray.

The poor King had prayed, all his life, latterly under a sofa. Whether he reached his God now in his cell, God only knew. On their wedding night the royal bridegroom had prayed aloud for heirs and the prayer had been granted, without stint; but what now? She herself would die without seeing a legitimate grandchild.

The snuff having faded in flavour, Charlotte jabbed with the knotting-shuttle again, narrowly watching her daughters' fingers busy likewise. Augusta would no doubt give her completed purse to soldiers' charities. She thought of herself as the widow of General Brent Spencer, despite the King's ban on royal marriages without royal consent. Oneself did not enquire, provided the outward proprieties were preserved. As for Sophia, she was upstairs, as usual in ill health. The King had never known of *that* matter; she, Charlotte, had contrived to keep it from him. It would have driven him mad much sooner, without doubt: only twelve years after the attack which

235

had almost led to a premature Regency. If that had happened, it would have been better for George Augustus, much better; his powers had been at floodtide then, in 1788. By the time of the final madness, he had been sapped by debauchery and waiting, forever waiting, with never enough given him as a rule to do. He had more talent than any of the rest put together, yet the King, who had promoted the younger sons in the army and navy, would give George, Prince of Wales, nothing more than the colonelcy of the 10th Hussars. It was cruel and unjust, but one dared of course say nothing. The Prince had made them an excellent colonel, however, taking intense care over every detail. In a way, he had used poor young Charlotte at times as if she were a recruit. It was natural, perhaps, with the mother being as she was. For Charlotte to have been allowed to go the same way would never have done.

The King had been fond of his grandchild, had wanted to bring her up out of the care of her father. That however was unnatural. About then—or was it earlier?—the King had been briefly in the care of Dr Willis, in the latter's house in Queen Square in Holborn. The episode was not much spoken of. It was perhaps only remembered at all because she herself, recalling certain delicacies the King liked, had briefly rented a corner house nearby whose cellar was cool enough to keep them until needed. The place had later become an inn and they had named it the Queen's Larder. Well, by then everything was known in any case.

Confined as he was now, it was extraordinary to think that her husband knew nothing of poor young Charlotte's death, of his sons' recent marriages, in fact of anything that had happened since the doctors had so tormented him with red-hot quackeries supposed to draw out the madness from his head, and the strait-jacket. They had promised him that if he obeyed them, and came obediently to Kew, he would be allowed to see her, his wife; but the promise had been broken. In any case, by then she herself was afraid, having run out in her night-shift for help at the time of the crazed hostile stare behind the candle. Madness was untidy, unaccountable; Charlotte's prosaic mind, for all its courage, could not encompass it. There was right and there was wrong, there was black and there was white, God arranged everything and the devil must be overcome. Despite all of that, and her own years of unceasing devotion, the King had cried out, in the last of his sanity, that he had always disliked her. That had hurt greatly. The King had added that he was in love with Lady Pembroke, a perfectly respectable woman about Court. It had sounded as if, deep in what remained of his mind, he was after all like his ancestors, the regrettable first and second Hanoverian Kings. To have trodden the path of virtue all his days, at least since her own arrival, must have been hard. She thought of it wryly, aware of her worn-out body.

As for the daughters, they had been as disobedient, despite her watchfulness, as the sons. Some years ago they had insisted on being allowed to ride openly to Parliament, to chaperone young Charlotte, while their father was afflicted with his disease. They should have remained as if in mourning, as she herself had done from the beginning. They had no proper feelings, no heart.

The venomous glance shot towards Elizabeth; she must soon fetch more snuff. She would have to grow even more greatly accustomed to the smell of tobacco if she married her German Margrave; they said he stank notably of it. Well, the matter was out of one's hands.

One must try to remember happier times; there had been a few, such as when the King had supervised each label on each separate jam-jar to fit up a fully appointed house for old Mrs Delany, who made such beautiful pressed paper flowers, exactly like the originals. Then there were the paintings they had collected together, and the concerts; 'Charlotte plays; she plays!' the King had said in his abrupt way to the Mozarts, father and son, when the little prodigy was brought to England. She had sat down and had played a duet obediently with the small Wolfgang Amadeus, though left to herself she would sooner by far have listened to him.

Then there was the King's precise drawing, like that of an architect or botanist: no one gave him credit now for excelling in that, but both Prinny and Elizabeth had inherited his talent and the taste, shared with herself, for art. Then there had been the famous evening walks together on the terrace here at Windsor, when the common folk had crowded to see them all, especially little Amelia at three years old, flourishing her fan and smiling at everyone. Amelia's birth had consoled the King for the loss of Alfred and, worse, Octavius. 'If it had been Octavius, I would have died too,' he had said at Alfred's death. He had not done so; better perhaps if he had; then Amelia herself had died later, not of a broken heart—that never killed anybody—but of tuberculosis, which had troubled her for years: the younger children were not strong. Amelia had been a sentimental young woman and had fancied herself in love. Had she lived, she could have petitioned Parliament to be allowed to marry. The man was a cold fish, an equerry. To say Amelia had died of a broken heart, as most put it, was nonsense. If broken hearts caused death, she herself, Charlotte Sophia, would not now be sitting here, waiting for the deadly water to rise.

Fifteen children, to a man who had always secretly disliked her. In their separate ways,

239

they had all turned out a disappointment, the children, except Adolphus. Adolphus of Cambridge was virtuous, like herself. He had had no affairs and no debts, and lived mostly in Germany though at present, with his new bride, he was resident in England. The Queen thought with pleasure of the pretty and innocent young princess Dolly had brought from Hesse-Cassel, and that that had been a love-match nothing could spoil. Clarence, hunting for a bride at the same time, had fancied young Princess Augusta for himself, but had generously taken Adelaide of Saxe-Meiningen instead when he learned that his brother was smitten. By now, Adelaide suited William, so everybody was pleased. Thank God for such an outcome, at last, in the family! The young Cambridges—Dolly had been given the dukedom when it was decided he was suitable to govern Hanover—were meantime at Kew. But for that blessing, it would seem by now as if all of them were accursed; as if it would have been better had she herself never written that letter long ago to the King of Prussia to beg him to spare her brother's state. Had that not been so, she would no doubt have been married to some minor German princeling, instead of to a man she had never, when one considered it, really known at all.

'Ma'am, a letter has come.'

It was Princess Augusta, who had risen to receive it from the bearer. One must hope it was not more bad news. To the rustle of Augusta's satins—she was overdressed as usual, and one gave the girls permission to sit in one's presence while engaged in some useful occupation—the Queen ordered the wafer to be slit open. Princess Augusta scanned the lines, her still handsome face a mask.

'It will not please you, ma'am,' she said presently in her forthright fashion. 'It is to say—well, you had best read it for yourself.'

'It is the King?' Perhaps, at last, he was dead. Charlotte seized the letter; it could surely not be that, there would have been some more formal announcement. It was merely to say—to say—

The Queen gave a gasping sound, then went into a spasm. Her daughter laid her back in her chair and summoned help. Then she turned to Elizabeth, who had watched moodily and without concern, having had much to endure from their mother.

'What is the matter?' she asked. It might only be some small thing; the Queen was always too strict for her own good. Augusta handed her sister the letter, and seeing the contents Elizabeth laughed, her plump face with its wide mouth suddenly like a faun's: the family called her Fatima, but soon now she would be married, and away from all oppression.

The fell news just received had been to say that the young Duchess of Cambridge, Dolly's

241

wife, had met Ernest's notorious Duchess by chance while out walking at Kew, and the two had embraced and talked together. It may kill Old Plugnose, thought Elizabeth with satisfaction. She herself had taken with a pinch of salt, at the time, the lurid tale Mary had imparted before her own marriage to Slice; Mary was a troublemaker. There was no proof in any case that Ernest's wife Frederica was a murderess, though she had certainly been divorced and had married the man implicated in her first husband's death; it could happen to anyone.

'This will kill me at last,' wheezed the Queen, recovering meantime. Dolly's pure young wife to be contaminated by that adulteress! It did not bear thinking of, and anything might happen as a result. She herself must die now. She could endure nothing more.

*   *   *

The old Queen did not in fact die till the autumn, by which time Elizabeth was heartlessly married to her tobacco-prone Margrave, to whom she made an excellent wife later on back in Homburg. Once Charlotte Sophia was dead, they opened up her wardrobes; and a multitude of moths came whirring out in a cloud from the disturbed fabrics, which they had long ruined over the neglected years. The Queen's death was hardly noted; society's gossip rather concerned Elizabeth's uncouth German bridegroom, who had not only had to be soaked in a hot bath three days running before he could appear at the altar, but had bent over meantime and burst his breeches, having to borrow the Duke of York's, who was providentially as fat as he was. Then he was sick in the honeymoon carriage; but love came nevertheless between fat bride and stout groom, and Elizabeth was to be happy with him in Germany for eleven years, till his death. That marriage, the Cumberland union, and those of the Cambridges and poor Charlotte, had meant happiness and fulfilment; also, William of Clarence came to adore his Adelaide, plain as she was; but their one surviving baby died, while the Fitzclarences lived on. As for the Cumberlands' only son, Frederica had given birth to a most beautiful slender boy with fair hair, the joy of their lives. While still very young he became blind. They said it was after an accident while playing with a watch-chain. Nevertheless both the King and his daughter Sophia were also, by then, long since without external sun. The phrase was Byron's, written from abroad in a scathing poem following the old King's death at last in 1820, *A Vision of Judgment.*

*   *   *

The King had lingered on for a further two years after his wife's death, of which he was doubtfully aware. He was eighty-one years old, deaf, blind and with a mind by degrees forced inwards. He had long ceased to be shaved lest he do himself harm with the razor if one should be available. His long white beard straggled thinly over the furred robe they had put on him to keep him warm. In the old days, he would not so have pampered himself.

The blind pale eyes stared into vacancy. The sparse furnishings of the room which had become the third George's world were familiar enough after so many years. Now and again, active as he had once been, he would get up and grope about, feeling first one object and then the next, coming at last to the harpsichord he could no longer hear himself play. Playing that, or a small organ, had been the last pleasure left, while the King's fine hands still strayed over the keys. They were an artist's hands: he had inherited a meticulous talent in such ways from his mother, who had loved botany and, like himself, loved Lord Bute. *Chacun à son Bute*, an impertinent lady-in-waiting had once said to Augusta, Princess of Wales: but there had, of course, been nothing improper.

The King's fragmented mind remembered, as the old in any case do, the things of long ago more clearly than those of the recent past, which were, inevitably, painful and best forgotten. He recalled his strait-laced mother now—'George, be a king!' walking with dear Lord Bute, with his magnificent silk-clad leg, in the gardens they had planned together at Kew and which would be their memorial. He himself would have obeyed Bute in anything; he had loved the man abjectly, lacking his own father early as it had turned out. Handsome and decisive as the Scot had been, he was a part of known and familiar things; there would have been no question of accepting the offer made by the disgraceful old King, whom one was seldom permitted to see, of a separate income and establishment. His mother and Bute had meant security; the world beyond was an untried place, and his young sister Caroline Matilda, when she was sent later on to Denmark as a bride, was treated shockingly by her husband; her early death was a mercy. He himself had resolved then that if he ever had daughters, they should never marry; no, never that; marriage enslaved and degraded women. His own mother was different, strong-minded, a widow who brought up her own family with strictness. He saw her face now, narrow and double-chinned, with beneath it a firmly upright tight-laced body, before the remembrance faded into the mists that, incapable of any discipline, came and went in his mind. Hannah Lightfoot's face came then instead, that of the young Quaker woman he had long ago been permitted, though not openly, to marry after Quaker fashion, as it could be discounted; and their two children he scarcely remembered. Those had been taken away, and he had afterwards been forbidden Lady Sarah; her family were Whigs, the worst evil to befall Britain, in whose name he, George, had said he gloried. 'Britain, Britain,' the confined man repeated to himself; they had misprinted that remark made at the time of his coronation, calling the word Briton. Someone had thrown down a gauntlet at that ceremony, or rather after it at the banquet, on behalf of the absent Stuarts; strange that that should come to mind, nothing more having come of it. The old Cardinal King, beggared by the Revolution, he himself had helped with money from a royal grandmother's Italian dowry, filched in 1688 by the government; it had been only right to let the poverty-stricken old man have it back. One had been rewarded, by the end, with the return of certain Crown jewels; there had been a sapphire, a stone said only to be worn by kings. 'George, be a king.' He had nevertheless lost America: his mother would not have approved of that. The colonists had however been stubborn. He himself would by no means submit to stubbornness, either in his family or in his subjects. He had shown firmness, after all. What had happened everywhere was unfortunate. A great deal had gone wrong, also at home. George III found he could not remember all of it, or the reasons.

246

There was a reason for everything, if one could find it. Here, alone, at least he had time to think, to remember, here and there, out of order like the time he had evidently talked to an oak tree and shaken it by the hand. They said he was mad, but what he remembered came, when it did, with fierce clarity.

Hannah. What had become of her? Pretty Sarah, Sarah Lennox. Lady Pembroke, lately, had reminded him of Lady Sarah, a little. For years there had only been ugly little Charlotte, with whom he had contrived to do his duty. Duty had meant the early advent of that other, the beautiful and damned. He, his father, had foreseen it, had tried again and again to whip the evil out of the heir, but there had been scandal later on with an actress, then still later a Papist. Of all things, to go through a form of marriage with a Romish widow, six years older! It had been denied, of course, in Parliament by Fox. Fox. The other devil, who had led his son astray. Fox, the kin of Lady Sarah and the reason for no marriage there: a Whig. His own son George had become a Whig to spite his father; of that there was no doubt. There had been women, sin, debt, all the things he, the King, had denied himself; he had lived sparsely, had lit his own fire early each morning, had hardly eaten lest he give way to the family tradition of corpulence. George Augustus on the other hand ate, drank, smoked tobacco, fornicated with others and abhorred his wife. She, his own niece Caroline, hadn't been so ugly; something could have been made of it, before the abandoned woman grew wild. The Queen had never liked her; the failure of the marriage was partly Charlotte's fault. A great many things were. He could see it all now, for years having deceived himself, pretending they were devoted.

Once, long ago now, he had got his hands round the heir's throat and would have throttled him. George Augustus was a coward; he had burst into tears. No man did that who was a man. The fellow was degenerate, unworthy to reign. If it had been York, there might have been hope; York had a good heart, still came to visit him, his father, here. No one else came, except when they brought food.

Food. He still didn't eat much. He felt his own arms under the furred robe, thin as sticks. If he were to stop eating altogether, he would die. Why had he never thought of it before? Amelia was dead; he would be reunited with her. All of his daughters had been beautiful; where were they now? Charlotte kept them from him. There was a great deal she had kept from him, after all; she was sly, always agreeing, always obeying outwardly, while doing as she chose in her own way.

Someone came in now, bearing food on a tray. The King smelled the cooked mutton and decided not to eat it. He was used to denying himself; it would not be so hard to eat nothing,

nothing at all, and to fade out of a life that was no longer worth living: deaf, blind, forgotten, cut off from his family, nearer the dead than the living; they beckoned now, Octavius and Amelia. He could see her staring eyes, her thin arms, so like his own now. 'Remember me,' she had said as she was dying. She had looked accusing then: what harm had he done her? She must know he, her father, had loved her above everyone: out of all his Cordelias, all, all, he had said so to them, and now—

It took him several days to die, but being obstinate he kept to his resolve. The reign of George IV, so long delayed, had begun; and the new King himself was old.

CHAPTER TWENTY-TWO

Lady Keith was being driven westwards, at commendable speed though not at a pace dangerous enough to spring the horses. If Mama was indeed dying, she was dying, and it was for Providence to decide whether or not one would arrive in time. There was no point in risking delay by injury to the bays, the coachman or, possibly, oneself.

Queeney permitted herself to lean back for once on the cushions, observing the passing of the landscape outside rather than paying heed to her maid, who had accompanied her and who sat opposite, with her back to the box. Georgy and the Admiral had not come. Lord Keith was not too well—his statement that Bonny was reputed to be at death's door on his island had aroused fear in Hester lest her husband might be hastening towards his own demise: that arranged meeting at last with Mercer again had told on him more than he would admit, and in any case he had avoided unnecessary dealings with Mrs Piozzi because of her regrettable second marriage. Also, he trusted her, Hester's, own common sense in dealing with the probable chaos of any existing will. Undoubtedly most of whatever was left to leave—so much had been needlessly squandered—would go to that ungracious young Italian, the late Piozzi's nephew, whom Mama, without any evident affection received in return, treated as her son, having adopted him formally and endowed him with the ridiculous name of Salusbury Piozzi Salusbury. The creature had taken her money shamelessly, and the latest swindle—it could be nothing else—concerned a hoped-for baronetcy in return for recent services as Member of Parliament for a part of Flintshire. Its purchase had at first been placed at £5,000 of Mama's money, then reduced to two-thirds of that sum; but Princess Charlotte's unfortunate death occurring just then, all such matters had of course been postponed. Now, with the coronation pending at last after the

whole disgraceful business concerning the Queen's unwanted return to England, the price had risen to £6,000, which by now must be almost all Mama had left. Even she had had to be persuaded to part with it, and there was still no sign of the pending baronetcy in the gazettes; no doubt the Italian had merely pocketed the money. Well, there it was; the poor old soul would soon be dead; and oneself was, thankfully, otherwise provided for.

Queeney surveyed her own prospects complacently, certain by now that Mercer de Flahault was no longer a threat as regarded one's own jointure and Georgy's expected inheritance; the title, of course, could not be alienated. There had been that attempt at reconciliation two years ago now, between Mercer and her father after the birth of little Emily in Scotland. She, Queeney, had remained adamant in refusing to receive de Flahault's wife at Piccadilly, and the Regent, in one of his erratic gestures of charity, had offered a room in which the father and daughter might meet one another in Carlton House. The Admiral had come home afterwards laconic as usual, saying little—one had of course asked no questions—except that Mercer herself had seemed well enough after the birth. He had then made it clear, a few days later, that his own intentions had not changed. 'Tulliallan, every stone of which is mine, and every penny I myself own will go to you,

251

Hester, and to our child after you. I will have no truck with any daughter of mine who has disgraced her social position and my own. She and he can manage well enough, I don't doubt, on her mother's money and Meikleour,' he had grunted. Queeney, rarely demonstrative, had risen and kissed his cheek, noting its pallor. Since then the Admiral had seemed to age greatly. It remained to be seen whether he or Bonaparte would go first. News came slowly from St Helena.

It came occasionally from Scotland; Mercer, on return there, still wrote dutifully, no doubt hoping for more than she would in the end get. By now she had given birth, almost yearly, to an increasing number of daughters; it was evident that the curse of Aldie prevailed. She, Queeney, was however content enough with her one dear biddable Georgy. Georgy must marry suitably in proper course. One must ensure that, whether or not her father was alive still, by never permitting her the unwise freedom allowed to her half-sister from a child: that had done harm.

Here was Bath already, with its dignified crescents; but they were driven to Conway's Sion Row house in Clifton, not the best quarter of town. Lady Keith emerged, handling her silk skirts cautiously. A second carriage waited already at the door; her sister Sophia's. It was unlikely the youngest, Cecilia, would make the long journey from Segroid; in any case Mama had seen her quite recently. What a pity the death had to take place in shabby lodgings! There was the newly decorated house in The Crescent; it would have been much more suitable.

* * *

Hester Lynch Salusbury Piozzi was indeed on her deathbed, and knew it. It was not as a result of a recent fall she had had at Exeter; she had recovered from that, a little, after slipping off a stool while climbing into some high strange bed or other. It had bruised her leg, but that was healing, though slowly. No, it was a general feeling of indescribable weakness, not unpleasurable, as if she were drifting off to sleep. She was aware of what was happening about her, in the room; of her daughter Sophia, a shadowy presence seated beside the bed, who kept assuring dearest Mama that Queeney would soon be here. 'Have patience,' Sophia kept saying. 'It will not be long now.' All her life—Hester Piozzi laughed inwardly—she had tried to have patience regarding Queeney, after the mistake of her own she now clearly recognised, that unfortunate hasty saying that Dr Johnson wouldn't want to be bothered with a child's stuff. The child in question had never forgotten it, had shown no affection since; and one had, sadly, loved her more than any of the rest, being the eldest born.

Perhaps now, as it was for the last time, there would be some unbending, some absence of formality, some sign of the possession of a heart. Queeney after all took after her father. Thrale had been the same; phlegmatic, not given to demonstrations of fondness. God knew the conception of twelve children and one dead before birth might have elicited a trifle at times: well, there it was, and there had been the mistresses, and Thrale's pox she herself had had to nurse. All of that was far back in the shades; she had no feeling now that Thrale waited for her. Piozzi was a different matter. Would her dear love come for her, or would his Romish Church—she had after all caused him to forsake it latterly in exchange for the Church of England—let him out of purgatory, which one supposed he was unavoidably in, and allow him to come? She so longed to see him again; surely even the keys of Peter would let matters be unlocked for the time. Love! Not everyone had experienced it as they had done together. It was different from any other she herself had ever felt; for her parents, for Lucy, her little girl who had died; for Harry, who had died also. Would she meet with him, her manly little son, and be told by him that she had been a bad mother? She hadn't understood, that time, that he had been in pain; he might have been teasing her as he often did. The tutor had wanted to whip him. Mercifully that had not happened; they had seen for themselves in time that the little boy was dying. Nobody knew why so many of her children had died. If she could have those years over again! But time never returned.

The past. It was gone; but early memory was with her now, of her mother and father, who had so loved one another. Mama had been an heiress who had married Papa, her cousin, knowing he was in debt and needed her money. All of that had been spent in paying the debts, and during one's childhood Mama had ironed and sewed and wielded a broom like a servant, all for love; and Papa had kept losing his temper because he knew he was useless, an unfortunate state for anyone to be in. He had gone twice on expeditions to Nova Scotia to try to make a fortune, and had come back both times poorer than before. *My life*, he had called Mama in letters. After his death Mama—there must have been some money saved by then, or perhaps old uncle Tom at Offley, from whom one had had expectations which were later disappointed, had lent some—Mama had had her portrait painted in widow's weeds by Zoffany, standing beneath a portrait of Papa himself, greatly resembling Piozzi. That was the extraordinary thing which had first caused her to notice Gabriel, that resemblance; but Piozzi himself had been of a gentle temper, had never lost it except towards the end when he was screaming day and night with appalling pain.

She herself had no pain now, merely this immense weariness. If only Queeney would come, she herself could go; was that the sound of carriage wheels?

There were surely others in the room to watch her die; after all, at eighty, she was a noted Bath-blue. It was in fact growing difficult to separate the living from the dead. Dear Sophia Byron was somewhere, her company having been missed for years; and dear Dr Collier, Hester's own early tutor, who had encouraged her to translate a life of Cervantes while still quite young, and who had been most cruelly taken away; evidently he had not forgotten her. Her eyes filled with joy; there was Sarah Siddons with her long nose, and dearest whimsical Mrs Garrick, and at last, at last a great lumbering figure in a dark coat and scorched wig and, no doubt, worsted stockings. Sam Johnson had forgiven her at last: there was only understanding and forgiveness where they were all going now. She wasn't afraid. She would even tell the good Doctor later on how he had spoilt the prose of little Fanny Burney, making it so ponderous Fanny's later books were never as popular as *Evelina*. Why had Fanny insisted on returning to her family at last from Streatham? 'She had everything she could possibly want from me,' thought the dying woman peevishly. Later, at the time of the Piozzi marriage, Fanny had betrayed her, the little serpent, secretly siding with Queeney who was already planning to take the other girls away. That had been difficult to forgive, but one must forgive everything now. Fanny had married a French *émigré* officer in the end, for all her coy gushing spinster's ways. One had thought of all that before.

Forgiveness. One was growing weaker now; soon it would be too late. She must forgive all pettiness, all spite: ungrateful Johnny, who hadn't come after taking all her money. It was more important to have loved Johnny than for him to have loved her in return. *It is more blessed to give.*

Someone had come into the room at last, a tall prosperous presence with rustling skirts. Queeney, her first little baby, born when she herself was sixteen! The dying woman stretched out a hand; it was all her strength would permit. Someone took the hand, and someone else the other. It no longer mattered after all who it might be; Hester Piozzi had to have her last little joke. She freed a hand and with it, sketched a coffin in the air. Then she died.

*   *   *

There was not much notice taken, as there was other and more important news at the time. The Cato Street conspirators, who had tried to murder the Cabinet, were executed in a row to the edification of watchers and gruesome reports in the newspapers. Meantime they buried Hester Thrale Piozzi beside her regrettable Italian husband in Wales, whose climate had killed him slowly; and while a wrangle was continuing with the unspeakable Sir John Salusbury Piozzi Salusbury about the possession, or otherwise, of a silver teapot, a suitable inscription was thought of for Hester Thrale Piozzi's tomb, causing the Streatham days, and her fame as a literary hostess, to be remembered by observers before all else: *Dr Johnson's Mrs Thrale.*

*   *   *

Emily Cowper, Lady Melbourne's daughter, had been married off in youth by her strong-minded mother to a husband almost as complaisant as William Lamb; everyone remarked on the Cowpers' second son's likeness to Palmerston. Emily had a kind heart, and her beauty and intelligent company cheered the King in his loneliness and, worse, embarrassment at the prompt return of Caroline, who among other impertinences had written to ask which gown His Majesty would like her to wear for the coronation? That was postponed until the enquiry in the Lords into Caroline's conduct abroad had taken place; like the Delicate Investigation, it came in the end to nothing, and the Queen—

unfortunately, she *was* the Queen—had had the bad taste to drive meantime in an open carriage wearing a wreath of fresh roses in her hair, like her dead daughter. She had never mourned Charlotte or pretended to: on receiving the news, unofficially, of the Princess's death she had been heard merely to state that she herself was Caroline, 'a happy, merry soul'. 'She is unfit for any decent human relationship,' wrote Lord Grey in disgust.

A section of the common people, egged on by certain newspapers, cheered Caroline wherever she went and had jostled her on arrival at Greenwich so closely that she complained loudly afterwards of her bruises. The enquiry abandoned—it was after all hardly a kingly concern if an Italian courier's semen had been found on shared sheets at an inn, with other such details—arrangements for the delayed coronation went steadily ahead for June of 1821. Emily Cowper was given, by the King, a favourable seat well away from certain stuffy peeresses who had by no means forgotten that the Lambs were nobody in particular. Emily, hungry with all the rest of the ladies as only the peers were, by some oversight, fed, remained avid to see all that went on, and a good deal did not, or not strictly according to the book. In the first place, she herself knew, as did certain other intimates, that Prinny was no longer entirely sound in his mind. It was probable that recent events had further unhinged it; for instance, he told her her mother had died in his arms, whereas he had never once visited poor Betsy's protracted deathbed: likewise, he had still convinced himself that he had led the field at Waterloo. Nevertheless he walked valiantly, beneath a covered canopy along a raised way, from the Speaker's House that day, gout or no gout, to Westminster; and had been cheered by everyone. The crowds knew it was his day and no other's; they struggled for a glimpse of the tall vast figure, its tremendous presence fortified by a twenty-seven-yard-long train of red velvet powdered with gold, followed by plumed and braided nobles and officials and, not forgotten, Little Edward Hodge, proud in his specially designed uniform. He was a child Prinny had virtually adopted after his father's death at Waterloo, and though he afterwards grew tall was known as Little Edward all his life.

Prinny was at his most royal on this greatest of occasions. A curled brown wig almost covered his shoulders: there was something almost mystical about the man who had waited so long, and in such defiant magnificence, for the throne. George IV entered the Abbey; and the ceremony began.

Em Cowper watched with her calm grey eyes. There was a certain sapphire gleaming above the considerable waist of Lady Conyngham, the King's new favourite, who since Charlotte's death had, with her maternal ways, displaced the rigid Isabella Hertford. ('Damme, our mother had best take riding lessons, or it's all up with us,' had remarked Lord Yarmouth, Isabella's unregenerate son, to his brother on observing, some time back, the stout pair the King and Lady Conyngham made cantering together in the Park.) The sapphire almost, as Em wrote later, put out Leopold's eye where he stood near the King. She knew a certain malicious satisfaction: few liked the Marquis Peu-à-Peu, though many aspiring young ladies hoped in vain to marry him. On receiving the coronation ring with its great ruby, His Majesty was seen to cast a glance up at his fat inamorata, as much as to say he would give her that as well if it could be done. Em took it all in with delight, forgetting her increasing starvation as the hours passed; and heard nothing of what evidently transpired outside the Abbey. The Queen had arrived, and had tried to gain entry by all three separate doors, only to be refused because she had no ticket. 'Go home,' the crowds hissed. Caroline went at last; and within three weeks was dead, not, as the opposition would have it, of a broken heart, but of a throat infection caught at the theatre. It was as though she had determined to have the last word after all.

None of the undignified attempts to force an entry meantime had been heard by those inside the Abbey, with the choir and the organ drowning all other sound. The occasion was one of solemn glory, the acme of Prinny's already factual reign. If anyone recalled dead Charlotte, it was Charlotte's widower; and as the King walked back, crowned, in procession to the banquet, there were no hisses for the first time since he had come among them long ago as Prince Florizel, powdered and in spangles, riding in splendid youth to Parliament.

*   *   *

The reign continued; it had after all begun ten years previously. By degrees, after he had visited Scotland, Ireland, Hanover, the King ceased to be seen; one reason was that his doctors forbade the continued wearing of his constricting stays. 'Prinny's belly has now reached his knees,' wrote the diarist Creevey spitefully. Increasingly George shut himself away at Windsor, at his Cottage, as the Lodge was fancifully called; entertaining a few intimates, fishing in Virginia Water, once taking his little niece Alexandrina Victoria, dead Kent's daughter, up for a ride in his phaeton to her remembered delight. He had refused to allow them to christen her Charlotte. She was a rabbit-mouthed little thing, subject meantime to her mother.

Mercer de Flahault, in Scotland, bore her husband five daughters over the years. The last was born almost as news came that Byron lay dying at Missolonghi, a marshy place in Greece, which suppressed and violated country he had tried to revive as a nation; it would become one because of this endeavour. They brought Byron's body home to England. The crowds lined the dock as the ship came in, clamouring for a drop of the brandy that had preserved the body in its cask. The ostracised lion had come home.

CHAPTER TWENTY-THREE

Mercer had changed her identity; she had become Meg de Flahault, laird of Meikleour and mother of five daughters, heir to the ancient curse of Aldie which denied her sons. By the time it had become evident that there were to be none, her health had suffered, but her ambition was rekindled; now, she could proceed with her plans for Charles to become, at last, Ambassador to St James's after his old father should die. London society would be forced to accept them: there could be no refusal.

Talleyrand meantime showed no signs of dying and continued to reign in Portland Place: but the prejudice against the Emperor's former officers in France was at last modified to allow Charles entry there again and, almost, toleration, though the Bourbons proper would never fully approve of his presence. There was, however, still the Orléans branch, whom Mercer-Meg—she became Lady Keith in her own right upon the Admiral's death in 1823—continued to cultivate, especially the charming eldest boy, named Ferdinand after his imbecile grandfather long ago in Naples. Meantime, shortly after that last disappointing and cold meeting with Papa at Carlton House, Meg travelled on alone to meet Charles again in Paris, leaving Emily with her nurse. There was enough diversion in the French capital to cause her to forget her mortification over the Admiral: as they said still, she had dropped twenty-three thousand pounds a year by her marriage, and was accordingly regarded with amazed favour by some, overt dislike by others; but that had always been the way wherever she went. Her mother-in-law, at any rate, liked her. They stayed, French fashion, on a floor of Adélaïde de Souza's house in the Grande-Rue-Verte and were hardly disturbed by her or by her agreeable, but by now slumberous and partly invalid, Portuguese husband. Adélaïde herself was both interesting and interested, as befitted a woman who had once even ensnared a fastidious, and aristocratic, bishop. Her shrewd eyes above the flaring passionate nostrils had summed up her son's rich wife, still so rich even on the mother's money! Here was a woman who would be as masterful as herself, which was necessary for

Charles, inclined as he was towards *laissez-faire*. Such a marriage was better in all ways than having continued to attach oneself to the dreary Hortense, who would never again be allowed to return after having welcomed the Emperor back at the start of the Hundred Days. In Madame de Souza's opinion and that of others, her imperial stepfather had been the only man Louis Bonaparte's unhappy wife had ever really loved; but one did not say so. At least, now, there was a beginning for Charles in the reconstituted society of Paris; already upstairs, Meg—a pleasant simple name, direct like its owner—was blossoming out as a hostess; the sound of their elegant parties was most encouraging. Once they had brought home, and had introduced, a small eager bright-eyed Irishman named Thomas Moore, a poet who had known the celebrated Byron and who was, like him, abroad for debt. He and Charles sang songs together full of nostalgic Celtic melody, foreign to Adélaïde, whose nature was practical: and had dinner.

Before that, Meg herself had made a certain discovery in the garden.

It was thick with roses and heavy with their scent, and she had wandered among them appreciatively, aware by then that she was with child a second time. By himself, sniffing a rose, she found a little boy. He was charming, and said his name was Auguste. There was, from the beginning, no doubt whom he resembled:

265

there were, for instance, the eyelids. Meg tactfully took the matter not to Charles himself, but to her mother-in-law. That lady threw up her hands.

'My son begged me to have Auguste sent out of the way for your visit, but truth to tell I cannot bear to part with him, and sooner or later you had to know. I adopted him soon after he was born. Queen Hortense was greatly embarrassed at being asked by the Emperor to hold the baby King of Rome at his christening, which of course was magnificent, in Nôtre Dame while she herself was almost about to give birth to Auguste. The affair had, naturally, been concealed from the Emperor. Charles says Auguste was conceived in the Pavillon de Flore on a certain evening. You understand such things. Somehow we managed not only to deceive Napoleon himself, but his terrible old Corsican mother, whose eyes were everywhere. Auguste was born secretly not much later on in the country, and Charles, who has a compassionate nature as you know, took special leave to be present at the birth. The baby—is he not handsome now?—was christened as belonging to a working couple named Demorny. The same ruse was employed, one understands, when your Princess Sophia gave birth to a son secretly; unreasonable of her father not to permit any of the daughters to marry except for the eldest, who was however much too fat.' She smiled, having wandered off the point on purpose, and patted Meg's arm. 'The whole thing is over now,' she said. 'Hortense is devoted to her sons by Louis, and will by no means acknowledge Auguste; I have difficulty in obtaining money from her for his upkeep, but I myself grudge him nothing. It will be best for him to go into the army, though God knows by then whom we will be fighting.' She rattled on, deliberately making the whole thing light and amusing. She was a very clever woman.

'I will help him also,' Meg said evenly. 'He seems delightful.' Jealousy had never been one of her faults, and had Charles not been attractive to other women he would not have attracted her either; so she assured herself. She was more than prepared to have little Auguste as a guest at Meikleour whenever his grandmother would part with him, or if that lady should fall ill or even die. At present both prospects seemed unlikely. She smiled. 'I am glad that your garden is full of roses,' she said. It was the right answer; occasionally, the woman who had been Mercer Elphinstone could show tact.

As time passed and the other daughters arrived one after the other, proving that the curse of Aldie was not even yet broken—Emily might break it later, she showed determination in all things—Auguste, by then an elegant youth, visited them often in Scotland. His half-sisters adored him, as every woman he met was to do all his life. As for Charles, he was so grateful to Meg for resolving what might have been a dilemma without making a single scene that he became greatly devoted to her, and in any case enjoyed the life they led at Meikleour, shooting, entertaining neighbouring lairds and their friends, and designing a garden there and, later, at Tulliallan, which Georgy, both before and after her two childless marriages, allowed them at any time to use. However Meg nursed her ambitions: now that her own childbearing days were done, she would be a diplomat's wife, not the rusticating Highland laird she had seemed to become. Charles in any case could not endure the sound of bagpipes; it was discreetly murmured that he must have heard too much of them at Waterloo. It was time to go abroad, in search of fame; she already, thankfully, had fortune.

*　　*　　*

She was never popular; the couple in fact were christened Les Megs. If she had known, even Tom Moore had come to dinner that time most unwillingly; he had said afterwards that he would rather have gone by himself to eat an ice at La Colonne; the hostess's constant politics wearied him, although he admitted he had enjoyed his dinner. The Duke of Devonshire, in after years, found Mercer wearisome in such ways also, although they continued friends and by then, made mock of one another's ugliness when they met. Lady Keith, as Mercer was always known in Paris, astonished society by capturing her husband's attention for two hours one evening when every other woman in the room desired to talk with him, but Charles sat by his wife, who lay, as by custom then, on her sofa. Nevertheless Meg was to accompany him valiantly to embassies in Vienna, Paris and, at last for a time, London, though she had refused to come to Berlin, a brief assignment. St James's was not achieved by any help at all from Old Talley, who had long sized up his son as pliable; the hardness of a diamond was needed in high diplomacy as well as a velvet manner and much bowing over ladies' hands. Les Megs however continued a devoted couple, with occasional lapses by Charles— Anna Potocka, remarried, was after all in Paris—into old age and death; this came at last in Paris also, on the eve of the Franco-Prussian War: Meg died first in bed, Charles followed in his chair, not long after.

*   *   *

Lady Caroline Lamb had herself died in 1828. She had known with unusual clarity, by then, that she was dying, because nothing seemed to matter any more, not even the arrangement of a centrepiece; she had once jumped on the table
269

to show the manservant how to arrange one, posing like a goddess among the imagined flowers. William had been sent for and had come and carried her gently away, saying only 'Caroline, Caroline!' He had always loved her, despite everything; despite his family, who had tried to separate them, but William had come back. He wasn't with her now; there was only one other presence in the room, that of her plain neglected sister-in-law, Caro George Lamb.

George had never loved his Caro the way William had loved herself, always, always. They had been out riding together here at Brocket when a funeral cortège was seen to pass by the gates, black plumes nodding, followed by many carriages, some empty. William hadn't told her then, not till later, that it was Byron's funeral, bearing his body north to Hucknall. She had fainted at the news. There were no mementoes of Byron left in her rooms, letters, portraits copied from the originals, miniatures, gifts they had exchanged at the time, she had burned in a bonfire and made the servants dance round it. There had never been a love like theirs, however, and lacking him she had become a shadow of herself, an echo, a skeleton. She had however, lived on brandy, whisky, laudanum, growing ever crazier, slovenly in her dress, ostracised like Byron himself. Now he was a hero and they had brought his body home. She knew his body better than anyone; oh, she could remember. She had written *Glenarvon* to punish him, and after that no one but William would endure her company. She was persona non grata. Dear William. When she was dead he would grieve; but he had his politics; he would certainly be great one day, perhaps Prime Minister. Poor Augustus had been kept for a time in a cottage with leeches to his head, like Byron at the end. She had heard about that afterwards; the fever, and the leeches, far away in a marshy place in Greece; and he had been in love by then again with a young man. She could understand it; Byron had been two people, in fact several. She had understood him very well.

Remember me . . .

Now she was going somewhere where they would meet again; how coldly furious he would be to see her always! It would be like the times she'd got into the Albany and he hadn't liked it. Heaven; the Albany, and Byron for ever and ever. William couldn't come yet, but later, later, they would all be together, loving, friends, together always all three. Love. So many had loved Byron, and he . . . had he ever truly loved anyone except himself?

Now she was floating on and up, having become something with even less weight than she had ever borne, and without care. It was no longer night or day, and one had forgotten the January cold beyond the windows. Everything now was a window; she saw past and future and the whole of time. It was peaceful. Nothing mattered any more.

Caro George Lamb only knew death had come when she saw the placid expression of the once pretty features: there had been a little sigh, no more. She rose, ignoring the cluttered brandy bottles, and sent for William to come as soon as he might, and of course to bring poor Augustus. No doubt it would mean nothing to the boy to look on the face of his dead mother, because nothing meant anything to William's only son. What a tragedy the marriage had been! In its way, it was worse than one's own.

CHAPTER TWENTY-FOUR

Prince Leopold was indulging in a dream, an exercise he did not often permit himself. Reality was too bitter; he had long accepted what his personal life had unavoidably become now for over twelve years. There seemed no demand for his talents of government; as Charlotte's widower he received a handsome enough pension from the English nation to continue in a life of ease and uselessness, something after the manner of his dead wife's father and her surviving uncles. The King was by now a crumbling wreck, unseen by many except certain intimates who did not include his son-in-law: chief among them was his brother the Duke of Cumberland.

Where were the hopes that had sustained him, Leopold, once, the happiness he had briefly known? Through his adored and adoring wife, he had looked forward to ruling this powerful country; now, all his hopes were buried in Charlotte's tasteless marble tomb at Windsor. One day he had asked to be allowed to join her there. Meantime, all he had contrived in the end was the marriage of his widowed sister Victoire to the Duke of Kent, who had died shortly after the birth of their daughter; that was one prospect, he himself could advise the young Alexandrina Victoria, perhaps, later; but she was meantime only a child of ten. There was no present outlet for his ambitions, the constructive and careful quality of his mind, the result of his carefully educated upbringing. At times his presence was remembered abroad: there had been offers of a crown from Greece, that country Byron had died to save five years ago now: but there were too many conditions attached, and it was too far from the centre of events in Europe, where Leopold's interests lay. He had still not finally rejected the Greek proposal; in his experience it was unwise to jettison anything until there was some alternative. There were stirrings in France, the returned Bourbons having as usual behaved stupidly and their adviser, Polignac, having already driven the country almost towards a second revolution; but he himself, as a Protestant, would be out of the running there if they were ejected, as might well happen again. There would certainly be changes, perhaps more upheavals, in a Europe that had never known freedom or contentment since the Congress of Vienna; but one man's lifetime was short, and he was already almost forty.

Twelve years, spent in idleness and remembered grief, with Charlotte's apotheosis, on a painted panel showing her with their child at her breast, borne upwards by angels in a bright cloud to heaven! It was not, after all, enough for a man still alive: he had consoled himself physically; women were willing, and some of fairly high station here had hoped to marry him. He had not gone as far; the memory of Charlotte would come between himself and any new face forever present at his table, in his bed. In his heart he was still, would always be, the brooding sable-clad figure shown in the sentimental souvenirs brought out all over England at the time of his young wife's death. For consolation he had kept the Lawrence portrait, which her father had demanded to have returned at the time the great sapphire was taken back as a Crown jewel, pertaining to the nation. 'I do not want to part with anything of hers!' the widower had written in a heart's cry: but the sapphire had to go, and George IV had bestowed it later on his fat mistress. That would not be forgiven; but he, Leopold, had contrived to keep the Lawrence, and looked at it constantly; the bright scooped-up hair, the happy eyes, the long neck and serene smile! He had done that for her, when all was said; yet she had had a presentiment of death, even then. *The bridegroom of a year! The father of the dead!* That was Byron, writing at the time from Venice in the midst of his debaucheries.

Charlotte. He had not yet allowed them to remove her bonnet and cloak from the back of the door where she had hung them after their last walk; her watch, which she had laid on the mantel, lay there still. Such things helped to console him, no doubt, yet reminded him of his grief. Charlotte.

Charlotte. Was he imagining that he saw her now, the bright and splendid hair, the graceful white arms that had so often embraced him, her very features? There were hissing footlights between. He was after all in a theatre. This could not possibly after all be Charlotte; but it was like enough to her to cause the dream to remain. Leopold knew who she really was; a young actress, Stockmar's cousin, good Stockmar who still served him faithfully. He had come here tonight for this reason, knowing nothing more than that and, vaguely, that, being German born, her name was Karoline Bauer.

275

He stared in fascination, listening to Karoline's pronunciation of English. Charlotte and he had used to speak German together; it might be similar. It could never, of course, be the same; that was not to be contemplated. Nevertheless after the performance, Leopold of Saxe-Coburg took himself round to the green-room, walking on cork-soled shoes. They protected his feet from damp.

*   *   *

Karoline Bauer herself was a young woman of proper sentiments, without undue illusions. She had been strictly brought up, and though she was flattered at the attention shown her by the widower of the late Princess Charlotte, anything of an irregular nature was detrimental to one's reputation and career now actresses no longer belonged of necessity to the *demi-monde*. Also, the Prince of Saxe-Coburg was not as handsome as he must surely once have been at the halcyon time of his marriage. He wore, she suspected, a wig, black in colour, and certainly had false teeth. Nevertheless it was a distinction to have been noticed by him, and his weighty manner reminded one of home. They conversed formally and pleasantly of Heidelberg, which was a place Leopold knew, and the rose-red castle on its rock, and the sunsets to be admired above the Neckar.

Karoline herself and her mother, who was of course always present, came from that city. It made a point of conversation. After the Prince had bowed himself out at the end of recurrent visits the two women, old and young, would discuss the whole matter in low-voiced German.

'He is wearing double-soled shoes,' remarked Karoline, who had noticed the thick cork additions.

'He is no doubt careful of his health in such a climate as England's,' remarked the elder lady equably. She would not be sorry to see Karoline settled, but it must be respectably; the box-office returns had been disappointing.

The Prince sent flowers. Karoline was pleased; there had not been many such little attentions in a country that still remembered Sarah Siddons and Fanny Kemble. To leave the unrewarding stage to other talent might, after all, be wise.

In the end, and in the circumstances as they were made clear, the Prince proposed. It was to be understood that it must be a morganatic marriage. Karoline's mother advised her to accept; it was after all necessary to consider one's old age. A small house was found in Regent's Park, with lilacs in the garden. When the blossom was in season, they could walk beneath them, no doubt: that would be pleasant. It was to be hoped that it would not rain too often, this being England.

*   *   *

As time passed, Karoline grew restless. Prince Leopold was by no means an ardent lover, and life, to use a newly minted term, was boring. When he called, Leopold mostly spent his allotted time at a fashionable occupation which had come about now that, with the long peace, officers' uniforms with their gold braid were no longer in full demand. The reduction of the gold to powder, which could then be transformed into something useful or decorative, was known as drizzling. One took braid and frogging and gold buttons and epaulettes and whatever else of the kind should offer, and proceeded to digest them by means of a machine placed on the table, which made a humming noise when operated. Leopold spent more and more time at this passionless occupation on his visits.

*   *   *

In fact, he was thinking of the future, which seemed to have improved in prospect; there was talk, no more quite yet, of a rival constitutional monarchy to Holland, that country being intolerant of Catholics. Karoline, sitting as earlier instructed under the light of a lamp which then fell becomingly on her hair, began to realise that whatever happened she would still be acting a part; that

278

of a dead woman. The thought made her shiver. Outside the rain beat down. She longed to be out of England, in some sunny place, to be received again into ordinary society. Here, she was shunned; one day not long ago she had been walking in Kensington Gardens, and a little girl had appeared at whom Karoline, who was fond of children, had smiled. A high-coloured lady in maroon satin had appeared, had pounced immediately, and had wrested the child away, saying: 'Drina, it is not suitable for you to look at such persons.' Drina, she had discovered, was Princess Alexandrina Victoria, the heir to the throne; and her high-coloured mother was the Prince's sister, by right one's sister-in-law.

It was unsatisfactory and unkind. Nobody in fact called except the Prince himself, also of course Cousin Stockmar.

*   *   *

Leopold by then had decided to become King of the Belgians if the offer should be made. It was a toss-up—that of course was the kind of vulgar term any of Charlotte's uncles might have used—between himself and one of the six sons of the newly established Citizen King of the French. The Bourbons had gone, as predicted, having learned nothing and forgotten nothing, and Louis Philippe d'Orléans had ridden in to the Hôtel de Ville

279

last year to the fickle plaudits of the nation. His Queen, Marie-Amélie—he had not been long in obtaining the quasi-royal title after calling himself Lieutenant of the Kingdom—and their numerous family had followed. There were two daughters, one of marriageable age. The prospect of forging a constitutional hereditary kingdom on the edge of the Channel itself was not only enticing, but probable. The marriage with Karoline must of course be annulled. He had long realised that there were no feelings between them such as had existed between himself and Charlotte. Charlotte! Her memory would inspire him all his life. He would take her portraits to Belgium, to be hung always before him there. A political marriage made no difference, except to produce heirs. From what he recalled of her as a child at Twickenham, Louise d'Orléans—he remembered her name, apt as he was at detail—had been a pretty enough child, with fair ringlets. He would not want an ugly wife. It was a tenable prospect: and the parents were fertile.

He continued to await events; the essence of success was patience. There would of course be initial rivalry with Holland to overcome; a neighbouring kingdom with similar commercial aims would be objected to. Slender Billy—his old father was by now king—and he would cross swords, if that was the way it could be described, once more. The thought itself was challenging. He had won Charlotte: he

280

would win the war also.

He had completed the drizzling, and caused all the collected gold powder to be melted down to make a handsome tureen to keep. The morganatic marriage, which had never been publicised, was duly annulled with objections from neither party. Karoline, with suitable *douceur*, retired to write her memoirs and to marry an Italian Count. There was no quarrel by anybody with her cousin Stockmar. That astute personage would remain as close adviser to King Leopold I of the Belgians and, later, liaison officer between him and the young Queen Victoria, whose Prime Minister meantime was William Lamb, Lord Melbourne. Later, much loathed for his by then stiff formalities—it was a long time since Charlotte had died—Stockmar became preceptor to Victoria's son and heir, the not noticeably grateful, or improved, Bertie.

CHAPTER TWENTY-FIVE

In a quiet house in Brighton in the year 1830, an old woman was waiting for news of the expected death of her husband at Windsor. They had not met for many years, although she had sent an affectionate letter lately with the offer to go to him now. No acceptance had come.

She was a beautiful old woman, the refinement of great age having made her features again as they must have been in youth, emphasising the clear-boned profile in the oval face, the great gently lustrous dark eyes beneath the close white cap she wore; in the old days, her plentiful silver-gilt hair had been a feature whether or not she wore it powdered as for formal occasions.

She wore a crucifix about her neck and another, larger, hung on the wall. Since the Emancipation Act of a year ago such things were no longer dangerous, but in any case Maria Fitzherbert had always kept them displayed in her houses. She was praying, as she had done daily since their marriage thirty-five years ago, for the soul of her husband, George IV, now at the point of death.

He had been young when they met, younger than herself by six years. That had been the least of the objections her enemies had used; that, and the fact that she had been married twice previously, both times to older men; and was a papist. For that reason alone, any union with him other than through marriage had been abhorrent to her; and yet, she loved him. It was impossible not to do so; even in later years, when he had grown stout and capricious, he had had those who never ceased to love him. At the beginning, though, he had been Florizel. She had heard of him before they met, and of his affair with the actress Mrs

Robinson, and his debts, and how he enjoyed boxing, and Whiggery, and driving fast greys. Afterwards she learned other attributes of his, not all of them bad; his love of art, of music, of fine things; his frustrated ambition to hold a high command in the army; his constant interest in happenings abroad. Young and headstrong as he was, and passionately in love with her, she, the older and wiser, had known the situation in which marriage with herself would involve him, the Prince of Wales. He would forfeit the crown if they were to marry; and he swore it mattered not a jot. How could she resist him? He was irresistible, her lover, when he set out to charm; and he had charmed her, widow Maria, then had forced her hand by pretending to wound himself with a knife, so that she found him pale as death with blood on his linen cuff, for lack of her; and by then she loved him so deeply, perhaps more like a mother than the wife she became, that she had yielded. He needed a mother; his own was occupied with childbearing, and intimidated by the King. The King hated him.

They had been mostly happy together after the secret marriage. At one time—Maria closed her eyes, remembering—she had borne him a dead child, her only one in all her life, not come to term. It had been after they had gone out to shelter the poor émigrés who had escaped from France and were washed ashore from their boat in a storm; he and she had provided food and warm clothes for them, had seen them housed. Later, there had been questions asked in Parliament about the marriage, and Fox, the Prince's evil genius, had betrayed her, made him, her husband, do likewise, denying the marriage as rumour and no more: had rolled her in the kennel, as she had said angrily, on hearing of it. She should not have yielded, should have kept her temper, should have endured—well, she had done so—his boisterous drunkenness, his unfaithfulnesses even with her personal maid. It was useless to remember all of that; only now, when he was dying, she must recall that she loved him; had loved and prayed for him all these years alone, except for Minny. Minny was certainly his daughter by another woman. That mattered nothing; she herself had been a mother to Minny and Minny a loving daughter to her, once it was permitted by the Seymour relatives, the child's own mother being dead. The woman to whom she had to be grateful for that permission was Isabella Hertford. Forget, forget. George had been fond of little Minny; it was the child herself who gave him the name Prinny. 'I'm Minny, you're Prinny,' she had said, laughing and seated on his knee. Little Charlotte should have been there as well, loved by her, Maria, because she was George's daughter by that poor German princess: but the cartoonists had got hold of her, the papist, as always, stout by then and hooknosed, dangling a rosary in front of the baby princess: and Charlotte had been kept away.

Damme, never saw the woman in my life. That had been the first betrayal. That had hurt; perhaps more than all the rest. But he had loved her still, and needed her; on the morning of his wedding to Caroline of Brunswick she had heard his desperate hoof-beats outside her window, having ridden from town at breakneck speed, but she had not opened the door. Later, she had taken the Pope's advice, and had returned to him, her husband.

There it was; and for years now, after he had tired of her in favour of Isabella Hertford, then discarded Isabella in turn, he had been a recluse at Windsor. Only last year, they said, he had shed tears at the signing, at last, of the Catholic Emancipation Bill. Strange man; yet he had never minded the undoubted fact of her own faith. Possibly the Duke of Cumberland, who had been with him a great deal lately, had emphasised the Protestant nature of the dynasty; George was said to have remembered, for once, their father, and said that the signing of the Act would kill him now, as it would have killed George III in his time.

'It will be a mercy for the poor Irish,' Maria thought. They had suffered in all possible ways; but the suffering now was not uppermost in her mind. Nor did she shed tears herself; the grief lay too deep. Once she had said, and it had been foolish, that she wished she had never been born. God decided that. Little Princess Charlotte was dead now, and her unfortunate mother. That so-called marriage had been for nothing, after all. And her own?

'We loved,' she said aloud, and her hand, bearing its wedding ring, touched the crucifix at her throat. 'I do not regret our loving, any more than Christ his dying. It is all of it God's will. May God have mercy on the King's soul who is passing, and on all the dead whose names are unknown.'

If she had the time over again, would she act differently? Never; she knew it. She smiled to herself a little; then heard a carriage draw up to the door. Word had come at last. Maria held her hands tightly together; it was not yet time to make the sign of the cross: perhaps, after all, he would see her.

A visitor was however announced, a lean man with a great beak of a nose nobody could mistake; the Duke of Wellington. His presence could only mean one thing. Maria Fitzherbert rose from her chair.

'He is dead,' she said. It was not a question. The Duke inclined his head. Slowly, Maria crossed herself.

'May his soul rest in peace.' She made herself say the words aloud; but how could there be peace yet for *him*, with so much laid to his charge? Yet there had been kindness in him. *You're Prinny*. The child had laughed then and so had he. They had all three laughed together;

286

and now, Prinny was dead. There would never be anyone like him again: never.

Wellington conveyed the accustomed condolences in his stiff way; everyone knew this was the late King's true wife. The fact that the marriage had been most inadvisable didn't mean it had not taken place, Royal Marriages Act or none. Mrs Fitz still wore the wedding ring openly. He forebore to dwell on the details of the King's death except that it had been merciful; and said nothing about the innumerable envelopes, each one containing a lock of a different woman's hair, they had found beneath the royal pillows. There was a thing to be said rather than that. He regarded the dead King's widow steadily.

'Madam, His late Majesty was found to have about his neck, after death, your portrait, in a miniature set round with diamonds. It lay against his heart. It is to be buried with him, as he would have wished.' He found himself speaking with difficulty; as always, he was unable to make his words sound other than dry.

Her eyes had lit up with sudden immense joy. It was as though the years dropped away, leaving her a young woman again. Yet she did not foist her emotions on him, a thing he constantly dreaded from Kitty, his wife, whom as a result he had avoided for the greater part of their years together; granted, there had been the campaigns. But the late King—how impossible it was as yet to think of George IV as dead! He would live forever—had been most fortunate in this woman. One could see why he had never forgotten her, had been faithful in his way; strange to think of such faith, in such a man.

'Many things have died with him,' he heard Maria say quietly. 'It will be a different age now.'

Wellington bowed, agreed—it was difficult to think of Tarry Breeks as filling the vacancy—and presently left her. With the foresight of the great commander he was, he had done his duty. As though it had been a projected battlefield, he could picture the scene in a few days' time, the great heavy coffin beneath its gleaming pall, the flare of numberless torches making it luminous against the dark: and the First Gentleman, of all those who had roystered through the old century and the new, laid to such rest as he might be permitted to enjoy, with staves broken and voices echoing in the shadows 'The King is dead'. It was true enough that there would never be another such. Capricious, untrustworthy in all ways he had been, except about the secret of the locket; extravagant, unfaithful, drunken, hated, loved; the Regent, to be remembered thus, having given his name to an age. Not far off, the appalling monument to the daughter he had both resented and loved reared everlastingly, yards of sculptured white marble forming an unending pall, a concealed young corpse and a fleshly resurrection which would have made the poor Princess smile. She would have been Queen now, and Leopold Consort, had things gone as they were intended; and yet, who could predict, or foresee the pattern of Providence? Perhaps little Vic would make a good queen, free of that mother. Cumberland, if he lived, would become King of Hanover at that rate, with Salic law over there; and Leopold was almost certainly to be invited to Belgium. Well, it remained to be seen what would happen next, except that he himself, at his age, was unlikely to live into the reign after this.

Even he did not foresee the great rolling of drums, the tremendous mourning crowds, the enormous triumphal car and lining of troops on the way of his own state funeral many years hence, in Victoria's reign. He drove back to Windsor thoughtfully, preparing meantime for that of the man who had made not one but two inadvisable marriages. There had been several of those made, including Wellington's own; but the two boys were healthy: young men by now. One must put trust in God, do one's duty, and not take time to ask why things happened; the fact remained that they did, and only God knew the answers.

There is a conscience in the most acquisitive, or else perhaps ghosts triumph. Some weeks after George IV's death, Lady Conyngham, who was not as a rule known to part with jewellery, returned the great Stuart sapphire to the Crown. She said that perhaps the late King ought not to have given it to her.

We hope you have enjoyed this Large Print book. Other Chivers Press or G. K. Hall Large Print books are available at your library or directly from the publishers. For more information about current and forthcoming titles, please call or write, without obligation, to:

Chivers Press Limited
Windsor Bridge Road
Bath BA2 3AX
England
Tel. (01225) 335336

OR

G. K. Hall
P.O. Box 159
Thorndike, Maine 04986
USA
Tel. (800) 223–6121 (U.S. & Canada)
In Maine call collect: (207) 948–2962

All our Large Print titles are designed for easy reading, and all our books are made to last.